ONLY ONE MORE LIE

TRUE CRIME JUNKIES
BOOK 9

CHRISTY BARRITT

CHAPTER 1
DECEMBER, LAST YEAR

nly one more lie, Juniper Burrows promised herself as she stood at the fence beside the snowy reindeer pasture. One more, and she'd be done.

She couldn't handle the secrets anymore—and she especially hated keeping things from her parents.

If anyone questioned her, she'd keep her secret safe. But this would be the last time. She couldn't go on like this.

"What are you thinking about?"

Juniper glanced up at the sound of a cheerful voice. She'd been so lost in her own problems that she hadn't even heard her friend approaching.

Her thoughts immediately shifted to the fact that Peppermint had come out in public—something her friend had vowed not to do. No one could know she was at the camp. The revelation would only create more tension.

"What are you doing out here?" Juniper glanced around. "Someone might see you."

"Anyone who sees me will think I'm a guest here. It will be okay." Peppermint stared at her as if willing Juniper to understand. Then she pulled her black cap down on her forehead and tugged her oversized white coat closer.

"Not my parents! They won't understand." Panic crept into Juniper's voice. She thought she'd explained this to her friend.

"Then I'll make sure they don't see me." Peppermint flashed a smile.

"Why did you come out?"

"Because I'm going stir crazy. I need to be around people!"

"Then maybe you shouldn't stay here. This isn't the place to be social. You're going to get me in trouble." She hated to be harsh, but sometimes Peppermint didn't seem grateful for the sacrifices Juniper had made to let her stay here.

"I don't want to get you in trouble. I promise you I'm being careful, and I'm trying to figure out my next steps. I know I can't stay here forever."

Her words eased some of the tension across Juniper's chest.

Peppermint shifted and leaned against the fence, looking so laid-back that Juniper felt a touch of jealousy.

"What were you thinking about when I walked up?" Peppermint asked. "You looked so preoccupied when I saw you over here."

"I'm thinking about what to get people for Christmas," Juniper lied and instantly chided herself for breaking her earlier vow.

Secrets and lies . . . two things she hated. Yet here she was engaging in them both.

But it wasn't just her. Her parents had been keeping secrets from her also.

Truthfully, she was miffed at them. She'd wanted to take some college classes in person in Fairbanks. They'd said they needed her here.

Then they'd had the nerve to tell her to stay away from the one boy she was interested in. They'd told her this guy was bad news—just like they'd told her that Peppermint was a bad influence because she was flighty and had a wild streak.

The disagreement made Juniper want to rebel. Made her want to date Caleb, even though she'd been forbidden. Wanted to make her gloat about Peppermint living at the camp right under their noses, though they were clueless.

She was an adult now! Why did they still think they could dictate all her decisions? It wasn't fair. How could she be so different from her parents?

Starla, her favorite reindeer on the farm, nudged Juniper's hand and pulled her from her thoughts. The creature clearly wanted more of the hay Juniper held.

She was surprised none of the other reindeer had run over to get some. Instead, they munched on their dinner from a feeding trough at the center of the pen.

"You're one hungry girl, aren't you?" Juniper murmured. "Is that because you're getting ready for your big flight on Christmas Eve?"

Juniper didn't really believe that, but she had fun thinking about it—and thinking about reindeer flying was better than thinking about secrets and lies.

Her family ran a reindeer farm forty-five minutes outside Fairbanks, Alaska. Visitors came from all over to stay here. To meet the animals. To take hikes through the boreal forest with the creatures.

Even though Juniper had practically grown up here, she still thought the experience was magical.

Even if her life here had been built on a lie.

"This is a great place to spend Christmas," Peppermint murmured with a glance around the property. "I've always been jealous of you being here, and I desperately wanted to visit, to step into your perfect life."

"It's hardly perfect."

"It's better than the way I grew up. My parents barely decorated for Christmas, and they didn't believe in presents. They still don't. They're such downers."

A lump formed in Juniper's throat. Her friend hadn't had an easy upbringing—and it wasn't just because her parents didn't have much money.

Peppermint's parents were never violent with their

daughter, but they were manipulative and controlling. Plus, her dad had major anger management issues.

Peppermint had needed to get away. Her mom and dad were even pushing for her to marry a family friend —as if this were the olden days of arranged marriages or something.

They wanted to force her. Peppermint had been terrified.

"Speaking of your parents . . . have you talked to them lately?"

She shook her head. "Nope. As you know, I ditched my old phone. They have no idea how to find me. That's the way I like it."

Peppermint's parents had moved without her to Seattle a couple of months ago. That was where a new career opportunity had arisen. That was also where the man they wanted Peppermint to marry lived.

Juniper knew of an old cabin on the property here at the camp where her friend could stay until they figured something else out.

One thing was for sure: Juniper couldn't tell her parents Peppermint was here. They were the kindest people on the planet . . . until it came to Peppermint's parents. Peppermint hadn't even been allowed to spend the night. That was how much contempt her parents had toward Peppermint's parents.

Their friendship had all been cloak and dagger.

"I wish I didn't have to spend Christmas in that cabin by myself." Peppermint frowned and rubbed Starla's face. "Not to sound ungrateful or anything. It just gets awfully lonely out there."

"I wish you didn't have to either."

A smile tugged at Peppermint's lips before quickly disappearing. "Maybe I won't soon."

What did that mean? Juniper studied her friend. Probably nothing. But something about Peppermint's tone made Juniper wonder if her friend had some type of plan she hadn't shared yet.

Juniper swallowed hard and glanced around, making sure no one was out here with them.

She didn't see anyone. But that didn't ease the tension between her shoulders.

It was just nerves, she told herself—anxiety about possibly being spotted with Peppermint.

Juniper's radio beeped, and her mother's voice cut through the air. "Juniper! We need you at home. Right now."

She grabbed the radio and squeezed the Talk button. "Be right there."

Her mother's tone sounded urgent. She and Juniper had gotten into an argument earlier today about college and Caleb, and now Juniper didn't feel like hurrying. Would she get back to the cabin only to have her mom ride her case about something else?

Juniper would take her time getting back, she decided. She deserved to make *some* decisions for herself. The move was passive-aggressive, but it gave her a slight sense of satisfaction.

"Wonder what lit the fire under her?" Peppermint raised her eyebrows, her voice turning cold.

Peppermint had never been a big fan of Juniper's mother.

"Beats me." Juniper placed the radio back on her belt and then tossed the rest of the hay on the snow.

Since the reindeer needed to eat about nine pounds of this per day per animal, this was merely a snack for Starla. With thirty-five reindeer at the camp, a lot of hay and pellets were needed to keep the majestic critters healthy and happy.

"I'm going to run." Peppermint stepped away from the fence. "We'll catch up later, okay?"

"Sounds great. Remember—stay out of sight. Please." The last thing Juniper needed right now was for her parents to discover she'd let Peppermint stay on the property. World War III would break out if they knew.

Trying to do the right thing was so hard sometimes. Doing right by Peppermint meant doing wrong by her parents and vice versa.

"I'll be a ghost," Peppermint promised, wiggling her fingers near her face as if to look like an apparition.

The problem was, Peppermint wasn't the quiet, ghostly type. She was more like a wrecking ball. It wasn't a coincidence that her favorite song used those words in the lyrics.

Her friend scampered away, skirting the edge of the property to avoid running into anyone.

Once she was out of sight, Juniper's lungs loosened.

She stepped out of the pen, careful to lock the gate behind her. She'd need to put the feed bucket away before heading inside.

That was okay. She wasn't in a hurry. She was still cooling off from their argument earlier.

Before she took another step, she paused and the skin on her neck prickled.

There it was again.

That feeling.

Like someone was watching her.

She scanned the landscape around her. Saw the snow-topped buildings and trees. The festive street-lamps. The cheerful Christmas flags.

Nothing that gave her pause.

But the eerie feeling remained.

Like someone was keeping an eye on her.

Did someone at the camp know her secret?

They couldn't. How would they?

She shoved the thought aside and headed to the small shed where they kept the reindeer food. She took her time placing her bucket there. She straightened up a few of the bins. Checked inventory.

When she'd sufficiently killed enough time, she trudged back outside.

Juniper glanced over the hill at the log cabin she called home. A rock-encased chimney complete with smoke snaking toward the heavens stretched high on one side, and a large porch welcomed visitors.

Her mom and dad had built this business from the

ground up six years ago. Before that, they'd been on the verge of bankruptcy after the diner they'd opened in Fairbanks had failed to thrive. They'd feared they might need to leave their little slice of heaven here in Alaska.

Instead, they'd started this reindeer farm. Had opened the place up to visitors. They'd added more attractions every couple of years. Some people in town had even started calling them the Comeback Kids.

Juniper paused at the cabin and glanced behind her one more time.

That feeling remained—the feeling of eyes being on her. But she still saw no one.

She wished she could shake the paranoia. But it stayed with her like the Ghost of Christmas Past.

She slowly climbed onto the wooden porch, the hollowness beneath the boards causing her footsteps to echo. She stopped abruptly as something new caught her eye.

A snowman stood on the porch, a weird blonde wig shooting out from beneath its top hat.

Who would have left this here? Not her mom and dad. And most guests didn't come near their cabin, especially since there was a sign outside marking it as private.

She'd ask her mom when she found her. There had to be a story behind this.

For now, Juniper stomped the snow from her boots. Tundra, her husky, barked inside, almost sounding agitated.

Sometimes Juniper thought she'd rather be with animals than with people, although she *did* like people. Just not the angry ones who on occasion stayed here.

Ninety-five percent of their guests were amazing. Unfortunately, the other 5 percent stuck in her mind, the ones poorly behaved.

Just last week a man, his wife, and son had been here. The man had been so upset that he'd screamed his head off. He'd demanded a refund because the sky had been too cloudy to see the northern lights. He'd thought they'd have more snow. And it was too cold.

Mom had refused to offer any money back. The man vowed to destroy their business through bad online reviews and social media callouts.

Despite that, her mom stood firm and refused a refund.

Juniper had been proud of her mother. People shouldn't back down to bullies. It only rewarded their bad behavior, making things worse in the long run.

But the man—his name was Bert Something or Other —had an unsettling look in his eyes, as if he wasn't used to being told no. Her mom even had to call the police on him when he'd shown up at the camp a couple of days later making more threats.

The whole confrontation had left Juniper uneasy. Hopefully, Bert wouldn't be back any time soon. He'd ruined the whole happy vibe of the camp.

Having a happy vibe was something her parents emphasized as very important to maintain. The family's problems should always be private and not take away from the overall experience of their guests.

She supposed the theory made sense.

As Juniper slipped inside the cabin, she inhaled the scent of freshly baked cookies and chili. She couldn't wait to eat both.

The smell of evergreen and cinnamon hit her next.

The aromas of Christmas. She loved them.

Tundra met her at the door, barking and whining. The sound made her gut twist. He wasn't usually this agitated.

"Hey, boy," she murmured as she rubbed his head. "I told you I'd be right back. Did you miss me? Is Mom mad because I took so long?"

She glanced around the living room, her gaze skimming the nine-foot-tall Christmas tree, one she and her dad had cut from the forest themselves. Three stockings hung by the fire—one for each of them. Garlands were strung across every doorway and the mantle.

Her mom went all out at Christmas. They spent an entire day decorating and baking and listening to Christmas music.

"Mom?" Juniper called. "Where are you?"

When no one responded, she paced across the knobby wooden floor toward the kitchen. Tundra remained on her heels, panting as if anxious.

She paused in the kitchen. Mom wasn't at the stove, even though chili still simmered, and a tray of fresh sugar cookies teased her from the counter.

A new scent hit her nostrils, and she stiffened.

Something . . . smoky.

Was something burning? That was when she noticed the oven was on.

She hurried toward it and threw the door open. Smoke billowed out, filling her lungs. She coughed and waved her hand in front of her face.

Wasting no more time, she grabbed a potholder. She snatched the pan from the oven and shoved it on top of the stove.

Cornbread. Black now darkened its edges.

She frowned as she stared at it. It wasn't like her mom to leave something cooking without being close. She was usually much more careful.

Juniper turned the oven off, more apprehension embedding itself between her shoulder blades.

Strange. Maybe Mom had gone upstairs.

Tundra stayed with Juniper as she searched the rest of the cabin.

Her mom and dad were nowhere to be found.

She grabbed her radio. "Mom, are you there?"

There was no response, only static.

It didn't make sense. Mom had radioed her less than thirty minutes ago. Where could she have gone in such a short amount of time?

Why would she leave if she'd asked Juniper to hurry home?

She remembered walking into their cabin two days ago to see her mom and dad whispering about something. They'd quickly shut down their conversation when they saw her.

Her parents had their own secrets. Maybe even their own lies.

She didn't want to think they might. But didn't everyone have aspects of their lives they kept hidden? That was what Juniper was learning.

Tundra whined beside her.

"What is it, boy?" Juniper rubbed the dog's head. "Do you know something I don't?"

Tundra let out another low whine and paced toward the back door.

Juniper followed and peered outside.

Three sets of footprints were pressed into the snow, leading from the house to the metal barn in the back, a place where the family stored farm equipment and personal UTVs.

Wait. Three sets of footprints?

Who did the third set belong to? Juniper hadn't seen anyone else approach the house. Employees knew not to come to the family cabin except for emergencies. Dad insisted their family should have a little separation between personal and business.

Juniper shoved her shoes back on, pulled her coat over her shoulders, and opened the back door. She would follow the tracks to the barn.

But the bad feeling brewing in her gut grew larger.

She should have come right away, she realized. Why hadn't she come right when her mom asked?

CHAPTER 2

DECEMBER, PRESENT DAY

FOUR DAYS UNTIL THE NEXT MURDER

Slasher was not the name of one of Santa's reindeer," Duke McAllister called over his shoulder with wry amusement in his voice. "Sorry to disappoint you."

"You're thinking of *Dasher*." Andi Slade turned from the front seat and looked at Mariella Boucher, who sat in the SUV behind her, her twin brother Matthew beside her.

"Wait . . . how did I mess that up so badly?" Mariella rolled her eyes at herself.

The four of them were playing a silly Christmas trivia game as they headed to their next investigation. Things would turn serious soon enough. For now, it felt good to relax a moment.

"Let's face it: our lives now revolve around murder," Matthew said. "Slasher is only appropriate."

"You've got a good point." Andi tugged her stocking

cap down lower on her brow, chilly despite the heat billowing into Duke's SUV through the vents at her feet. Christmas music played on the radio—"Jingle Bells." The lyrics about dashing through the snow seemed especially suitable right now.

"I *so* wish we were coming here under other circumstances." Mariella peered out the window at the winter wonderland around them.

As Andi followed Mariella's gaze and observed the snow covering every visible surface around them, she couldn't help but agree.

Though Andi normally boasted about enjoying tropical vacations, she might make an exception for this place. At least, she might if she weren't here to hunt a killer.

But Andi and her team had come to the Borealis Reindeer Camp for work, and they couldn't lose sight of that. Someone's life depended on it.

A moment later, they spotted the sign for the camp.

The sprawling, five-hundred-acre resort was in the subarctic boreal forest. It had started as a reindeer farm and had grown into a family vacation destination.

The camp had twelve cabins, a large lodge with ten rooms, and a dining hall. Twenty-two people were employed here, and more than ten thousand guests came through each year.

Some of the cabins had glass ceiling tiles so visitors could see the northern lights over the White Mountains. In the winter, they offered snowmobile rides, campfires, and ice fishing. In the summer, they took guests on UTV rides to the Arctic Circle, hikes, river rafting trips, and panned for gold.

Andi had researched it before coming.

The camp seemed like such a lovely place for such a horrible thing to have happened.

Andi's throat clenched at the thought of it.

This was where the December Dismemberer had claimed his last victims.

For the past six years, the killer had struck on the same date in various locations around Fairbanks. He slit his victims' throats and then built a snowman . . . leaving various body parts on the snowman as his calling card.

There was no rhyme or reason to his chosen victims. They shared nothing in common.

That made the man even more terrifying. And people in the Fairbanks area hadn't forgotten. Andi had heard customers whispering about the upcoming date in the grocery store. She'd read news articles in the local paper. She'd seen social media posts where people proclaimed they were leaving town on the date, just to be safe.

Residents of Fairbanks shouldn't have to live in terror.

But maybe that was what this guy wanted.

December 6 was quickly approaching.

Andi and her team had only four days to stop this guy before he continued his murderous spree this year.

Juniper Burrows, the daughter of the most recent victims, had personally reached out to them—to Simmy, specifically—to ask for their help. She wanted closure.

She'd actually approached them much earlier, but they had too many other cases they had been tied up with. Unfortunately, they were now down to the wire.

Two and a half months had passed since the team had brought oil tycoon Victor Goodman down.

Since then, Ranger and Simmy had gotten married and moved into a nice home in Fairbanks with Ranger's daughter, Anastasia. They would live there during the school year but utilize another cabin Simmy's father had left her in the summer. The three of them seemed so happy together. They had a live-in nanny, Karen, who helped take care of Anastasia when they were on trips like this.

Mariella was mostly living in Anchorage, partially so she could be closer to her boyfriend, Jason Somersby, who lived farther south in Salmon-by-the-Sea.

Matthew had moved to Anchorage with his sister. The two of them managed the day-to-day operations and production schedule for their true crime podcast, *The Round Table*.

Then there were Andi and Duke.

Andi glanced at Duke's strong profile as they slowed near the entrance of the camp.

Duke with his wavy, dark hair and barely there beard and mustache. The former Army CID investigator had given up his Alaska tour agency in order to go full time with the podcast.

But really, the only reason he'd started the business was so he could find his fiancée, Celeste. He'd accomplished that, and now he'd moved on.

Not just career-wise either.

He and Andi had officially been dating for more than two months.

She'd never been happier.

Duke stopped in front of a large log cabin, and Ranger and Simmy pulled up behind them. They'd driven separately so they'd have two vehicles on hand, just in case. Plus, the newlyweds probably wanted some alone time.

Andi glanced at the camp in front of her.

Black light poles lined the road, each draped in evergreen. In the dim light of the midafternoon winter day, colorful Christmas lights twinkled on several buildings in the distance, including a large one at the center.

That must be the lodge.

On the other side of the property, dipping low on a hill, she spotted a fence with several reindeer behind it.

This was the perfect Christmas village, wasn't it?

Car doors slammed before they all began trudging through the snow toward the owner's private cabin.

A young woman stood on the porch. Andi recognized the nineteen-year-old as Juniper Burrows. She'd looked up her picture before coming. A middle-aged man stood beside her. Based on their body language, they were in the middle of a heated exchange. The woman's hands flew in the air, and the man crossed his arms as he shook his head.

He looked at their vehicles, scowled, and then stomped down the steps away from them.

Interesting.

Andi turned back to Juniper and observed the woman a moment. She wore an oversized white jacket with a red-and-white knit cap that reminded Andi of a candy cane. The tall, slender woman had fair skin and curly blonde hair that came past her chin. Snowflakes had landed on her long eyelashes as she stood there staring at them.

Andi climbed the porch steps. "You must be Juniper."

Behind her, Matthew filmed their meeting. They liked to add video clips of their interviews to supplement their podcasts. The feature had been a real hit with their fans, who often went online to find more information about the cases they talked about. They'd already asked Juniper if it was okay to record everything, and she'd given her permission.

The rest of the team stood on the ground behind Andi, somberness on their faces as they prepared themselves to dive into this latest case. All talks of Slasher the Reindeer were forgotten.

Andi held out her hand. "It's nice to meet you."

Juniper shook Andi's hand and then glanced at the rest of the team. "It's a real thrill—and honor—to meet you all. I'm a big fan. Of course, I wish the circumstances were different."

Andi cast her a tight smile. "We do too."

"You're Andi—the brains of this podcast."

Her eyebrows shot up. "What was that?"

Juniper shrugged. "You're the brains. Duke is the instinct. Mariella the face, Simmy the heart, Ranger the muscle, and Matthew the logic."

Andi rocked her head back and forth as she thought through the assessment. The woman wasn't wrong. In fact, she'd pretty much hit the nail on the head.

"That's the first time we've been described like that," Andi said.

Juniper shrugged again. "I analyze things too much sometimes. It's one of the hazards of living so far away from civilization and having limited contact with the outside world."

"Thank you for having us here and letting us record everything," Andi continued. "I know this interview won't be easy for you."

"People thought I was crazy when I decided to keep this place open after . . ." Her voice trailed, and she swallowed hard. "Anyway, I know that's what my parents would have wanted. I just have one rule: no snowmen."

"Makes sense to me." Andi stomped some of the snow off her boots.

"Anyway . . ." Juniper drew in a deep breath as if mentally shifting gears. "It's cold out here. Eleven degrees last time I checked. How about if I get you guys inside? I just made some peppermint hot chocolate. Really, I'm not trying to be a cliché. But Christmas is kind of what we do around here."

"That sounds amazing," Andi murmured.

"My friend Pepper—I call her Peppermint—has started a whole business based on the flavor," Juniper continued. "She makes candy, hot chocolate, candles, etc. She even crocheted this hat I'm wearing."

"She sounds fun." Andi instantly envisioned what the woman was probably like—eccentric but driven.

They walked inside the cabin, shedding their shoes and coats at the door. A husky greeted them, and they all rubbed his head.

The place smelled like evergreen and cinnamon. A tall tree with sparkling lights stood next to a large window, reminding Andi just how close Christmas was.

She really needed to do some shopping. With everything going on and all her recent therapy appointments, she hadn't had the chance. She wasn't exactly in the holiday spirit, despite all the answered prayers in her life.

Everyone gathered around a large stone fireplace, finding seats on the forest green couches and tawny brown chairs. Juniper served them hot chocolate, which had been kept warm on the stove, along with a tray of sugar cookies.

"I like your necklace," Matthew murmured. "It's an Evenstar pendant, isn't it?"

Juniper touched the chain at her neck. "Oh, this? Thanks. I'm a closet *Lord of the Rings* fan. My parents always said I liked to read too much. I always responded by asking if it was even possible to read too much? Not in my book."

"Beautiful place." Duke's gaze swept the cabin.

"Thank you." Juniper glanced around also before smiling sadly. "My parents built this themselves. They even gathered all the rocks used on the fireplace from a nearby river."

"It looks like quite the operation you have going on." Mariella picked up a cookie shaped like a star.

Andi noted there were no snowmen sugar cookies. Only Christmas trees, wreaths, bells, and stockings.

"I read the reviews," Mariella continued. "People love it here."

"I'm glad. I've been doing some stuff on Instagram, and the posts have become super popular. People are finally seeing what I've found special here for so many years."

"Sounds like you're in a good place, despite everything that happened." Simmy held her mug closer, letting the steam hit her face. "When we do something we love, it doesn't feel like work at all, does it?"

Juniper practically beamed as she glanced at Simmy. "My mom used to say that too. She also used to insist on having cookies and hot chocolate for every guest who came into the lodge to check in for their stay. I've tried to carry on that tradition."

Juniper paused, and her smile faded as she let out a long breath—as if she dreaded what she knew was coming.

Reliving what was undoubtedly the hardest, most horrible day of her life.

Andi licked her lips, trying to be sensitive and choose her words carefully. "Do you want us to jump in with questions? Because we can wait if we need to."

Juniper shook her head, her expression suddenly tight. "No, we don't have any time to waste. This guy is going to strike again in four days unless we find some answers. We can't let that happen. I don't want another family to go through what I have. What happened last year haunts me every single day."

"I can only imagine." Andi glanced at the rest of her team. "If y'all are okay with it, then we can set up and get started."

"That would be fantastic." Juniper rubbed her hands on her jeans, showing her first sign of nerves. As if sensing Juniper's anxiety, Tundra sat beside her near the fire.

Andi stared at the questions she'd written on a piece of paper. She held it in her hands as she waited for Matthew to finish setting up the sound and cameras.

A few minutes later, he gave her a thumbs-up.

It was showtime.

Juniper licked her lips as she prepared to begin.

But before the first question left her lips, Juniper's radio crackled. "Juniper . . . I need . . . your help. Now!"

———

Duke heard the urgency in the man's voice and rose.

"Emmett?" Juniper put the radio near her lips. "Where are you?"

"The reindeer . . . pen. Come . . . now."

Juniper raced to the door, Duke on her heels.

They quickly threw on their shoes and coats before flooding outside. The whole gang hurried across the icy snow, down the road, and paused beside a UTV parked near a fence.

Duke's eyes widened when he saw a man lying in the snow, spilled containers of hay beside him as he writhed with pain.

Juniper rushed toward the man, who was probably in his early sixties with a salt-and-pepper beard and large belly. "Emmett . . . what happened?"

"Don't worry . . . about me." His expression tightened.

"Of course, I'm worried about you." Juniper fell onto her knees in the snow beside him. "Are you hurt? What happened? It's slippery out here."

He shook his head, though clearly in pain. "It's . . . not me. It's . . . her."

Emmett pointed inside the reindeer pen.

Duke walked toward the wooden fence and peered over it.

His eyes widened at what he saw.

A young woman lay frozen in place, partially

covered by drifting snow. Based on the blue tinge of her skin, she was dead.

Juniper climbed to her feet and ran to the fence.

She glanced down.

A soft cry escaped, and then she screamed, "No! Peppermint!"

CHAPTER 3

ndi resisted the urge to run toward the woman, to check her pulse.

The woman was clearly dead. Her face was blue and covered with snow. Her body lay unmoving.

Peppermint . . . the friend Juniper had mentioned earlier.

What had happened?

Juniper climbed the fence, landed in the snow, and fell on the ground beside the woman. Tears tried to roll down her cheeks but froze before escaping her eyelids. "No . . . not Peppermint. No!"

Andi grabbed her phone to call 911. The police needed to come ASAP.

As Juniper sobbed beside her friend, one of the reindeer walked over and nudged her.

Juniper sniffled as she glanced up at the creature.

"Oh, Starla. Why do bad things keep happening? This is my fault, isn't it?"

The reindeer rubbed her nose against Juniper's face.

Andi stared at the woman buried in the snow. She looked young—Juniper's age—with pale skin and long, dark hair. Her cheeks and nose were frosty, but she almost looked peaceful despite that—in a sickeningly serene sense.

"When was the last time you spoke to your friend?" Andi asked Juniper softly.

"She called me at eight this morning. She said she was going to stop by and talk to me about something. I couldn't figure out why she wasn't here yet—" Her voice cracked, ending with another sob.

As Juniper dug her hands into the snow, Andi realized she could be ruining evidence.

Duke seemed to pick up on that also. Instead of jumping the fence like Juniper had, he walked around to the gate, went inside the pen and gently tugged Juniper away from her friend. As he did, Simmy crept closer to the fence and placed her hand on Juniper's shoulder.

"What could have happened?" Juniper whispered, her voice hoarse with emotion.

Andi observed Pepper. The woman had probably only been dead a few hours if her calculations were correct. She saw no blood or bruises—no signs of how the woman had died.

Someone had clearly left her like this. People didn't

just die in a pasture, perfectly laid out in the snow with their arms folded across their chest.

"We'll get to the bottom of this," Andi murmured.

Juniper sniffled again. "And why would she be here with the reindeer? She usually comes to my place. She's my—was my—best friend."

As another round of sobs began, Simmy entered the pen, moved closer to Juniper, and wrapped an arm around her.

Then something caught Andi's eye. She knew she shouldn't touch the body.

But . . . was that a paper in her hands? The white slip blended in with the snow and Pepper's white jacket and gloves.

She glanced at Duke and saw he had gone back to check on Emmett. Upon finding Pepper, the man had temporarily been forgotten.

With Duke occupied, Andi was on her own.

After a moment of contemplation, she stepped through the gate and leaned closer to Pepper's body. She used her sleeve to brush away some snow.

Yes, it was definitely a paper in Pepper's gloved hand.

Andi didn't want to mess up any evidence, but she knew how to be careful.

She picked it up and turned it over.

The words on the other side made her blood go cold.

I told you this would happen.

What in the world did that mean?

This wasn't the start Andi had envisioned for this investigation.

Not even close.

————

Duke saw Andi's expression. Saw the paper in her hands.

He stood from where he'd been kneeling near Emmett. "Andi . . . ?"

She showed him the note, and his breath caught. What did that mean?

Andi turned toward Juniper. "Any idea what this is about? It was in her hand."

Juniper looked at it, and her face went pale. "No, I have no idea. Peppermint was holding that?"

"She was," Andi said.

She practically collapsed into Simmy. "Why is this happening to me?"

As Emmett moaned, Duke turned back to the man, who still lay on the ground. The man had clearly fallen and hurt himself, even if he tried to deny he was in pain.

"Your name is Emmett, right?" Duke started.

He grimaced but nodded. "That's right."

"You're the manager?"

"Been here five years. I was making a run to the reindeer shed when I thought I saw something in the snow. I took a closer look and . . ." He grimaced again. "I wasn't expecting to see Peppermint. Suddenly, I was lightheaded and then . . ."

"Then what?" Duke looked him up and down for any clues. He wore a heavy black snowsuit that made it hard to see much.

"I slipped on the ice and heard a snap. I think I may have broken something."

Duke knelt beside the man. "What hurts?"

"My leg." Emmett reached for his right calf and winced.

Duke gently felt along the man's leg, pausing at a protrusion. "Your fibula is definitely broken. I'm no expert, but it feels like a compound fracture."

"Don't worry about me." Emmett's face pinched with pain. "I'll be okay. It's Juniper I'm worried about. Her parents would want me to watch out for her."

"You won't be okay if you don't seek medical attention," Duke told him. "This isn't going to heal on its own—not properly, at least. A doctor or nurse will need to set the bone and check for tissue damage. Plus, you don't want infection to set in."

Emmett opened his mouth as if about to argue again. Then he closed it and nodded with resignation. "You're right."

"Matthew." Duke looked behind him to where Matthew stood, trying to stay out of the way. "Let's see if we can get him out of the snow and somewhere warm until help arrives. We'll need to be careful with a break like this and secure it first."

"I'll stay with the ladies," Ranger said before quietly adding, "just in case."

Duke knew what that meant. Foul play was involved.

No one should be left alone, not until they knew what had happened to Pepper.

The note made him especially curious.

It took some effort, but Duke and Matthew managed to get Emmett inside Juniper's cabin and onto the couch.

"Before the ambulance gets here . . ." Emmett winced as if each word was agony. "I need to tell you something."

Duke leaned over him as he sprawled on the couch. "Whatever it is, it can wait."

He gripped Duke's arm, his eyes widening with intensity. "You don't understand. I need . . . to tell you . . . something. Something—important. Couldn't say . . . in front of Juniper."

"What's on your mind?"

His face wrinkled with pain. "Someone . . . did this."

"Did what? Broke your leg?"

"No . . ." Emmett pressed his eyes closed. "Killed . . . Pepper."

"Emmett . . ." Duke paused. "Did you see something?"

He shook his head, appearing to give the motion every last ounce of his energy. "No, but . . . maybe."

"What do you mean?" The man wasn't making sense.

"I mean—" Before Emmett finished his statement, his hands jerked forward. He clutched his heart and let out a moan. Sweat spread across his forehead as his eyes widened.

This man was having a heart attack, Duke realized. He checked for a pulse but found none.

Wasting no time, he began CPR.

CHAPTER 4

hankfully, the paramedics arrived on the scene twenty minutes later—fast for the Fairbanks area. Matthew had left the cabin just long enough to tell them what was going on with Emmett.

Andi had been praying for the man since she'd heard. Now the medics could take over and get Emmett the help he needed.

Five minutes after that, an Alaska State Trooper SUV pulled onto the scene.

Andi's old friend Logan Gibson climbed out. The man was tall with a chiseled face and short hair. Tattoos beneath his shirt hinted that he hadn't always been on the straight and narrow, though he never talked about his past.

He'd proven himself to be an ally throughout their investigations, however.

Andi met him halfway, anxious to talk.

"A dead body?" Gibson started. "And you were close by when it was discovered? I guess I shouldn't be surprised."

"I tried not to touch anything, despite the fact I was very curious."

"I appreciate that."

"Except the note I found." She handed it to him. "But I was wearing gloves."

She frowned apologetically.

He read the words there, and his eyes widened. "Interesting."

"I thought so as well."

He slid the paper in an evidence bag and placed the bag in a plastic box he'd brought with him.

Then he paused and glanced at the body in the snow. "Let's take a look."

As Gibson edged closer to the body, Andi stayed with him. Suddenly, the biting cold didn't matter as much, though she'd be happy when she could warm up.

Before Gibson touched anything, he documented the scene by taking pictures. When he was done, he snapped on some latex gloves and began to gently brush the snow from Pepper's face. Fresh flakes had fallen since the initial discovery of her body.

Andi's heart lurched into her throat at the sight of the woman's face.

Someone this young didn't deserve to die. Not that older people did. But Pepper's death was such a shame.

And how heartbreaking for Juniper that she had to go through another loss.

"I don't see any obvious signs of foul play—no blood or bruising." Gibson studied Pepper's face with a compassionate frown. "But the medical examiner will need to do a more thorough investigation."

"Someone her age doesn't just drop dead for no reason. Not to mention she wouldn't have dropped dead in this position, holding a note like that."

"Agreed. Something went on here. I'm going to need to question everyone and see if they saw anything."

Andi nodded toward Juniper, who still stood with Simmy. "Juniper was Pepper's best friend. If anyone knows anything, it's probably her. Her parents owned this place, but they were both killed last year."

Realization rolled across Gibson's features as he rose to full height. "The December Dismemberer."

Her throat tightened. Even the man's nickname was creepy and unnerving. "You didn't work that case by chance, did you?"

"No, but I've definitely heard a lot about him."

"He's who we're here to investigate."

Gibson's eyes narrowed as he nodded slowly, thoughtfully. "I hope you find some answers. Every time I go somewhere in town, I hear people talking about him. They're scared."

"I know. You don't think . . . ?" Andi glanced at Pepper again.

She didn't want to finish the statement. Not in front of Juniper.

"You didn't find a snowman nearby, did you?" Gibson asked.

"I did not. I can honestly say I didn't look either."

"This murder, however, wouldn't fit the December Dismemberer's MO."

"Is it really that out of the question to think a killer might have changed his MO?" It was an honest question. Did killers always follow the same pattern? Or were there circumstances that caused them to mix things up sometimes?

"This would be a lot of changing." Gibson rubbed his jaw as he stared at Pepper, his gaze clouded with thought. "Wrong date. Wrong method of murder. Striking the same place twice. It just doesn't fit if you ask me."

"I agree. But it could still be an idea worth exploring."

Gibson glanced at Pepper again. "Then I guess it's a good thing I have you guys here to help."

———

Emmett was still alive when the paramedics took him away. Duke was thankful for that.

One of the assistant managers at the camp accompanied him.

As soon as the ambulance left, Duke found Andi.

Something was going on with her lately, something she hadn't opened up about.

She'd been more distant, more preoccupied. Some evenings, she disappeared, saying she just needed some time alone.

He was all for giving her the space she needed. He only wished Andi wouldn't lock him out.

She'd been through a lot. They both had. And they needed each other to get through it.

He turned his gaze from her and scanned everyone around them.

Gibson was here and questioning Juniper. Two other police officers were on the scene, helping to manage the situation.

He paused beside her. "Anything I need to know?"

"Gibson doesn't know how Pepper died yet. But the medical examiner is on his way. Maybe he can at least give us an approximate time of death."

"Any details would be helpful."

Duke glanced at the people who'd gathered and spotted the man Juniper had been arguing with when they arrived. The man still looked angry as he stood on the edge of the crowd.

What was up with him? Duke needed to find out, and there was no better time than now.

He excused himself from Andi and strode toward the man. The man was probably in his mid-thirties and lean with dark brown hair, black glasses, and a round face.

As soon as the guy saw him, his scowl deepened, and he shifted.

"I'm Duke," he started. "You mind if I ask you a few questions?"

"You're not officially on this case, so I'm under no obligation to answer."

"No, you're not. But we're here to help, not to hurt." Duke paused. "You mind if I ask who you are?"

"I'm Tim. Tim Burrows."

Facts clicked in Duke's mind. "Calvin's brother?"

Calvin was Juniper's father—and the most recent victim of the December Dismemberer.

"That's me." Tim said.

That could explain the tense discussion Duke had seen between this man and Juniper when the team had first arrived. "How long have you worked here, Tim?"

His jaw stiffened. "Three years."

"Why don't you want us here?" Duke crossed his arms as he cut to the chase.

"Who said I didn't want you here?" Tim's gaze held a challenge as he stared at Duke.

"It's pretty obvious."

He scoffed. "I looked upset earlier because I *was* upset. But not about you. If you really must know, I was upset because I had to kick a guest out today."

The man's explanation could make sense, but Duke wanted more information first. "Why is that?"

"He heard you guys might be coming, and he's obsessed with Calvin's and Mary's murders. It was all I could do not to punch the guy." His face reddened, and he shook his head. "Calvin and Mary were family. They deserve better than to simply be a headline, to be someone's sick fascination."

Duke nodded slowly. "I get that. We don't want to glamorize this, if that's what you're thinking. We want justice."

"I'm afraid more and more people are going to come just because they have a morbid curiosity. Any chance Juniper has of healing will disappear faster than daylight in December."

"And you think the podcast will only make this worse?"

"Absolutely. Look at what happened today."

Duke glanced back to where Pepper had been found. "You think her death is connected?"

"I think Pepper was nothing but trouble. She was always running around camp like she owned the place. Apparently, she lived here secretly for a couple of months before Calvin and Mary were murdered. They wouldn't have wanted her here."

Duke tried not to show his surprise. But he wanted to hear more about Pepper's secret residency sometime.

"Why wouldn't your brother want Pepper here?"

"Because they didn't like her or her parents. But she was Juniper's best friend. She needed a place to live when her parents moved to the Lower 48 so she wouldn't have to go with them."

"And after Calvin and Mary died? What happened then?"

Tim scowled again. "Then Juniper insisted Peppermint should move into the staff housing. She had a whole cabin to herself. I kept telling Juniper she needed to make her leave, but Juniper wouldn't listen. And Juniper has the final say in these things now that she's in charge."

Duke hadn't been expecting that tidbit. "I guess that won't be an issue now."

Tim shrugged, his expression softening but still annoyed. "I guess it won't."

A lot was going on here at this camp, much more than Duke had initially assumed.

CHAPTER 5

wo hours later, Andi and the gang watched as the medical examiner took Pepper's body away.

Juniper stood outside on the porch with them, still grief-stricken.

But as the ME pulled away with Pepper, Juniper turned to them, something changing in her gaze.

Her grief now had flares of anger.

"I want to go on with the interview," she announced.

Simmy stepped closer, her gaze soft with compassion and concern. "Are you sure you don't want some time to process what happened first?"

Juniper nodded a little too adamantly. "I'm positive. I need the person who killed my parents to be found. I need the person who killed Peppermint to be found also."

Andi nodded slowly. "If you're sure . . ."

"I am."

"Okay then," Andi said. "Let's get started."

Andi hoped she could concentrate. Not only was she thinking about Pepper and the note left in the dead woman's hands, but Duke had also told her what Emmett said.

He'd implied that someone had killed Pepper.

Had Emmett seen something? Before he could share whatever that was, he'd had a heart attack. What had he been about to say?

The man knew something.

She prayed he pulled through—for the sake of those who cared about him, but also so they could figure out what happened to Pepper.

At Juniper's direction, they headed back inside the cabin. Gibson and his crew were wrapping up outside and getting ready to leave. The state trooper had already dismissed them and said he'd be in touch.

The gang took their places around the fire. Juniper sat in the front where they could all see her. The woman was still visibly shaken with her pale face and dazed expression.

At least the fire was warm. Ranger had added wood each time it started to die down.

Andi tried to shift back into podcast mode.

The Arctic Circle Murder Club had covered a lot of cases. But this one . . .

What kind of killer cut various body parts off his victims and left thus-said parts on a snowman? What kind of killer struck so close to Christmas? What kind of killer seemingly had no rhyme or reason to his murderous schedule?

The families and friends of these victims needed closure. Andi didn't take on these cases for the glory or because she liked learning more about the horrible things that happened to people. Not at all.

She participated in these true crime podcasts because she craved justice and closure. That was what she tried to give others. That was where her satisfaction came from.

She felt as if it was her God-given calling in life to do this—as well as being an attorney. She'd just gotten back her license to practice law in Texas and had found out last week that she passed the Alaska Bar Exam also.

She did these podcasts for the sake of Robin Carson, the first victim. He'd been a utility worker who lived near Eielson Air Force Base.

For the sake of Kaine Smith, the second victim. He'd worked for the planetarium in Fairbanks and had lived in Moose Creek.

For the sake of Robert Elon, who'd owned a gift shop in North Pole.

For the sake of Brianna Jenson, a nurse who worked the NICU and lived in Badger.

For the sake of Anderson Carswell, a gardener in Chena.

And finally, for the sake of Calvin and Mary Burrows, who'd owned the Borealis Reindeer Camp.

———

Duke leaned closer, watching Juniper as Andi began her interview.

He had the distinct feeling the woman was hiding something. But what?

Andi shifted in her chair and glanced at the paper in front of her. "Can you tell us a little about your parents?"

"They were wonderful people." Juniper clasped her hands together in her lap. "They had a lot of friends. Even when they were homesteading, my parents believed in the importance of community. So they would go back into Fairbanks pretty often, and they were involved with a church as well as the local Caribou Club."

"Caribou Club?" Andi asked.

"It's a community-oriented service club, much like the Moose Lodge or the Rotary Club," Juniper explained.

Duke took a mental note of that. Anyone Calvin and Mary had interacted with could be a suspect, so they would need to check out the couple's connections with the club.

Their podcast team only needed to link one person to all the victims. Then they should figure out who this killer was.

In theory, they could stop him before he struck again. That was Duke's prayer at least.

"My dad was more of the quiet, no-nonsense type, but over the years he learned to be much better in the customer service space," Juniper continued. "Still, his preference was to work behind the scenes."

"What did he do here at the camp?" Duke asked.

"He basically designed and built this place. He was an amazing handyman and good at everything—electricity, plumbing, woodwork, car repair. I never quite trust anyone to fix things like my dad could." Her voice caught. "That's the thing with this place. When it was a family operation, we all pitched in. But now it's just me, and I have trouble doing everything by myself."

"How about Tim?" Duke continued, remembering his earlier conversation with the man. "What's his role here?"

"He's my dad's younger brother, and he's the director of operations here. In other words, he oversees our UTV tours and other excursions. He and my father were never especially close. Truthfully, Uncle Tim got into quite a bit of trouble when he was younger. Nothing violent or anything. But he did some drugs and hung with the wrong crowd. It created some bad blood between them." Juniper paused, and her eyes widened. "If you wouldn't include that last part in the podcast, that would be great."

They agreed, but Duke made a mental note to check out this guy's background.

"How has this place been holding up since your parents died?" Andi continued.

"We've been very blessed with a lot of business. I can't complain in that regard. Of course, I wish my mom and dad were here to see it." Her eyes misted.

Andi leaned forward, her expression turning more serious. "Could you tell us what happened on the day your parents died?"

Juniper's hands began to tremble uncontrollably.

Then she started the next part of her story.

CHAPTER 6
DECEMBER, LAST YEAR

uniper stepped into the winter twilight outside, still curious about the three sets of footprints. Something about the situation felt off.

Tundra barked beside her, urging her to keep moving.

A bad feeling brewed in her gut, and her throat tightened as she walked across the snowy field toward the cold, gray barn. The frigid wind brushed her nose until it tingled. If she wasn't careful, the tip would dry out and start to peel.

"Mom!" Juniper called again, her voice disappearing with the wind.

The shout had been useless but worth a try.

The footprints ended at the barn, just as she'd suspected.

At the door, she hesitated. Something internal told her to stop. To turn around.

To run.

But she couldn't. She had to know where her parents were. If they were okay.

Maybe this was all just a big misunderstanding. Maybe she would open the doors and find her parents working on a special Christmas project. They'd talked about creating Santa's sleigh, something majestic the kids visiting would love.

That was probably it.

Maybe they'd brought one of their workers with them to help with any heavy lifting—which would explain the third set of footprints.

That was the most logical explanation.

Juniper wanted to laugh at herself. She'd most likely gotten worked up for nothing.

Mom had probably just been distracted and forgotten about the cornbread in the oven.

Silly, Juniper.

It wouldn't be the first time her imagination had gotten the best of her. Her parents liked to say she had an active fantasy life. She needed *something* to do out here in the middle of nowhere.

Tundra barked again, as if reminding her to hurry.

Juniper shoved the doors open and stepped out of the icy breeze.

Her eyes took a moment to adjust to the darkness inside.

Blinking, she glanced at the ground and saw the footprints didn't continue. Of course. There wasn't any snow in here. Only a tractor, two UTVs, and some old furniture her father couldn't bear to part with—despite her mother's protests.

Tundra ran inside, his bark turning even more furious.

The tension across her chest pulled tighter.

"Mom?" Her voice sounded weak as fear spread through her. All the earlier reassurances she'd told herself disappeared.

As Tundra ran toward the other side of the building, Juniper squinted at something in the shadows.

Were those . . . were those feet? And legs?

Her heart pounded out of control as she crept closer.

She sucked in a breath.

Her mom and dad were sprawled on the ground toward the back of the barn, behind the UTVs.

Juniper fell to her knees between them.

A scream caught in her throat when she saw their faces. When she knew for sure it was them.

When she saw the blood.

No!

"Can you hear me?" She stared at her mom's face, hoping to see movement or hear a moan.

Something. *Anything.*

But there was nothing.

Juniper knew the truth.

Both of her parents were dead.

Her vision narrowed. She couldn't breathe. Everything began to spin around her.

Was this her fault? Did this happen because of her secret? What if she'd come right away when her mom had asked her instead of dragging her feet?

Sobs shook her shoulders.

Juniper prayed what she'd done hadn't gotten her parents killed.

CHAPTER 7
DECEMBER, PRESENT DAY

Andi's stomach roiled as she listened to Juniper. She couldn't even begin to imagine the horror the woman must have felt after finding her parents dead like that.

She swallowed hard, dreading the question she had to ask next. But she had to be thorough. Skirting around difficult topics wouldn't help them find any answers.

"Juniper, I hate to ask you this." Andi licked her lips. "I really do. But . . . their hair . . ."

Tears glimmered in Juniper's eyes. "It had been cut off at the scalp and placed on a snowman. The memory of that . . . it's probably what haunts me the most."

That was this killer's pattern, hence his nickname as the December Dismemberer. He always cut off part of his victims—their hands, ears, feet, eyes, or hair. He then built a four-foot snowman and added a real body part. It was his calling card of sorts.

Profilers had tried to detail why someone might do that. The thought was gruesome and strange, most likely meant to send a message more than anything else.

Andi shifted as she carefully considered her next words. "I've read the police reports and the newspaper articles, but I'd like to hear this next part from you directly. Is there anyone you think could be guilty?"

Juniper let out a long breath before inhaling deeply. "That's all I've been thinking about for the past year. Who could have done this? I mean, it had to be someone familiar with my parents and where they lived."

"Do you feel as if they were targeted in particular?" Duke asked. "There were guests here at the time. This guy could have chosen anyone. Was it just chance he chose your parents?"

"I thought about that too." Juniper frowned and rubbed Tundra's head as the dog sat faithfully beside her. "I really do believe my parents were targeted."

"Why do you think that?" Andi asked.

She sighed. "I don't know, really. Maybe it's instinct. Maybe it's the fact that this killer came all the way out here, to the middle of nowhere, to execute his crimes. I'm not sure, really."

"This may or may not be relevant." Andi leaned forward. "But did they have any enemies that you know of?"

She knew her question was a longshot. If this crime had been a one and done, then yes, maybe one of Juniper's parents' enemies was responsible. But what were the chances that all seven victims had the same enemy?

It didn't make sense.

However, Andi had a hard time believing these victims were all chosen randomly. Clearly there was *some* type of connection—no matter how random—between the victims.

Andi and her team just had to figure out what.

This location was so secluded . . . it seemed odd to think that a stranger would come all the way out here, commit the crime, and then get away without being caught or seen by anyone.

Especially since there was a lodge and other cabins nearby with staff members and guests.

Why take such a risk?

Juniper slowly released her breath. "I suppose my parents did have a few enemies. The ones who come to mind are the Klinkharts."

"Who are the Klinkharts?" Andi stored that name away.

"Peppermint's parents."

Andi's eyebrows shot up. "I see."

"Her parents used to be best friends with my parents. From the time I was born until about six years ago, we did everything together. Peppermint is . . ." Juniper's voice faded. "Peppermint *was* their daughter."

Her face crumpled with grief.

Andi swallowed the lump in her throat. "We can

take a break. No one will blame you, especially after what happened today."

"No, I want to keep going." Juniper drew in a shaky breath as she composed herself. Then she blew the air from her lungs and started again. "When my parents decided to open this place, the Klinkharts wanted to go in with them. In fact, my dad discovered this property while he was hunting in the area with Heath—Peppermint's dad. There were caribou here, and my dad's imagination started running wild."

"He visualized what this place could become, it sounds like," Andi said.

"Yes, he did. My dad loved Christmas and thought they could bring it to life here."

"So why not go in with the Klinkharts?" Duke crossed his arms as he waited for her answer.

"My parents thought it was a bad idea." Juniper blew out a breath. "From what I understand, it was partially because they didn't believe in mixing business and pleasure. But I also heard my parents talking once about how Heath, the father, didn't make wise money decisions. And Claire, the mother, was a bit of a gossip."

"I can see where they'd want to decline," Andi said.

"When my parents told the Klinkharts they wanted to go solo, the news wasn't received well. I think Heath and Claire thought they'd be shoo-ins. From what I understand, they were having some financial issues and saw this camp as a solution to the problems they'd created. They were really upset."

"What did they do?" Andi asked.

"They cut off their friendship with my parents and started badmouthing them around town. It was ugly. I remember my mom was especially upset about how quickly Claire had turned on her. She'd considered her a sister."

"Are the Klinkharts still in the Fairbanks area?" Andi asked.

"No, they moved down to Seattle a few months before my parents were murdered." She shrugged. "They took their screen-printing business and opened shop down there, saying they could work anywhere."

"You haven't seen them since then?"

"Not really. I did hear they come back to visit sometimes. Someone said they were asking around town about Peppermint. But Peppermint didn't want to talk to them."

"Things were pretty ugly between them, huh?"

"They fought all the time." Juniper shrugged. "I know that might not be much help, but they're really the only ones I know of who had a beef with my parents."

That really wasn't much to go on, especially if they were in Seattle.

Andi had one theory brewing in her mind. This place employed seasonal employees. Many who worked at places like this could be found on a webservice that was targeted at young people who wanted to travel. Ski resorts, lodges, national parks even, utilized this service to find workers.

She only knew that because of a friend of hers while growing up in Texas owned a dude ranch. That was how her family had found the help they needed.

What if each of the victims had some type of interaction with a seasonal worker? One of the victims had actually been a guest here at the camp three years ago.

However, only two victims had traveled to any resorts in recent years.

This whole case felt like a wild goose chase. But Andi liked a good challenge, and that was exactly what she was getting right now.

Just then, Tundra let out a low growl.

———

Duke slowly turned to glance behind him.

What was the dog growling at?

He saw nothing.

"Tundra, it's okay," Juniper murmured.

Though her words sounded reassuring, her skin looked pale again, and her arms shook.

The dog's reaction had scared her, even if she didn't admit it.

"Let me go check things out," Duke said. "Just to be on the safe side."

Ranger joined him, heading toward the bedrooms.

They quickly perused the downstairs of the house but saw no one.

Then Duke glanced outside.

Again, he saw no one.

That was good news, he supposed. But still, the dog's reaction was unnerving.

What did Tundra see that they couldn't?

"I don't see anyone out there," Duke told everyone as he stepped back toward the group.

Juniper let out a breath. "Good to know. See? I told you, Tundra."

Andi seemed to pick up on the fact that Juniper needed a break. "What if we get back to this again later?"

Juniper didn't argue. "Yes, maybe we should do that. I need to show you where you're staying. Then I probably need to manage a few things here at the camp. I've gotten some text messages, and several of our guests and employees are upset. I should handle that."

It was a lot of pressure for a nineteen-year-old. Duke hoped the woman's uncle would help her.

But he didn't envy the position she was in. Not at all.

CHAPTER 8

Juniper gave them directions to the cabin where they'd be staying, as well as the code for the front door.

Duke welcomed the break.

After packing up their equipment, the team headed there with their overnight bags.

This particular cabin was located toward the back of the property. It featured three bedrooms, which worked out perfectly. Ranger and Simmy could stay together. Andi and Mariella would be in the second room. Duke and Matthew would take the third.

Duke and Matthew weren't exactly kindred spirits, but they would make it work.

Duke took a better look at the cabin. The place had already been decorated for Christmas with a large tree in the corner and a garland on the railing. In other circumstances, he might enjoy himself here.

"Why don't we all unpack and then regroup?" Mariella suggested. "Plus, dinner is in thirty minutes. I don't know about you all, but I'm starving."

That sounded like a plan to him.

But it was crazy to think it was already dinnertime. The window of daylight they'd had for the day had now disappeared into the eerie glow of the sunless sky around them.

It didn't matter how long Duke had lived in Alaska, he never got used to the winter in Fairbanks. At the shortest, on the winter equinox, the area had less than four hours of daylight.

But even when the sun sank, its light wasn't totally gone. Instead, it lingered low on the horizon in a civil twilight.

As he deposited his bag in his bedroom, he paused.

A footprint marred the floor—a large one, probably from someone wearing a boot. It was near the window, heading away from the exterior and into the cabin.

Normally, he might not think anything about a footprint. Maybe the cleaning staff had left it.

But this footprint looked fresh.

He surveyed the room but saw nothing of concern. Yet something about the print bothered him.

He kneeled and touched the edge of the shoe mark.

That was when he realized the sediment left behind was still damp.

Someone *had* been in here recently.

Duke supposed it could have been someone in maintenance or housekeeping.

But he'd keep his eyes wide open just in case it wasn't.

In the meantime, he tried to put the footprint out of his mind as he continued looking around.

Matthew set his bags on the floor on the opposite side of the room.

Then he paused. Duke could tell he had something on his mind.

Matthew pushed his plastic framed glasses up higher on his nose as he turned to Duke. "Look, I've been waiting for a good opportunity to talk to you one on one. I wanted to tell you that I'm really sorry about what happened on our last case."

Duke's gut tightened. He knew what Matthew was referring to.

Matthew had dated a girl who turned out to be working for one of their enemies. She'd been sent to get information, and Matthew had trusted her entirely too much—despite numerous warnings from the team.

His decisions had almost gotten the murder club killed. He'd been blinded by love and tricked by a beautiful woman. He wasn't the first man in history to do so. He wouldn't be the last either.

However, ever since then, Matthew hadn't quite been acting like himself. He'd been more aloof and withdrawn.

"You don't have to apologize." Duke paused beside one of the two sets of bunkbeds in the room.

"But I do. I was stupid." Matthew shook his head, his eyes downcast. "I just wanted to find what the rest of you guys have. A partner. I'm the odd man out here. Sometimes the loneliness gets to me."

"A relationship will happen when it's supposed to happen," Duke said. "There's no need to rush things."

He wasn't usually one to counsel other guys on dating. After all, Duke was in his early thirties and had never been married. But he had Andi now. However, based on the walls she'd been putting up lately, things weren't perfect between them either.

Matthew shrugged and backed up until he leaned against the wall. "I know. I'm not in the easiest position to meet people right now, if you know what I mean. I work at home by myself, and when I'm not doing that, I'm traveling with you guys. That's why I decided to give online dating a try. I won't be doing that again."

"You never know when the right woman will show up." Duke stepped closer to drive home his point. "Just hold tight and be patient. You don't need to apologize anymore."

"Thanks for being so understanding." Matthew nodded at the door and sighed. "I guess we should get to dinner."

"Probably."

They headed into the small living room area to meet the rest of the team.

Everyone waited near the fireplace.

Duke's gaze went to Andi as she hovered near the fire.

She was not only beautiful with her white-blonde hair and trim figure, but she was intelligent and spunky as well.

If Duke had his way, he'd never take his eyes off her. She was amazing, and he was so thankful to be with her. It had been a long journey to get to this point, filled with too many ups and downs—and near-death experiences. He hoped most of the danger was finally behind them, though he wasn't naive enough to think that was true.

Andi spotted him, and her gaze lit. "I don't know about y'all, but I'm starving. Investigating murder can really work up an appetite."

"Then by all means, let's go eat." Duke was rather hungry himself.

Maybe some food was just what they needed to clear their minds.

———

The gang stepped outside into the darkness.

Andi and Duke walked side by side through the snow toward the lodge.

Soon, they'd need to dive deeper into their investigation. But for now, they'd eat and get a feel for this place. She hoped they might have a chance to see Pepper's place later and check for any clues there. But right now, the police had cordoned it off and given strict orders for no one to go inside.

She would try to respect that.

"Why would someone leave that note on Pepper?" Mariella asked, looking like a snow princess in her white coat, pink hat, and sparkly earrings.

That was typical Mariella for you. She liked to add a little sparkle wherever she went.

"Was that a message for Pepper?" Mariella continued. "Or for someone else?"

"Excellent question." Ranger tugged his black stocking cap down over his ears as the breeze picked up.

"It said: I told you this would happen." Andi jammed her hands into the pockets of her black down coat. "It almost sounds like someone warned her and wanted to make a statement."

"This investigation could be a lot more interesting than I anticipated," Duke murmured. "It's certainly started with a bang."

"You think the person who killed Pepper is still here at the camp?" Simmy asked.

"It's worth considering," Ranger told her.

"I just feel so badly for Juniper," Simmy said quietly. "She's carrying so many burdens for someone her age."

Andi knew Simmy had been through a lot of loss also. If anyone could understand, it was Simmy. Her compassion made her a valuable part of this team.

"Should we ask Juniper about it?" Matthew asked.

"I'd think she would volunteer that information if she knew more," Simmy said.

"Unless she's hiding something." Duke slid the words into the conversation.

Andi glanced at him. "You think she's hiding something?"

He shrugged. "I do."

"But she asked us to come here," Simmy reminded them. "Why would she ask us to come if she's not going to share everything?"

"Because everyone has secrets," Mariella murmured. "Everyone."

No one denied her words.

Instead, Andi glanced around at the festive light poles, at the colorful Christmas lights.

Life continued on after loss and tragedy.

But that didn't mean things returned to normal. It was a lesson Andi was learning for herself also.

CHAPTER 9

he gang continued trekking through the snow, following the vintage-looking light poles that lit their path.

Andi shivered as she walked. The place appeared so peaceful . . . but it wasn't.

Horrible things had happened here. A killer—or two—was still out there.

It would be hard to relax knowing that.

She knew the truth. If Andi and her team failed, someone else might die. Her throat tightened at the thought.

They did have one ace up their sleeve, however. On the last episode of *The Round Table*, they'd hinted that they'd be looking into this case. Andi hoped that might be enough to draw this guy out—to either make him nervous or make him arrogant enough to slip up.

However, what if that had backfired? What if

Pepper's death had something to do with the fact they were coming to investigate?

They reached the lodge and stepped inside. Twenty or so people were seated at small, round tables in the dining area to their left. Many of them spoke quietly, whispering nervously to each other—probably about the rumors of the body found here.

Andi had no doubt some people would try to leave earlier than planned. Christmas and death didn't mix, nor did vacation and murder. She wasn't sure what Juniper had said to her guests to reassure them or to explain things. Publicity-wise, this had to be a complete nightmare.

The scent of something savory—probably some type of beef—teased at Andi's senses and made her stomach rumble.

The place was nice, not like the basic dining hall at the summer camp she'd grown up attending. Andi wasn't sure why she'd pictured this place being like that. Probably because the rustic resort called itself a camp.

But this dining hall had a pitched ceiling lined with rich-looking beams. The tables each had burgundy tablecloths covering them and small, decorated Christmas trees as centerpieces. Huge windows lined the north side, where the aurora might be spotted on dark nights.

Juniper met them near the door, Tundra beside her.

Her eyes still looked glazed with tears, but she held herself together.

"Good news," she started, her voice lackluster. "It looks like Emmett will be okay. I mean, he's still critical right now, but the doctor thinks he'll make it, that we got help to him in time." She glanced to Duke. "Part of that is because you did CPR, so thank you."

"I'm glad I could help," Duke said.

She released a breath, and then tensed as if her lungs froze again. "I'm sure you're hungry. We have a buffet tonight with beef tips, mashed potatoes, and green beans. We also have some freshly baked rolls and an assortment of drinks."

"Sounds delicious." Simmy tilted her head in that sweet manner she was known for. "Thank you so much for your hospitality. But if you want to take some time for yourself, I'm sure everyone would understand . . ."

"I'll do better if I can keep myself busy."

Andi understood that.

The murder club gathered at a table in the corner. As they all took their seats, Andi glanced at everyone in the room.

Most of these people were guests, but a few people appeared to work here—she could tell by the jackets and long-sleeved shirts they wore boasting the camp's name.

How many of today's staff were here last year as well? Who was here when the murders had occurred?

They would need to talk to those people.

They needed to figure out what connected the victims. It was the only way they'd find any leads.

As of right now, they didn't have anything.

The FBI had released only a few clues about who the murderer might be and even those were iffy. They believed he was a male in his twenties. They thought he might have driven an old green Toyota Corolla to one of the crime scenes. He dressed in blue-collar work pants, boots, and a thick jacket.

According to some reports they'd read, cops had narrowed their suspects down to a man named Jesse Burbach. The man *did* have a connection with two victims. But on the night of one of the murders, he had a solid alibi. For that reason, the police had taken him off their suspect list.

That left investigators with nothing and no one.

Their drinks were served, and they were told to help themselves to the buffet.

The rest of the team headed that way, but Andi and Duke didn't get up right away. Instead, she glanced across the room again.

Was the killer here? An eerie feeling washed over her.

She swallowed hard, not liking that thought.

Andi's gaze stopped at a fortysomething woman sitting at a nearby table. Her food was untouched as she stared at something in the distance.

Andi followed her gaze. The woman was staring at Juniper as she talked to a tall, blond man wearing an official camp jacket. The two met in the corner and, based on how close they stood, there was more between them than a professional relationship.

The man touched Juniper's shoulder as if trying to offer comfort.

"Are you thinking what I'm thinking?" Duke whispered in Andi's ear.

"I'm thinking the two of them are together."

Whoever that guy was, Andi wanted to talk to him.

As she continued watching, the man suddenly took a step back. He shook his head as if Juniper had said something he didn't agree with. Then he scanned the room before his gaze stopped at their table.

Andi watched as his nostrils flared.

He clearly looked upset about something, maybe even something pertaining to the team.

What could that man have against the murder club? Did he not approve of them coming? Was that what his reaction was about?

Andi didn't know. But he was someone she'd keep her eye on.

———

Duke had thoroughly enjoyed his food. But despite the late hour, the team still had work to do.

Before leaving the dining hall, they divided up the tasks they needed to accomplish. Mariella and Matthew would go back to the cabin and work on some admin duties, as well as adding more info to their murder board. The visual helped them to keep their thoughts organized, plus they'd begun to feature graphics of it in their episodes.

Ranger and Simmy would check out the barn behind Juniper's cabin. They had a couple of things to wrap up before they walked over. The team didn't expect to find anything new, but it would be good to see the place where the last crime had occurred. They would also take some pictures so the rest of the team could see the spot where Calvin's and Mary's bodies had been found.

Duke and Andi would check the Burrows' office for anything that may have been missed during the police investigation. He didn't have high hopes there would be any clues there, but they needed to be thorough.

Juniper drove them to her place now. Apparently, she'd moved the contents of her parents' office into the family home after her mom and dad had died. Then she'd set up a new office space for herself in the lodge.

Juniper escorted them to her parents' bedroom and unlocked the door. That reminiscent look flooded her gaze again as she observed the space. Duke had a feeling she didn't like to come into this room very often. Today had already been an emotional day for her.

He peered inside. The master bedroom was located on the first level of the house. A rustic-looking bed sat in the center of the space, a red-and-green quilt covering it. There was also a matching dresser and chest of drawers.

The contents of their old office had been moved into

what had most likely once been an empty corner. A couple of old, mismatched filing cabinets stood there, and a metal desk with several knicks on the side had been shoved against the wall. A fake leather chair had been shoved beneath the desk, with a piece of duct tape on the corner of the peeling green cushion.

Several pictures filled the wall above the filing cabinets, mostly photos of Juniper when she was younger.

They looked like a happy family.

Still gripping the door handle, Juniper turned toward them. "Go through whatever you need to look at. I don't care what you find. I want to know who did this to them, even if it stirs up more questions."

"Thanks for giving us access," Duke said.

"I hope you find some answers." She turned to leave.

Before Juniper walked away, Andi called her name, and she paused.

"One question." Andi openly studied Juniper's face. "Who was the man you were speaking with in the dining hall?"

Duke was also curious about the man and his strange reaction.

"You mean Caleb?" Surprise flooded Juniper's eyes. "He works here."

"What does he do?" Andi settled against the door jamb as she waited for Juniper's response.

"He's in charge of our UTV excursions and manages that team for me. He officially works under Uncle Tim."

"How long has he worked here?" Duke lingered in the doorway also.

"He started as a seasonal employee about a year and a half ago, but then asked if he could be brought on full time. I said yes, of course. Caleb's very helpful." Juniper paused. "Any reason why you're asking about him?"

"We'd love a list of employees who worked here last December so we can talk to them," Andi said. "And also a list of the guests here at the time of the murder."

"I can do that for you. Like I said, whatever you need, I'll be happy to provide if it's at all possible."

"Perfect." He nodded to the office. "We'll get busy then."

"Good luck." Juniper glanced back one more time and frowned. "I'll be back in a while to check on you in case you need anything."

After Juniper left, Duke and Andi stared at the filing cabinets in front of them, ready to dive in. Duke felt as if they were about to go spear fishing, but they had no idea if they were even swimming in the right pond.

They were about to find out.

They each decided to take a filing cabinet to search. It was the best place to start.

They both grabbed a handful of folders and sat on the bed to scour through them.

Only fifteen minutes into their search, a crash sounded close by.

Duke looked up to see a bookcase in the hallway

cascade to the floor in front of the door and a masked figure dart away.

CHAPTER 10

ran through the woods, desperate to get away.

They weren't supposed to be there.

I'd gone into the cabin only to do one thing, and they'd almost ruined that.

Thankfully, I'd gotten what I came for.

But they were going to regret sticking their noses into this.

I would make sure of that.

I jumped onto a snow machine I had stashed out of sight. They'd never catch me now.

I didn't like to play games. Games were for amateurs. Games were for people who didn't want to be taken seriously. And I most certainly wanted to be taken seriously.

No games for me. Instead, I gave warnings.

I tried not to follow anything being reported on the news about me. There was no need.

I'd been listening to some of my favorite true crime podcasts while I showered every morning. They were my guilty pleasure.

I'd stumbled upon *The Round Table* podcast not long ago. I was particularly interested in it because the investigators took on cases from Alaska.

A surprising amount of crime happened in this state, which was actually the third least populated of all the states, despite its vast amount of land.

Then I'd heard a preview of one of their upcoming cases.

It would focus on the December Dismemberer.

Why in the world had the media chosen such a stupid moniker for me? How would anyone ever take me seriously with a name like that?

They had no idea the depth of my anger. Reports made me sound as if I were a villain on *Scooby-Doo* or something. Those characters were cardboard cutouts! Pathetic! I was the real deal, someone to be feared.

I would not be mocked.

Hatred for the media made my blood boil.

In reality, there were very few people I didn't hate. However, I couldn't let that show. Most people thought of me as being rather affable, and I wanted to keep it that way. Facades were essential in my line of work.

My line of work being a serial killer—something most people couldn't say.

I smiled at the thought. I'd never set out to do this.

But I didn't realize murder could bring me so much satisfaction.

Until I tried it.

Soon, I'd strike again.

I pulled off the trail, ready for a break. I was safe and secure here. They'd never catch me. I was so much smarter than they were.

Then I reached into my pocket and pulled out a picture.

The picture of my next victim.

Yes, I'd already picked out the perfect one.

My blood raced. I could hardly wait.

However, what if these podcasters messed things up? I couldn't let that happen. I needed to deter them.

If anyone could find answers, it would be these guys. These amateurs had been on a streak of good luck, and that bothered me. I needed to end the streak. I'd remained hidden in plain sight all these years. I needed to stay that way.

I couldn't let these pitiful hobbyists ruin my plan.

But now I wondered if I should change course. Too many unexpected things had happened, making my plans riskier.

No, I decided. I wouldn't do that. I'd stick to my original plan—with some modifications.

I'd simply add a new plan on top of the old one. A plan to stop them from whatever they were thinking about doing.

These silly podcasters had no idea what they'd

unleashed when they'd announced their next investigation. I didn't like it when people cramped my style.

But I'd figure this out. One way or another, I would stop them.

Those *Round Table* fools were going to regret the day they ever murmured the words, "December Dismemberer."

My next victim was practically dead already.

CHAPTER 11

A ndi watched as Duke hurdled himself over the fallen bookcase as he took off after the intruder.

She climbed over much more gingerly, her heart racing.

She reached the hallway in time to see Duke disappear out the front door. But would he be too late to catch this guy?

Who had been inside this place with them?

Based on his actions, someone who was up to no good. Why else try to trap them in the room before running?

The deeper they dug into this case, the less she liked it.

The old Andi would have relished the challenge. The new Andi didn't feel like herself. She didn't feel quite so brave anymore.

Still, what was she doing just standing here? Duke might need her.

The spot on the top of her head began to throb like it did recently whenever she faced any type of stress or danger.

Andi tried to force herself from her spot, but her feet felt as if they'd taken root to the floor.

Duke could need you, she reminded herself.

It took several minutes to work herself up to taking the first step.

The rest came more easily.

She reached the door and propelled herself outside.

But she didn't see Duke anywhere.

There was only a set of footprints through the snow.

Please, Lord, let him be okay. Please.

———

Whoever the intruder was, the man was faster than Duke had anticipated.

Before Duke had even reached the front door, the man was already outside and headed past the barn and toward the woods.

As soon as Duke reached the trees, he paused.

The footprints disappeared.

Where had this guy gone?

The hairs on Duke's neck rose.

What if this guy had stopped and was watching him now?

Duke had so many questions, but there were no answers. Not yet.

Instead, he grabbed his gun and took a hesitant step forward.

People didn't just disappear. There was a reason there were no more footprints.

He just wasn't sure what.

He walked deeper into the woods, determined to catch this guy.

But there was no sign of him.

Whoever had been inside Juniper's cabin clearly knew this area well. It was the only way Duke could explain his quick getaway.

He searched several more minutes but still didn't find the man. Now he wanted to get back to Andi to make sure she was okay.

With a scowl, he started back to the cabin.

Something was going on here. Something he didn't like.

They needed to get to the bottom of this before anyone else got hurt.

CHAPTER 12

ndi set the files she'd been scouring on the bedspread before leaning against the headboard and sighing.

This research hadn't gone as they'd planned.

Thankfully, Duke had come back, and he was okay.

But they had no idea who that man was.

They'd spent the first fifteen minutes simply picking up the bookcase and placing the items back on it.

Then they'd begun to look through the rest of the files.

"Anything?" Duke glanced over at her.

"No. I figured this might not lead anywhere. But what Juniper said was correct. There's nothing suspicious in these files. Everything looks like business as usual."

"That's too bad."

"The only things that grabbed my attention were

these two items I found at the bottom of the drawer." She held up the items. "One is Juniper's birth certificate. Normally, that wouldn't be weird. But it was under a false bottom in this drawer, almost like it was hidden."

"Anything look strange about it?"

"Not really. Then there was this." She held up a partial photo of Juniper's parents. "This was taken around the time this place opened. There's a date in the lower right corner. But, as you can see, someone was torn out of the photo."

"Maybe it was Heath and Claire Klinkhart, their former best friends."

"That's what I was wondering also. But tearing people out of a photo seems immature. And why keep this picture at all?"

Duke looked it over. "Maybe Mary liked the way she looked in it, although she didn't strike me as the vain type—from what I heard about her, at least."

"Maybe. I'm going to hang on to this and the birth certificate, just in case. I'll return them both when this is over, of course. And I'll mention it to Juniper."

Duke set his own stack of files on the bedspread and leaned back also. "At least we can mark this task off our list."

"At least. But my fear is that there's absolutely no connection between these victims."

"There has to be *some type* of connection, even if it's vague. This guy didn't simply pick his victims out of the phone book and go kill them."

Andi shrugged. "He could have. I mean, what do we know? People have done stranger things for stranger reasons. I can't help but think there's some type of method to his madness. We just need to figure out what that is."

Before she could say anything, footsteps sounded in the house, and a shadow moved in the distance.

Duke bristled and rose to his feet.

Was their earlier intruder back again?

And, if so, what had he come to do this time?

Then she saw a familiar face.

Caleb. He didn't appear to know Andi and Duke were there.

Strange that he'd just walked right into Juniper's private residence.

Or maybe it wasn't.

"I know an opening when I see one." She scrambled to her feet and headed toward the living room.

Caleb flinched when Andi stepped out of the office, clearly startled by her presence. He stopped near the stairway and stared.

Where had he been headed? It almost looked as if he was walking to the bedrooms upstairs. But why would he go there?

"Can I help you?" He narrowed his eyes suspiciously.

"We're here investigating the murders that happened at the camp last year."

"I know. I saw you earlier in the dining hall." He

shoved his hands into his pockets and waited for her next move.

"You weren't in here earlier, were you?"

He narrowed his eyes. "No. Why would you even ask?"

"Just curious." Andi studied his face, searching for the truth. "You don't think having us here is a good idea, do you?"

He pressed his lips together as if he didn't want to answer. Finally, he said, "Not really. I told Juniper we should try to put what happened behind us, not stir up bad memories through the podcast."

"And she didn't listen to you." Andi was curious about how deep Juniper and Caleb's relationship went.

They were clearly more than friends. Were they close enough that Caleb helped her make decisions around here? Andi didn't think so. But that was almost how it sounded.

He shrugged. "Juniper tends to be a bit of a Pollyanna. I try to guide her in the right direction."

Whose right direction? Andi didn't ask the question out loud. But why would Caleb think he knew better than Juniper? Than Tim?

"I thought that was what Tim did?" Andi finally asked.

Caleb's gaze darkened. "Tim just wants to take this place over. He's waiting for the moment Juniper cracks so he can move in. I'm trying to make sure this podcast isn't the opening Tim has been looking for."

That was an interesting way of viewing things.

She crossed her arms as their conversation continued. "Why do you think the podcast would be a crack?"

"It will bring more attention to the murders—and the camp. I think we should put that behind us, not dwell on it more. It's bad publicity."

Andi could see his point, although some people would say that any publicity was good publicity. She wasn't sure that was true, however, especially not when it came to vacation destinations.

"Were you working here last year at this time?" Andi continued, determined to get some information from him. She didn't like how squirrely he was acting.

Realization seemed to wash over the man's face. "You mean when Calvin and Mary were murdered?"

"Yes, when they were murdered."

He ran a hand over his face and shook his head again. "You don't think someone working at the camp is behind their murders, do you?"

"It's a theory—something we need to rule out, at least."

He swung his head back and forth in disbelief. "That doesn't fit with this killer's MO. He picks random people. Why would someone here at the camp kill five other people in other locations before finally deciding to kill Mr. and Mrs. Burrows here?"

"That's what we're trying to determine."

His eyes narrowed, and he shook his head again. "Well, you're looking in the wrong direction. No one here did this. It was a stranger. A psycho. Not a friend or coworker. The idea is ludicrous."

"If no one here did it, then no one here should mind us asking questions. And now there's Pepper . . ."

His eyes closed as if her words brought him pain.

Andi frowned at Caleb's reaction. He'd almost been defensive. But now he also appeared sad.

Was that because he was protecting Juniper? Or was he protecting his own secrets?

———

Duke straightened the files, all while listening to the conversation on the other side of the door—just to be safe. But Andi's talk with the man sounded harmless.

As soon as Caleb left, he stepped out of the office and spotted Andi still standing in the living room, looking deep in thought.

Duke stepped closer. "That guy definitely doesn't want us here."

Andi snapped from her thoughts and turned toward him. "No, he doesn't. He doesn't want Juniper to have anything to do with us. I think it's because he's hiding something."

"I don't know what's going on, and right now it's getting late. But first thing in the morning, I want to talk to everyone who was here on the night of the murder."

"I agree," Andi said. "Even though the police conducted interviews, there's still a chance someone saw something and didn't even realize what they saw. I'm not just talking about Calvin's and Mary's murders, but Pepper's also."

Duke nodded slowly. "It's also a possibility that the killer posed here as a guest just so he could strike."

"I think so also," Andi said. "People would notice if a stranger showed up. It's not like the other murders that took place in a community or neighborhood. In the other locations, someone could have come and gone without eyebrows being raised. That's not the case here."

"We need to look into each of those guests. Maybe we'll find something the police missed." Duke stared at the door, where Caleb had just disappeared. "I'm definitely keeping my eye on him."

"I don't know why exactly he raises my suspicions, but he does. He looks like an all-American guy. But I have a feeling there's a lot more to him."

"We could run a background check," Duke suggested.

"Run a background check on who?"

They turned to see Juniper and Tundra standing in the doorway. Juniper stared at them with a look of confusion across her face.

Before either of them could respond, Juniper filled in the blanks. "You're talking about Caleb?"

Duke chose his words carefully. "We'll be looking into everybody who was here when the murders occurred."

Juniper paused in front of them and crossed her arms, almost appearing offended with her tight expression and narrowed eyes. "But the police already did that."

"Of course," Duke said. "But we want to be a second set of eyes, just in case anything was missed."

She rubbed her arms before shaking her head. "Caleb probably told you he doesn't want you to be here."

"He did mention that," Andi said.

"But I'm the one who's calling the shots." Her voice hardened as if she were trying to prove herself. "This is my decision."

Andi tilted her head before softly asking, "You're seeing him, aren't you?"

Juniper's eyes widened. "How did you know?"

"Your body language gave it away," Duke said. "The way you both stood close to each other, almost leaning toward one another. The low tone of your conversation. It shows a familiarity."

Juniper frowned, biting down on her lip. "I try to keep that quiet. I don't particularly want my uncle to know. I mean, he's not stupid. I'm sure he knows something. But Caleb and I have been seeing each other for a while. We're more serious than he thinks."

"Why don't you want Tim to know more?" Duke asked. "You don't think he'd approve?"

Her lips tugged down in a frown. "He and Caleb don't see eye to eye on things."

Duke stored that fact away. "Why not?"

Sadness filled her gaze. "I'm not really sure. I've always assumed it was a personality difference, and neither of them have told me anything otherwise. They've never mentioned any fights or disagreements that led to them disliking each other."

Duke and Andi needed to get to the bottom of this conflict. Maybe that truth would provide them with some of the answers they needed.

For now, they'd get back to the rest of the team and see if the others had discovered anything.

He and Andi bundled in their coats before starting back to their cabin. The brisk wind made the temperature feel at least ten degrees cooler and prevented much conversation. The air was so cold that breathing it made a person's lungs ache.

Finally, they reached the cabin, and Duke opened the door to allow Andi inside. As he did, something tumbled from the storm door.

He glanced down and sucked in a breath.

It was a hand . . . complete with fresh blood on the severed wrist.

CHAPTER 13

ndi stared at the hand as horror washed over her.

No . . . it couldn't be.

Had something happened to the members of her team while she and Duke had been in the office?

Panic raced through her at the thought.

She started to reach for the door so she could rush inside and see for herself.

But Duke squeezed her arm to stop her first. "It's fake."

Andi blinked, unsure if she had heard correctly. "What?"

He pointed at the bloody appendage near the door. "The hand is fake, even though it was designed to look real, all the way down to the blood."

She stared at the hand again, unsure if Duke was

correct. But as she took a closer look, she realized his words were true.

Based on the weight of the appendage when it had fallen from the door to the way it moved upon hitting the ground, the hand was a high-quality replica of a real one.

This wasn't just a cheap foam Halloween prank gone astray. Someone had to have this ready to use when the time was right. Maybe it had been used at a haunted house or something, given its realism.

Why was this the right time? Did someone—maybe the killer—want to scare the murder club away? Did the killer fear being caught? Or maybe this even connected with the message the killer had left in Pepper's hands.

"Whoever did this is sick," she muttered.

Duke's jaw visibly tightened. "Very."

Just then, the door flew open, and Ranger appeared, a questioning look on his face. Andi hadn't even realized he and Simmy were back already after looking at the barn. She was surprised their paths hadn't crossed.

"I thought I heard you guys out here." Ranger squinted. "Were you locked out?"

His gaze followed theirs, and he glanced at the ground. His eyes widened when he saw the hand lying in the snow.

"What the . . . ?"

"It's fake," Duke quickly assured him.

"Someone either has a sick sense of humor or they want to send a message." Ranger's jaw hardened.

The rest of the gang appeared around Ranger, all gawking at the hand.

"That had to be placed on the door after we went inside." Mariella wrinkled her nose with disgust. "It wasn't there when we arrived."

"I didn't hear any unexpected visitors out here," Simmy added.

Andi glanced above her, searching for any security cameras. But at places like this, security cameras could be seen as a breach of privacy. Guests didn't like them.

Just as she suspected, none were within sight.

"We need to tell Juniper about this." Andi shivered, suddenly realizing how cold her face felt, despite her surge of adrenaline. Her nose had gone numb already, and her lungs ached as the cold air filled them.

"Yes, we can see if she has any idea who might have done this," Duke agreed.

"Do you think it was the killer?" Simmy's voice came out just above a whisper. "Do you think he's here still? That he hasn't left the camp?"

"Which killer?" Andi's throat burned as she asked the question. "The Burrows' or Pepper's? Or both?"

Her questions hung in the air.

Andi wanted to say that those things weren't possibilities. But she knew better.

Anything was possible, especially when dealing with a killer with a warped mind.

———

"I don't know who would have done this." Juniper shook her head as she stared at the hand.

She'd come right over when they called. In the meantime, Duke had taken a plastic bag and placed the hand inside in case there was any evidence they needed to preserve.

Then they'd all moved into the living room, where Duke had set the bagged hand on the coffee table. Everyone had gathered around it to stare some more.

"Is there anyone here on staff who'd see this as being a horrible joke?" Duke paced toward the door, on guard.

The person who'd left this could still be close—a thought Duke could hardly stomach.

"I want to say no." Juniper swallowed hard and rubbed her throat as if the action hurt. "I mean, most people working here were pretty freaked out by what happened. Some wouldn't even stay. They just quit on the spot and left because of the horror of it all. The ones who did stay were loyal."

"Are any of your new hires fascinated with the macabre, by chance?" Andi was unable to sit still so she stood, occasionally pacing near the couch.

Juniper thought a moment before shaking her head, a lost and almost dazed look in her eyes. "Not that I know of. I mean, if they are they haven't made it obvious to me."

"Do you do background checks on people before they're hired?" Duke asked.

"I do. I don't hire anyone with a criminal history."

Juniper sighed and brushed a hand through her hair. "This is just sick. I don't know what else to say, and I'm so sorry you guys had to encounter this. What should we do? Call the police?"

"If it makes you feel better, this isn't real blood." Ranger shrugged nonchalantly.

"Are you sure?" Mariella's voice trembled.

"I'm sure. It smells sweet—like corn syrup and food coloring. You want to smell?" Ranger held out the bagged hand toward them.

"No, thanks." Mariella scrunched her nose again. "I'll take your word for it."

"We should let Gibson know," Andi agreed. "At least that way it can be on record if anything comes of this. But I think this is a sick, elaborate joke—nothing more. We can probably wait until morning. It's not an emergency."

Duke knew the truth: None of them were willing to face any other reality.

Because that reality would mean the killer was here at the Borealis Reindeer Camp and was sending them an ominous message.

That wasn't something any of them were prepared to deal with right now.

CHAPTER 14

The rest of the team had slowly trickled to their bedrooms to turn in for the night.

But Andi and Duke remained in the living room. They sat on the couch in front of the fire with a red-and-black-plaid blanket covering their legs.

With the craziness of today it would be nice to have a few minutes to decompress alone.

"I have a bad feeling about this deep dive." Andi stared at the dancing flames, mesmerized by them. "I don't know if it's because of how gruesome the crimes were or what, but there's something about this investigation I don't like."

"The murders were gruesome. The fact we know this guy will be striking again in four days doesn't do much for my peace of mind."

"Same here. This is like searching for a needle in a

haystack. I usually like to be more optimistic, but I guess I'm feeling overwhelmed."

Andi's therapist had talked to her about those kinds of feelings.

She'd been going to therapy after the deep dive they'd done on Celeste, Duke's former fiancée. At one point, Andi had been captured, and a mad scientist-like doctor had been about to do brain surgery on her.

Andi had been tethered to the operating table and, only moments before having her skull cracked open—while she was fully awake—Duke and the gang had saved her.

For the longest time, Andi had thought the event hadn't affected her. She tried to stay busy and not think about the horror of the moment.

But her psyche had different ideas.

One of the effects of Andi's recent trauma was anxiety. She'd never had to deal with it before in her life.

But now she did.

She often woke up in the middle of the night in a panic, covered in a cold sweat with her heart racing.

Through her therapy sessions, Andi had realized she had a lot of issues to work through. The realizations had been humbling and eye-opening, but necessary.

The anxiety that had hit her felt debilitating. Yet she didn't want others to know that or to think she was weak. One of her mentors in law school had always told her that leaders didn't show weakness.

For some reason, she was having trouble letting Duke see the severity of her trauma.

She sucked in a slow breath. Instead of sharing her thoughts, she decided to focus on the case. There would be time to talk about her anxiety issues later. Right now, they had less than four days to get this figured out.

The top of her head began to ache again.

She pressed her eyes closed, trying to quell her panic.

She couldn't have an anxiety attack. Not now.

Please, not now . . .

———

Duke sensed Andi had something on her mind and waited for her to share.

He'd noticed her breathing become more labored, her body become tense.

She said nothing.

After a few minutes, he murmured, "You okay?"

She nodded a little too quickly. "Just tired."

He didn't believe her, but he was trying to give her space. When she was ready, she would talk. But he hated being in the dark.

He only wanted to help her. He'd do anything for her. She knew that, didn't she?

"I just . . . I just want to not talk for a moment," she finally said.

His heart sagged with disappointment, but he accepted her request. "Whatever you need."

As Andi leaned against his chest, Duke planted a kiss on top of her head.

If Duke had his way, he'd propose to Andi now, and they could pick a wedding date in the near future. Andi was the woman he wanted to spend the rest of his life with. He'd known it for a while and, now that he had resolution with Celeste, there shouldn't be anything holding them back.

Except there was.

Whatever was going on with Andi, Duke would wait for her as long as necessary. He hated to see her struggling. However, he hoped she'd come out stronger in the end. Until then, he'd be there for her whenever needed.

He also dealt with some guilt. Andi would have never been in that situation with an extremely misguided doctor if it hadn't been for him. They'd been following those leads because of his desire to gain information about Celeste.

His actions had put Andi in danger—and could have ultimately ended her life. He thought about that fact often.

Several minutes later, Andi stirred and murmured, "I should go to bed."

"You do need your rest."

She glanced up at him, and her gaze softened. Then, the next instant, the walls went up again.

She stood abruptly, her gaze fluttering. "I'll see you in the morning."

Duke wished she could stay in his arms, where he could keep an eye on her—especially until he knew what was going on at the camp—and what was going on in her mind and heart.

CHAPTER 15
DECEMBER, THIS YEAR
THREE DAYS UNTIL THE NEXT MURDER

ndi awoke with a start.

She'd heard something. She was sure of it.

Cold sweat covered her forehead.

What if the killer was here?

Her gaze skittered to the clock beside her. Three-thirty a.m.

She reached for Mariella and shook her. "Mariella? Are you awake?"

Her friend blinked before stirring. "What is it?"

"I heard something."

Mariella sat up and glanced around the dark room, her eyes widening. "What did you hear?"

"I . . . I don't know. Maybe a footstep."

"In the room?" She pulled her blankets closer.

Had the noise come from inside the room? "No . . . not the bedroom. Maybe the living room."

"Matthew probably just got up to get a snack or something."

Andi's heart slowed a minute. Mariella's explanation made sense.

Why had she jumped to worst-case scenarios?

"You're probably right." Andi took a deep breath. "That's all it is."

Mariella turned toward her, studying her face. "Why don't you call Duke? Have him check things out, just to give you peace of mind."

"That's a good idea." Andi knew she wouldn't be able to go back to sleep until she did. She picked up her phone and couldn't deny how badly her hand was trembling.

Before she could dial Duke's number, Christmas music began blaring from the living room.

She froze and glanced at Mariella. Some of the reassurance she'd just seen in her friend's face disappeared.

Everyone in their group knew better than to start blasting Christmas music at this hour.

Movement sounded in the room beside her.

Duke's room.

Then a door opened.

Then nothing.

Except the music.

What was happening out there?

She and Mariella gripped each other's arms as they waited and anticipated.

Just breathe in and out, Andi told herself. In and out.

She couldn't let panic take over. She couldn't let it win.

Because if it did, she would be rendered powerless. Even worse—she'd become a liability.

The top of her head began pounding at the thought. The pounding turned into an ache.

Andi squeezed her eyes shut and began to pray.

———

Duke heard the music and jumped out of bed. Just to be safe, he grabbed his gun.

What was going on out there at this hour?

He hurried to the door and cracked it open, peering out to make sure danger wasn't waiting on the other side.

He saw nothing.

Still, he remained cautious as he edged his way out and glanced around.

The living room appeared empty.

He didn't see anyone—until Ranger opened his bedroom door, also holding his gun.

They nodded at each other, silently agreeing to split up and search the rest of the cabin.

A few minutes later, they determined that the main living areas and bathroom were clear.

Wasting no more time, Duke rushed toward Andi's

room and knocked. The door flew open, and she stood there looking breathless and disheveled. Her eyes were wide with fright.

"Are you okay?" she rushed.

He nodded, hating to see her so worried. "I'm fine. You and Mariella?"

"We're okay. Just shaken."

The whole gang drifted from their room and gathered in the living room. Music still blared, the happy sound a contradiction to the tension stretching across Duke's chest.

"Where is that music coming from?" Duke grumbled as he surveyed the room. He didn't see any obvious source of the music.

Ranger walked to a HomePod and hit the button on top. "From here."

"How did that even get turned on?" Mariella ran a hand through her hair, leaving blonde strands standing on end.

"Good question." Andi wrapped her arms across her chest, and her skin glistened with a layer of perspiration.

Duke tried not to stare. But he wasn't used to seeing her so shaken. She'd been through far worse than this. However, the walls she'd put up prevented him from digging deeper into the inner workings of her mind.

"Those things can be remotely controlled." Matthew paused beside the device and studied it a moment. "That's probably what happened."

"Probably," Duke agreed. "But I don't like the fact it happened tonight. Don't like the fact it happened here."

"A few minutes before the music started, I thought I heard someone walking around out here," Andi said. "Then I wondered if it was just a bad dream."

Duke hurried toward the front door and opened it, searching for telltale footprints in the snow.

There were too many to distinguish, however. Too many people had recently been in and out of the house.

The team couldn't catch a break. Danger and trouble followed them everywhere.

He turned toward Andi as she stood by the Christmas tree staring at something. Based on the tension in her shoulders, something was wrong—something no one else had noticed.

"Andi?" His question almost sounded hesitant.

She pointed to an ornament. "I don't remember seeing this on the tree before."

The gang gathered to look at whatever she'd seen.

Duke's eyes widened when he saw the ornament was a painted wooden snowman.

What was Juniper's one rule? No snowmen here at the camp.

So was this placement just an oversight? Had Juniper been joking when she'd said that?

He didn't think so.

Because even though Duke hadn't fully examined this tree since they'd been here, he didn't remember seeing this ornament either.

What were the chances that some random person had broken into the cabin, left this ornament, and then started the Christmas music?

Considering that the song that had just been playing happened to be "Frosty the Snowman," Duke knew the chances were slim to none.

CHAPTER 16

ndi woke with a start the next morning.

She glanced around, uncertain where she was or what time it might be.

Then she realized she'd fallen asleep in Duke's arms.

No wonder she'd slept so well. Being with him always made her feel safe.

After the events of last night, she hadn't been able to calm down. So the two of them had talked on the couch. She must have drifted to sleep in his embrace.

She settled back against him now, not ready to start the day.

The skies outside were gray, which probably meant it was morning and the sun was hovering on the horizon.

Slowly but surely, Andi was becoming accustomed to the Alaskan way of life. Endless snow, the midnight sun in the summer, and hours of darkness in the winter, seeing the northern lights . . . those things felt like home.

She leaned into Duke. She felt bad that they'd come so far in their relationship and overcome so many obstacles only for her to take a step back. But she knew it was the right thing.

Before she committed to any type of relationship, she needed to make sure things were as right as possible with herself. Not that things would ever be perfect or that she'd ever be without flaws or issues needing to be addressed.

But the trauma she'd gone through needed to be dealt with. The last thing she wanted was to carry that baggage with her into a long-term, committed relationship. She needed to handle the emotional struggles that came with her trauma, so she didn't end up taking those issues out on those around her.

Duke had been so patient with her in the process.

At the thought of him, she turned to study his face. The strong lines. The barely there beard. The slight wave to his dark hair.

He was so handsome. The man of her dreams, really.

His eyes fluttered open as if he sensed her looking at him.

Andi loved that sleepy look in his gaze. She truly hoped that one day they could wake up beside each other for the rest of their lives.

She just needed more time first.

He blinked before raking a hand through his hair and sitting up.

"Hey." His voice sounded hoarse and throaty.

"I guess we fell asleep out here." She glanced around, and her gaze stopped at the dining room table.

Ranger sat there with a cup of coffee in his hand, the man practically a shadow. She hadn't seen him earlier. She hadn't looked.

"Sorry," he muttered nonchalantly. "Didn't want to wake you. But I didn't want to wake Simmy either, so I just tried to make myself a ghost."

Andi stood and stretched. "Don't apologize. We stayed up late talking."

"I understand," Ranger said. "It was a long night."

She shivered when she remembered hearing the music begin blaring. When she remembered finding that snowman ornament.

She rubbed the sleep out of her eyes as she trudged toward the kitchen. "You have enough coffee to share?"

"Of course." Ranger nodded toward the pot behind him. "Help yourself."

As she grabbed two mugs, she prepared herself to get busy. They had a lot of work to do.

She glanced at the table and saw Ranger had papers spread in front of him. As her vision cleared, she noticed it was a list of current camp employees, a list of employees who'd left in the past year, and a list of all the guests here on the day of the murder.

Leave it to Ranger to always do his homework. Juniper must have sent this over either late last night or early this morning.

Duke joined her at the table, and Andi handed him his coffee.

Andi took a seat and glanced at Ranger. "Have you found anything of note on these lists? I assume you've been examining these names already."

"I'm just getting started." Ranger rubbed his beard. He'd trimmed it and kept it neater now that he'd gotten married. He used to have a much gruffer, mountain-man look. "But so far, there *is* one person who stands out."

"Who is that?" Andi took another sip of her coffee, relishing the warm liquid as it washed over her tongue and down her throat.

She waited to hear what Ranger had discovered, hoping it was a lead, something that might guide them to finding answers.

———

"This is Bert Sims." Ranger pushed forward a piece of paper with the picture of a man with a long face and a mop of curly, dark hair. "He was a guest at the camp on the night of Calvin's and Mary's murders. He currently works as a mechanic for the city of Fairbanks."

"Why did he catch your attention?" Duke examined the man's picture. The guy appeared harmless. But his looks didn't necessarily mean anything.

"I did a quick internet search on him and found a

couple of mentions," Ranger said. "He has some anger management issues. I found a couple of charges against him for assault and battery. That's a red flag. But he was also very vocal about how unhappy he was about his stay here at the camp. He ranted about it, posting on several places, like he wanted to ruin the reputation of this place."

"Definitely sus." Andi took another sip of her coffee. "Where is this guy now?"

"From what I can tell, he currently lives in the Ester area near Fairbanks."

"Maybe a couple of us can head out to chat with him today or tomorrow," Duke suggested.

"That's a good idea," Ranger said. "We have a few other things to figure out first—starting with digging into the backgrounds of each of these staff members and guests."

They continued to quietly sip their coffee and review the lists.

Several minutes later, the sound of a vehicle coming toward their cabin filled the air. Andi peered outside and saw Juniper pull up in a UTV. Andi hurried toward the door to let her inside.

Juniper paused in the doorway and raised a basket in her hands. "I have breakfast. I thought you might want to eat here so you can work."

She set the basket on the table and pulled out two glass containers—one with biscuits inside and the other with sausage gravy. The savory scents of the rich gravy floated through the room, making Andi's stomach grumble.

She also brought some fruit and muffins.

"Looks perfect," Andi said. "Thank you."

"You're welcome." Juniper's voice sounded lackluster.

"How are you today?" Andi asked.

"Peppermint's death keeps hitting me. I think I was in shock yesterday, but now it's becoming real." She shrugged. "Anyway, I guess I'm hanging in. In other news . . . did you all find anything?"

"Not yet," Ranger said. "But we're still combing through things."

"Of course. If you need to talk to anyone on staff, let me know, and I'll make it happen."

Andi stepped closer. "Listen, last night . . . something strange happened."

They told her about the music.

"That's eerie." Juniper rubbed her arms as if suddenly chilled.

"Any idea who might have access to the HomePod?" Duke took a sip of his coffee as he waited for her answer.

Her eyebrows shot up. "We don't monitor it. So every guest who uses this place can sign into it and should also sign out. I . . . I really don't know who would have done something like that."

Then Andi carefully picked up the snowman ornament. "Do you remember this?"

Juniper's face went pale. "Where did you get that?"

"It was on the tree last night," Andi explained. "But I don't remember it being there earlier."

"Put it down."

Andi blinked, confused by her response. "What?"

"Put it down. I don't want to see it."

Andi set it on the table, still confused. "You recognize the ornament, don't you?"

"It belonged to my parents. My dad whittled it himself. After they were killed, I put it in the attic. I never wanted to see it again."

Then the truth hit Andi. What if the person who'd broken into Juniper's house yesterday had been in the attic? What if he'd grabbed this ornament?

Was someone playing some kind of twisted game? That was how it seemed.

Shivers raced up and down her spine.

Duke shifted in his seat. "Is there anything you want to tell us, Juniper?"

"Someone is determined to make my life miserable," she blurted. "To take away the people I care about. To ruin any good memories I have of them. There's nothing else to tell."

"Honey . . ." Andi stepped closer, tapping into her inner Simmy.

But Juniper scooted away. "I'm sorry. I don't like to get emotional. I . . . I just don't understand."

"We're trying to get to the bottom of things," Ranger assured her. "That's all."

"I know, and I appreciate that." She took another step back and swallowed hard. "Listen, I have a lot to do, so I'll let you guys eat. But I'll be in touch later."

They barely had a chance to thank her before she hurried from the cabin.

What was with that reaction? Duke wondered. Juniper knew more than she was letting on, didn't she?

Right now, he and Andi needed to talk to Tim. He hoped they might be able to see Pepper's place as well.

The countdown for murder was on, and they had to concentrate on stopping a killer. That was their first priority.

CHAPTER 17

ndi and Duke met with Tim Burrows. He sat across the kitchen table from them inside Juniper's place. Juniper had insisted they'd have the most privacy there.

Juniper wasn't with them. She had some paperwork to do, she'd said, and she'd gone back to her office in the lodge.

Andi studied the man a moment. Fortysomething Tim had a thick blond and gray beard, a nearly balding head, and red cheeks. He was on the heavier side with a rounded belly and hooded eyes.

Before they even started, Tim volunteered, "I appreciate the fact you're here looking for answers about my brother's and his wife's murders. But I'm not sure what exactly you're expecting to find out by being here."

"As you know, if this killer continues to follow his

pattern, another murder is imminent." Duke remained undeterred in the stiff, wooden chair. "We're trying to do whatever we can to prevent that from happening."

"You guys really think you can do something the police haven't?" Tim squinted, not bothering to hide his doubt. "Sounds arrogant to me, like you all have an inflated view of yourselves."

This guy was blunt. Andi wasn't sure if she admired that quality or despised it.

"We're trying to do *something*." Andi let her statement hang for a moment.

"Don't make no sense to me," Tim said. "Juniper wanted to pretend like none of this happened, to stick her head in the sand. Then out of the blue, she suddenly wants to bring all this attention to her parents' murders? Why the change of heart?"

"Maybe she realized with the anniversary of their deaths coming up that this guy was going to strike again," Andi said. "Grief goes through different stages."

"I suppose." He still looked unconvinced, like he had a chip on his shoulder.

Andi locked gazes with the man. "So, are you willing to help us? Or are you ready to let the murders of your brother and sister-in-law go unsolved and the person responsible to remain walking free?"

Her words seemed to make him loosen up a little. "Of *course* I want to help. I mean, if I thought I could help, I would have done something a long time ago. But I don't know anything."

"We've already talked to Juniper," Duke said. "She told us about her parents. But sometimes kids don't know everything about their mom and dad, not like peers might. Do you know if Calvin or Mary had any enemies?"

"They were good people, and their whole lives revolved around this camp. I can't imagine they were targeted because of something they may have done."

"So they had no enemies?" Andi clarified.

"Not really." Tim blew out a breath and leaned back as if thinking about the question more seriously. "Well . . . there *is* one person I can think of. A guy named Edwin Standard. Calvin and Mary knew him from the Caribou Club."

Andi perked up at the possible lead.

"Why was Edwin an enemy?" Duke asked.

"My brother thought something shady was going at the Caribou Club, and he began to distance himself from the organization. When I asked him about it, he said some of the money the club raised was being spent on parties the organization put on for members instead of being given to the intended recipients—people in need."

That sounded shady, Andi mused. "Tell us more."

"I guess there's always a small operating cost taken out from these fundraisers, right?" Tim blew out another breath. "But this money they'd collected was supposed to go to victims of a local wildfire, victims who'd lost everything. Instead, the club had this huge party. Said they'd gotten stuff donated for the event, but Calvin knew that wasn't true."

"What did your brother do?" Duke crossed his arms as he settled back in his seat to listen.

"He called the leaders out on it." Tim shrugged. "That, of course, made them mad. Edwin was the president at the time, and he actually booted Calvin and Mary out of the club."

"Did they leave kicking and screaming?" That was how Andi pictured the couple, especially Mary. She didn't seem like the type to walk away with her head down.

Tim frowned and twisted his neck. "Not even close. That was the surprising thing. For some reason, Calvin and Mary left quietly."

"I wonder why." Andi tapped her lips as she stored that information away. Maybe it didn't amount to anything. But it was worth looking into.

"I wondered that too. It was almost like the club had something on my brother and Mary that forced them to keep their mouths shut."

Duke shifted in his seat. "You know where this Edwin guy is now?"

"Unfortunately, he died about two months ago."

Andi leaned back, suddenly deflated. Tim could have mentioned that earlier.

She hoped he might have something else helpful to offer.

———

"Is there anyone else at the club who was involved in that situation?" Andi asked, still determined to find some answers.

"Not that I know of," Tim said. "I know that's not helpful. But that's all I've got."

"What about Heath and Claire Klinkhart?" Andi crossed and then uncrossed her legs again as she tried to shift her thoughts. "Juniper brought them up earlier. Do you remember anything about them?"

"I know those two had a big falling out with my brother. But I think once they went their separate ways, they were gone for good." Tim shrugged. "At least, that was what I heard. I haven't seen them in years. I know Pepper was estranged from them, though I never asked why. I try to stay away from drama."

Duke shifted before asking his next question. "Did you have any theories about what happened to your brother and his wife?"

Tim didn't miss a beat. He'd clearly thought this one through. "Really, I think this killer is psychotic. For all I know, he throws darts at a map of Fairbanks, and wherever that dart lands is where he'll strike next."

That thought was chilling. Not that Andi hadn't already considered that option herself, although not exactly in those terms.

"What about Emmett?" Duke asked. "Any thoughts about him?"

"Emmett?" His voice rose with surprise. "He does a decent job here. He was visiting his mom in California when the murders occurred, if that's what you're wondering. He's not your guy."

"Good to know." Andi leaned closer, trying to make sure Tim was locked into this conversation. "I hate to ask this, but I have to. Do you resent the fact that Juniper took over this place instead of you? After all, you're older and more experienced."

Tim's expression remained tight. "Those were my brother's wishes, so what can I do? If I had a child, I'd do the same. I do think Juniper is in over her head, and the fact she doesn't like to listen to any of my advice can be infuriating."

"I'm sure it can be frustrating." Duke tapped a finger against the tabletop. "What about you and your brother? Did the two of you get along? Did you have any beefs with him?"

Tim bristled. "What are you implying? That I killed him? Why would I do that?"

"I'm not implying anything." Duke's voice remained calm as he skillfully deescalated the situation. "I'm just looking for answers."

Tim's shoulders loosened ever so slightly. "No, we got along just fine. He was my older brother, and he was always there for me when I needed him. After I got divorced, I didn't know where I'd end up. My wife got our son and the house. I wasn't in a good place mentally, you know? He offered me a job here, and it saved my life. I had no place to go otherwise. So, I guess you could say I owed my life to my brother."

"Good to know," Duke murmured.

"Anything else you want to add?" Andi asked before they wrapped this interview up.

Tim let out a long puff of air. "I've had this one idea that's been nagging me for a while. But I've never bothered to voice it aloud because I know it will sound crazy."

Andi leaned forward, anxious to hear what his theory might be.

But before he could start, someone pounding on the door interrupted them.

———

Duke bristled at the sound of the heavy knocking. Who could be here?

He rose and strode toward the entrance of the cabin, Tim beside him.

When he threw the door open, a man he'd never seen before stood on the other side.

"Can I help you?" Duke asked.

"I'm looking for *The Round Table* podcasters," the man muttered. "I heard they were trying to get in touch with me."

Duke squinted as he tried to place the man. "And you are?"

"Name's Bert," he stated, underlying anger in his

voice.

Tim let out a low growl. "I remember you. You're the guy who tried to get this place closed down."

Bert shrugged as if he couldn't care less. "It's not my fault you guys don't live up to people's expectations."

"There's no need to get upset right now." Andi stepped forward, ever the negotiator. Her gaze turned to Bert. "Why did you come all the way out here?"

"I got a message saying you guys wanted to talk to me and that you were at the lodge investigating this murder. I wanted to know what it was about."

"A phone call would have sufficed," Tim muttered with narrowed eyes.

Duke really wished Juniper's uncle would stay quiet. His reactions only served to stir up more emotions.

"I prefer to have my conversations face-to-face," Bert muttered. "So what did you want to talk about?"

"We're actually in the middle of something right now," Duke said. "But I can get one of my colleagues over here to talk to you."

"Are you going to talk about how this place should be shut down?"

"Why would we talk about that?" Andi kept her voice even and calm.

"Because it *should* be shut down," he stated. "It's nothing but a tourist trap."

"You came here," Tim barked. "You obviously thought this place had appeal."

"My kids begged me to come, and we were all sorely disappointed. Now, I want the world to know to stay away. It's been my mission ever since I was asked to leave." His nostrils flared again. "Nobody *ever* asks me to leave. Nobody."

CHAPTER 18

ndi couldn't believe the nerve of this guy. Did he think the world revolved around him?

Was Bert a killer? She couldn't say for sure. Not every guy with a temper was also a murderer.

But he'd shown up quickly, and he really did seem to hate this camp.

She'd already texted Ranger, asking for his assistance. He was on his way.

"This place set off a whole train of bad events in my life." An undertone of a growl rumbled in Bert's voice. "My wife said she didn't like how I acted. Then she left me. She left *me*! Vacation was supposed to bring us closer."

"I'm sorry to hear that." But Andi could see his wife's side of it also. The guy was a hothead. She could only imagine what it would be like to be married to someone like him.

"I'm a bit of an influencer," Bert continued. "People usually go out of their way to get my stamp of approval on things. But not Calvin and Mary. No, money was the most important thing to them."

Andi had a hard time seeing this guy as having a strong following. He was too gruff and unpolished. Plus, he didn't have a face for the position. It was too uneven and gawky.

She kept those thoughts silent.

"You're saying all this because Calvin and Mary didn't give you a refund?" Duke clarified, a touch of disbelief to his voice.

Bert's eyes narrowed. "I was entitled to one. They didn't live up to their guarantees."

This guy really was too much, and Andi couldn't wait to get him out of here. He only appeared to be slowing down their investigation.

He'd come here to rant. To let everybody know he was unhappy.

She could be wrong, but she didn't get the sense he was a killer.

———

Ranger successfully took Bert off their hands.

Then it was the three of them again—Duke, Andi, and Tim.

Tim had been about to say something before Bert showed up.

They all took their seats in the living room, and Duke reminded them where they'd left the conversation —Tim was about to say something.

"That's right. I think you should look at Caleb Brinley." Tim's jaw and eyes hardened at the mention of Caleb's name.

Duke wasn't surprised. Caleb had already shot to the top of his list of suspects.

But he was interested in hearing Tim's take on it.

"Why do you think we should look at Caleb?" Duke asked.

"My brother didn't like him. In fact, I heard Calvin saying something that indicated to me they were considering firing him."

"Why would they want to fire Caleb?" Andi tilted her head as she waited for his response.

"At first, I thought it was because he was interested in Juniper," Tim said. "My brother was protective of his little girl. Then I overheard Calvin saying something about some missing money."

"Missing money?" Andi's voice lilted with curiosity.

"Yeah, I asked him about it. He said they couldn't definitively pin the loss on Caleb, but he was their number one suspect."

"When did they discover the missing money?" Duke asked. "And where was it missing from?"

"A few days before they died. They had a cash box in their office."

Duke's eyebrows shot up. The timing was definitely incriminating. He couldn't deny that.

"Did your brother confront him?" Duke studied Tim's face, interested in getting his take on the situation. The way his jaw tightened and his cheeks remained red indicated he was still angry.

"No, he didn't. Not as far as I know. I think he wanted more information first, but he hadn't found it before he died."

Andi stared at Tim, appearing ready to start another cross examination. "Did you tell the police all this?"

Tim didn't bother to hide his frown. "No, at the time it didn't seem like a big deal, I suppose. I assumed this killer was someone *not* affiliated with the camp. But since then, I've started to wonder if Calvin and Mary were killed for some other reason and their murders were set up to look as if the December Dismemberer had struck. Maybe that psycho had nothing to do with this at all, and it was just a copycat crime."

Duke knew that could be a possibility. But there were some holes in that theory. "If that's the case, no one else was found dead on that date. So either his streak was broken or—"

"Or the victim wasn't discovered . . . or maybe this guy died." Tim shrugged. "Who knows?"

Duke supposed any of those options could be correct. He didn't think they were, however.

"Does anybody know if Caleb had an alibi during the time of the murders?" Andi asked.

"I looked into that myself." Tim's gaze darkened. "It turns out he was patrolling one of our UTV trails. We do that every day to make sure they're safe."

"Where does this trail run?" Duke asked.

"On the backside of the property. The police didn't find any tire tracks leading to the barn, but that doesn't mean someone didn't park a UTV somewhere, walk through the forest to my brother's cabin, and lure Calvin and Mary to the barn."

Tim had clearly thought everything through.

Duke had to admit the man's theory did have some plausibility. He and Andi would need to talk to Caleb again.

"What about Pepper?" Andi asked. "Any idea what happened to her or who would want to hurt her?"

His expression remained solemn. "Not really. She was kind of annoying and had a strong personality. But I never heard anyone say they didn't like her. I have no idea who would have wanted to kill her."

Just then, a yell sounded in the distance.

They all rose from the table and rushed out the door to see what was happening.

Four or five people scrambled toward UTVs parked near the lodge. They jumped into the seats and sped into the forest.

Something else had happened, Duke realized. Something bad.

Did this event tie in with the case? That was the question.

CHAPTER 19

ndi, Duke, and Tim darted from Juniper's house toward the commotion in the distance.

They paused when they reached Juniper. She and Tundra stood outside the lodge, and Juniper wrung her hands with a worried look on her face.

"Juniper?" Tim started. "What happened?"

She seemed to snap out of her shock as she turned to them. "Caleb was fishing with four of our guests when the ice broke and one of the guests fell through."

"What?" Tim muttered. "I told you that lake wasn't ready for ice fishing yet."

"Caleb said it was." Juniper's conviction died a little with every word.

"Caleb doesn't know what he's talking about!" Tim snapped.

"You guys can argue about that later." Duke stepped

forward as if to referee. "What's the current status of the situation?"

"They pulled the woman out. I already called 911, and an ambulance is on its way. Again," she added feebly.

"Is this common around here?" Andi hated to ask the question, but she had to. "All these accidents?"

Juniper glanced at her uncle, a shadow darkening her gaze.

There was clearly something the two of them knew that they weren't sharing, and Andi wanted to know what it was.

"It's becoming more common." Tim narrowed his gaze at Juniper. "All because of poor decision making. I've told you before, and I'll tell you this again. You're not cut out to manage this camp, Juniper. You don't know a thing about safety."

A surge of protectiveness rose in Andi as she glanced at Juniper and saw the doubt flash through her eyes.

Andi wanted to stand up for the woman. To tell her she could do this.

But she didn't know enough about what had happened at the camp to say that with confidence. Maybe Juniper really *wasn't* cut out to manage this place, not when so many risks were involved.

"The team is headed out there to help bring her back right now," Juniper finally said, her confidence wavering. "We followed all the procedures set in place in case something like this happened."

Tim stared at her with what could only be described as contempt before taking a step back. "I'm going to monitor everything out there myself, something *you* should be doing. As the owner of this place, *you* should have been one of the first people on the scene."

Juniper squeezed the skin between her eyes and lowered her head.

The words had been like a physical blow to her—which was, no doubt, exactly what Tim intended.

Without saying anything else, Tim stormed toward a UTV in the distance and jumped behind the wheel. Andi and Duke stayed with Juniper.

Andi definitely had more questions.

She hoped Juniper would answer them.

———

Duke and Andi escorted Juniper back inside and into her office in the main lodge.

People had begun to stare at Juniper, and Duke wanted to get her out of public view. She was the face of the camp, and if she looked panicked, everyone else would panic.

They had some hard-hitting questions to ask—preferably before Tim got back to demean her anymore and before the ambulance arrived.

Duke figured they probably had fifteen minutes tops.

He leveled his gaze at Juniper. "You need to tell us what's going on."

Andi kept a hand on Juniper's arm as she lowered her into a seat in the corner. Andi then knelt in front of her, probably not wanting to move far away.

Duke got a better look at Juniper under the bright fluorescent lights. Saw her red eyes. Her shaky limbs.

Self-doubt was written across each and every action.

His heart panged with compassion for her. But maybe she was in over her head. Plus, she was dealing with a lot of grief right now, and grief could cloud a person's judgment. She should have stepped back after Pepper's death and let Tim take over for a few days, at least.

"This wasn't supposed to happen." Juniper's voice trembled.

"What do you mean it 'wasn't supposed to happen'?" Andi questioned, her eyes narrowed.

"I know you were here yesterday when Peppermint was found. Now you're here today for this incident. It seems as if things are escalating."

"Have there been more people injured or put in danger recently?" Duke was concerned for everyone here if that was the case.

"I promise you I'm following all the rules. I'm trying to do everything with the utmost safety of the guests in mind. But it seems like Tim is working against me. He wants me to fail. He wants me to think this is my fault.

Maybe it's starting to work." Tears rolled down her cheeks.

"What are you talking about?" Andi cocked her head to the side. "If you want our help, then you need to tell us what's going on."

"I should just sell this place . . ."

"Who would you even sell it to?" Duke asked.

"I have a man—Dudley Something or Other—who keeps calling me and making me offers," she said. "I keep turning him down."

"So what's been going on here, Juniper?" Andi waited for an answer.

Juniper grabbed some tissues from a nearby box and dabbed her eyes. "The truth is dangerous things keep happening here at the camp, and I almost feel as if someone is trying to sabotage us."

Duke didn't like the sound of that. "What else has happened?"

"Really, they're things that seem simple at first glance. But when you add them all together . . ." Juniper swung her head back and forth before blowing out a shaky breath. "We had a small kitchen fire one day after a burner was 'accidentally' left on. One of our families got lost in the woods for five hours after the trail markers somehow got switched. A UTV flipped, and we discovered later that air had been let out of two tires. Thankfully, in each of those cases, everything turned out okay. But they were still scary."

"It sounds like it," Andi murmured.

"Then some of the guests thought they saw people in the woods."

Duke sucked in a breath. "What do you mean?"

"It's probably nothing." Juniper closed her eyes and shook her head. "Just some hunters who didn't realize where our property lines were. But it's unnerved some people and made them feel unsafe. Maybe I should see if this Dudley man is still interested . . ."

Duke ran a hand over his face. The truth was, they could be dealing with multiple mysteries here: The mystery of who killed Pepper. The mystery of who was trying to sabotage this camp. And the mystery of who the December Dismemberer was.

These events may or may not be connected.

But they were all dangerous and posed a serious threat.

CHAPTER 20

Just like yesterday, the rescue squad came.

Andi stood outside the lodge, her coat pulled close, and watched as paramedics loaded the injured guest onto a stretcher and carried her to the ambulance. Caleb walked with them, explaining what had happened.

As they walked by, Andi glanced at the woman and sucked in a breath when she recognized the woman's bluish face.

It was the woman Andi had seen in the dining hall yesterday, the one who'd been watching everyone.

Andi had been curious about her. The woman didn't seem like the typical relaxed vacation guest here to have a good time. Instead, she'd appeared on edge.

Why was that?

A man and a teenage boy, probably family members, trailed behind the stretcher. They had to be worried sick.

How had this even happened? Had someone weakened the ice on purpose? Had this woman discovered something she shouldn't have, and had someone tried to kill her in order to keep a secret?

And the even bigger question: Was that person Caleb? Tim? Or someone else entirely, someone they hadn't even met yet?

Someone here had secrets. Secrets that may have gotten Pepper killed. Secrets that might even relate to the deaths of Calvin and Mary.

There was much more going on here than met the eye, Andi realized. They had to get to the bottom of this, and they had no time to waste.

A mental timer was ticking in her ears as she turned to Juniper. "I want to see that lake."

"What?" Juniper blinked as if surprised. "Why?"

"I need to know if this was truly an accident or not."

"So you think this accident wasn't so much of an accident?" Duke whispered to Andi as they walked toward the lake, Tim leading them.

He'd had the same thought, so it wasn't really a surprise.

"Someone wants to ruin this camp's reputation. Or ruin Juniper. I'm not sure which one."

Duke remembered their earlier confrontation with Bert. He'd been here at the property when this accident had occurred. But Duke didn't think the man could be guilty.

No, the one who appeared responsible for this was the woman who'd been injured. After all, she'd insisted on ice fishing.

That was Caleb's story at least. Otherwise, planning for something like this would have been difficult. It would have had to be someone who knew the schedule and how the camp usually operated.

Tim was muttering beneath his breath as he tromped through the woods toward the lake. Duke couldn't understand what he was saying, but he didn't pay much attention either. He figured the guy was most likely just blowing off steam, and Duke couldn't blame him for that.

"My brother and his wife wanted a whole houseful of children, you know?" Tim called over his shoulder. "They had trouble conceiving but were finally able to have Juniper. They doted all over that girl."

"I'm sure they did," Andi said.

"They wouldn't want all this for her. It's a lot of responsibility for someone her age. People think I'm just on a power trip or something. But I'm not. I've screwed up and made my fair share of mistakes. But at least I have some experience with management."

"It is a lot of responsibly for a nineteen-year-old," Andi agreed.

"Mistakes like this are unacceptable. I'd quit and

leave this place, but then I really fear for what would happen."

Finally, the trees cleared, and a beautiful, frozen lake appeared. Several chairs and fishing rods were still out on the icy surface.

"Tell us a little bit about ice fishing here," Duke said as he pushed a branch out of the way.

"It usually starts in November and lasts until early April. We look for about twelve inches of clear ice first. You have to be careful and watch where you set up. We try not to go very far out at this time of the year because it's not fully frozen in the center yet."

Duke glanced across the lake and saw an area where the ice was broken. That had to be where the accident occurred.

"Can we walk closer?" Duke asked.

"Of course," Tim said. "We just need to be careful."

"You said this is a little farther out than you would usually go at this time of year?" Andi clarified, taking another careful step. The ground was slippery, and it was only going to get worse.

"That's right. We try to stay closer to the edges of the lake right now. I'm not sure why Caleb let that woman talk him into going out farther. It doesn't make much sense."

They paused close to the break in the ice, and Duke knelt to examine it. He wasn't an expert on this type of thing, but he wanted a better look.

"We use an auger to drill these holes." Tim remained

standing and nodded toward the ice. "We're very careful about the locations we choose. Safety first . . . unless Caleb is in charge." He scowled.

Duke didn't ask. He already knew how the man felt about Caleb.

Something on the ice seemed to catch Tim's eye. He knelt down and squinted as he examined something.

"What is it?" Duke asked.

"This mark right here . . ." Tim ran his gloved finger over a nick in the ice. "It looks like someone came out here and drove something into the ice in several places."

"Why would someone do that?" Andi frowned as she stared down at the small holes.

"It doesn't make any sense. The only reason someone would do this would be to weaken the ice, to compromise its safety." Tim stiffened as if his thoughts had just caught up with his words. "And if that's true . . ."

Tim didn't have to finish his statement.

If that was true, then someone had come out here and compromised the ice on purpose . . . hoping someone would be hurt.

The action could have had deadly consequences.

Maybe that had been the intent.

CHAPTER 21

uke and Andi left the lake, armed with new information.

They headed back to the cabin to check on the rest of the team and give them an update.

"All of these . . . all of these crimes and tragedies . . . they seem like too much of a coincidence," Andi murmured as her feet sank into the snow and her breath came out in icy puffs.

"I agree," Duke said. "Caleb *was* in charge of this excursion. Maybe he has more to do with this than we assumed."

"I definitely want to talk to him." Andi used her no-nonsense voice, the one Duke imagined she usually reserved for the courtroom. She was fully invested in this case now.

"We still need to figure out how everything is

connected or even if it *is* connected." Duke tugged his stocking cap down lower on his ears as the wind picked up. "I'm still not quite sure about that either."

Andi frowned. "There are definitely a lot of moving pieces."

He tilted his head. "It seems like there always are when we work a case."

"We do like to take on the complicated ones."

Just as they reached their cabin, the door flew open, and Bert stormed out. His nostrils were flaring and his cheeks red.

Obviously, the talk he'd had with the gang hadn't gone well.

"I'm going to tear this place apart!" he called behind him. "Mark my words!"

He jerked to a stop when he spotted Duke and Andi.

"Is there a problem?" Duke rose to full height, his shoulders broadening.

"I should have never come here." Bert swung his head back and forth. "I had no idea you guys would accuse me of murder!"

"You're saying you're angry about your stay here, but you weren't angry enough to murder someone?" Andi stared up at the man.

"Of course I wouldn't murder someone!" He snorted as if she were the crazy one. "I just wanted money."

"Like you wanted money back from other places you stayed?" Duke raised an eyebrow as he waited for the man's response.

"What are you talking about?" The man's face went pale.

"Do you always find reasons to complain about the places where you stay?" Duke continued. "Maybe you even brag on social media about how to get vacations at a discount. That's how you're an influencer, isn't it? You basically teach people how to scam others."

Bert's eyes narrowed. "You don't know anything!"

Then he stormed past them, headed toward a lone red truck parked off the side of the road.

When he disappeared, Andi turned toward Duke. "Impressive. How did you figure that one out?"

"My brother mentioned something to me about people who did stuff like that once." Duke shrugged. "And I did a little research after I talked to Gibson."

"With everything going on, I'm glad you thought to check out his social media content."

"Me too." Duke frowned and shook his head. "Bert's not a good person. However, I don't think he's a killer either."

Andi let out a long breath. "Unfortunately, I think the same thing."

———

As Duke and Andi stepped inside, the gang looked up from the kitchen table, where they'd gathered.

"That guy is a real treat, huh?" Mariella quirked an eyebrow, a fluffy pink turtleneck sweater consuming her neck. A coffee mug—also pink—rested in front of her.

"He sure is," Duke muttered. "I take it you didn't get anything useful from him?"

"Just a lot of self-righteousness," Simmy murmured with a roll of her eyes.

"I even found a camera on him," Matthew said. "He was recording all of this, probably in hopes of garnering more attention for himself."

Duke shook his head, aggravated. Some people . . .

"Did you learn anything new from Tim?" Ranger asked.

Duke exchanged a glance with Andi. Then they both took a seat around the table and updated the team on what had happened.

Just as Duke thought, from their position here, they hadn't heard the ambulance or the commotion. They'd had no idea what had transpired on the other side of the camp. The gang looked just as surprised by everything they shared as Duke had felt when they were discovering the information.

He grabbed a handful of cashews from a bowl on the table before asking, "How about you guys? Anything new? Or did Bert consume all your time?"

"I wanted to let you all know that I talked to the family of one of the victims earlier today," Mariella said. "Anderson Carswell. They live in Chena."

From what Duke could remember, Anderson was the

fifth victim. He was fifty-four, married with one son, and he worked at a garden center.

"They're desperate for answers and were thrilled to learn we're looking into this," Mariella continued. "They offered to drive out here so we could talk to them. I figured that was a good idea since it would save us the travel time. They're coming this evening."

"Sounds good," Duke said.

"I discovered one thing I thought was really interesting." Ranger pushed a photo toward them. "The state police sent these over, and I printed them off this morning."

Duke winced when he saw the image. It was from one of the December Dismemberer's crime scenes, and the details were gruesome, not something most people should see.

Several other pictures of the dead bodies were spread across the table . . . as well as the mutilations.

Andi glanced at the pictures and quickly averted her gaze. As she did, Ranger angled the pictures away from Simmy and Mariella, protecting them from seeing the horror.

"What is it about this photo in particular?" Duke looked away, giving himself a mental break from the horrific image. "Did you notice something?"

"I examined all the photos from the various crime scenes," Ranger started. "It wasn't fun, but someone had to do it. I noticed an unusual injury on Calvin and Mary, something I didn't see on the other victims."

"What was that?" Ranger had Duke's full attention now.

"This right here." He pointed to the photo and Duke leaned closer, hoping to see something that would help them.

CHAPTER 22

here appears to be hesitation marks on their neck." Ranger pointed to several small cuts on Calvin and Mary's skin. "To me, it looks like the killer started to kill them but stopped. He seemed to second-guess himself before finishing the deed."

Duke picked up the photo and studied it more closely. Ranger was right. Barely visible cut marks stretched across their skin.

"It could be because this was the first time this guy killed two victims at once," Andi suggested. "Maybe that threw him off his game."

"Maybe." Duke's jaw tightened as he stared at the photo. "It almost looks like he changed his mind. But why would he do that?"

"Maybe the killer knew Calvin and Mary personally." Ranger let his words linger in the air. "That could make him rethink his methods and do something less gruesome."

Duke nodded slowly. "You may be onto something. Maybe the killer had a personal connection with Juniper's parents."

"Or with this place," Simmy suggested.

"This location feels different than the others," Duke said. "It feels more personal, as do the murders of Calvin and Mary. Plus, there's been some strange stuff going on—mostly Pepper's murder. We'd be foolish not to consider the idea that there's a connection."

"But why would the killer wait six years, striking other people and locations, only to strike here where it's more personal?" Matthew asked.

"That's a great question," Andi said. "Until we figure out his motivation, we might not know."

"So where do we go from here?" Simmy asked.

"I want to dig a little deeper into both Tim's and Caleb's backgrounds," Andi said. "Caleb was actually there ice fishing when the woman fell through."

Ranger frowned and leaned back in his seat, a thoughtful expression on his face. "If he truly is the killer—the December Dismemberer—it seems as if he would have been more careful and not been on the scene."

"I agree with that," Duke said. "Maybe he's not the serial killer we're looking for. But I wonder if he might be behind some of the incidents happening here, especially if he was on the verge of being fired right before

Calvin and Mary were killed. He could have staged the murders to look like the December Dismemberer, just as Tim suggested."

"That's a good point." Andi sat up straighter and nodded. "We need to talk to Caleb again."

"I agree," Duke said.

Right now, Caleb had risen to the top of his list of suspects.

————

Caleb wasn't in the lodge. Juniper told them that, after the accident, he'd stomped off—he'd probably gone back to his cabin to sulk.

Instead of tracking him down there, there was something else Andi wanted to do first.

"I want to talk to Gibson and see if we can look inside Pepper's residence here," she announced. "He said yesterday we should stay away, but I'm hoping he might be more lenient today."

"It can't hurt to ask," Duke said.

"I think that sounds like a great idea," Mariella said. "I know Matthew and I have some things to work on here for the podcast. Maybe the rest of you guys could go?"

Duke glanced at Ranger. "How about if you and I talk to Gibson, see if we can take a look at the cabin where she was staying?"

"What about me?" Andi wondered exactly what

Duke was thinking because she wanted to see Pepper's place too. The whole thing had been her idea.

"I was actually hoping you and Simmy might talk to Juniper," he said. "She seems pretty upset, and I still feel as if there's something she's hiding. Maybe you guys can get more out of her."

Andi glanced at Simmy and shrugged. "It seems as if it could be worth a chance."

"Then let's do that," Simmy said.

With that decided, they all got moving. Duke called Gibson. He told them Pepper's place had been released, and they were free to go inside with Juniper's permission. Duke called Juniper, who gave them the go-ahead. She said she'd send Tim over with the key.

Meanwhile, Andi and Simmy bundled up to visit Juniper.

As soon as Andi stepped outside, she paused and glanced around.

Something didn't feel right.

Why did she feel as if someone were watching her?

As she scanned everything around her, she didn't see anyone except . . .

She squinted as she stared into the woods.

She'd almost thought she had seen a mound of snow moving. But that thought was ridiculous. Snow didn't move unless it was blown by the wind.

What did she think? That the snow was alive or something? She chided herself at the thought. It was ridiculous.

She touched the top of her head as that ache formed again.

The mad scientist who'd tried to do surgery on her wasn't here. Wasn't hiding in the snow.

She had to remind herself of that fact entirely too much.

"You ready?" Simmy stepped outside beside her.

Andi forced herself to smile. "Of course. Let's go find Juniper."

CHAPTER 23

s Andi and Simmy veered toward the dining hall, Duke and Ranger headed to the small cabin where Pepper had been living. After hearing Gibson approved of the visit, Tim said he'd meet them there to unlock it.

True to his word, he was there with the key. Duke was thankful Tim didn't try to squeeze his way inside also. Instead, he unlocked the door and then left them alone.

Duke hesitated before pushing the door open and stepping inside. He wasn't sure exactly what he expected to find. But he hoped that it might be something.

The first thing he noticed was the scent of peppermint. As he looked to his right, he saw a long table set up. Clear vials lined the space, probably filled with peppermint oil, if he had to guess. There were also candy molds, bags of sugar and corn syrup, spools of yarn, and boxes and bags of all sizes.

While Ranger headed to the closet, Duke went to the dresser.

He went through the drawers but saw nothing of note.

Then he searched her bed. Again, nothing caught his eye.

Maybe coming here had been unnecessary. Searching her phone or computer would probably be his best bet of finding out information, but the police had taken those.

He paused in the middle of the room and looked around.

What were they missing in here?

"Check this out," Ranger muttered as he stood in front of the closet, looking inside.

Duke walked over to him and peered at the shoes on the floor.

That was when he saw two pairs of slippers, one larger than the other.

"Most people don't have two different sizes of shoes," Ranger said. "I think Pepper had a second pair for a friend who might visit her here."

"Based on the size, I'd say that friend was a male."

"Bingo." Ranger nodded slowly. "I don't think a boyfriend has been mentioned yet, has he?"

"What's the chance Juniper doesn't know about this

boyfriend? Otherwise, why would she keep it quiet? The police should question him."

"I think we need to meet up with Simmy and Andi. Then we need to ask Juniper some more questions."

———

Andi and Simmy didn't find Juniper in the dining hall, but one of the employees told them he'd seen her walking toward the reindeer pasture.

Andi and Simmy headed that way, hoping to find her.

Sure enough, when they reached the area, they spotted Juniper inside the fence, feeding one of the reindeer.

They quietly stepped inside the enclosure, closing the gate behind them. Then they trudged through the snow toward Juniper.

"This is where I come when I like to think." Juniper didn't even turn to look at them. But she'd clearly been aware of their presence.

Andi was glad Simmy was here with her. Simmy truly did have a natural, nurturing way about her.

She was also glad Ranger's daughter, Anastasia, had Simmy. Andi knew Simmy had always wanted to be a mother. In fact, they'd recently learned she'd been a surrogate when she was younger, even though she never had any kids of her own.

"Did you know that reindeer are protective of each

other?" Juniper asked, still staring at the reindeer in front of her. "Sometimes, they even form something called a reindeer cyclone."

"What's that?" Simmy asked.

"When one of the reindeer is in danger, the rest of the reindeer start walking in a circular formation around it—almost in a tornado-like swirling pattern. When they do that, it throws the predator off and confuses them."

"That's real?" Andi said. "I thought it was fiction."

"No, it's real. I've only seen it once when a grizzly came into the camp. It was amazing to witness." She paused. "We all need a community like that who will gather around us and offer protection, don't we?"

"I'd say we do," Andi said. "For sure."

"The children who visit the camp are the best, especially the ones who still believe in Santa Claus," Juniper continued. "We always go through a spiel about how Santa only chooses the best reindeer to do his runs on Christmas Eve. We tell them that on occasion Santa had even chosen some of the reindeer here at the Borealis Reindeer Camp."

"I love that," Simmy said.

"Some of the kids even ask if this was where Rudolph came from."

"What do you tell them?" Andi reached forward to stroke the reindeer's head.

"I always laugh and tell them Rudolph came from another farm farther north, but that I'm not allowed to disclose the location for privacy's sake."

"Smart thinking."

A few minutes of silence passed.

Simmy touched her shoulder. "And how are you holding up, sweetie?"

Juniper shrugged and swallowed hard. "I'm not sure."

"I take it that your talk with Caleb didn't go well?" Andi asked.

Juniper pressed her eyes closed and didn't say anything for several seconds. "He doesn't even seem like the same person I initially met. I don't know what's going on with him. He's been especially moody the past couple of days."

Andi wondered if what was going on with Caleb was that he was a cold-blooded killer and afraid the podcast team would catch him. But she didn't say those words out loud.

Without knowing him, Andi couldn't really say.

But he still took first place on her list of suspects.

CHAPTER 24

ndi had more questions for Juniper.

"Do you know anything about the guest who was injured while ice fishing?"

Juniper gave the reindeer one last pat before turning toward Andi. "What do you want to know?"

"Her name? Occupation? Did she ever give you a hard time?"

"Barb is her name. Caleb said the woman was insistent they ice fish at a certain spot, and he tried to tell her it wasn't a good idea. He said Barb swore she was an expert and that it would be fine. I told him even if that *is* what happened, the guests should never have the final say when it comes to something that's a matter of safety. We're the ones liable for accidents like this."

"Is Barb a first-time guest?" Andi asked.

"She is. From what I understand, she's a nature

photographer. She and her family came here from Kansas."

"Has she given you any problems?" Andi continued.

"Not really." She shrugged.

"She was acting suspiciously when I saw her in the dining hall yesterday," Andi said.

"I know she kept going on walks in the woods alone. I thought it was a little strange, but she said she felt one with nature."

Andi stored that information away.

When she glanced across the camp, she spotted Duke and Ranger walking toward them. Had they found something?

The men reached them a few minutes later and joined them in the reindeer pen.

"You're coming from Peppermint's place." Tension stretched through Juniper's voice. "Did you find anything?"

"Not much," Duke said. "But we do have a question for you."

"What do you need?"

"Was Pepper dating anyone?"

"Dating?" A crease formed between Juniper's eyes. "No. Why would you ask that?"

Duke and Ranger exchanged a glance. "We found two pairs of slippers, and based on their size, we wondered if one belonged to a man."

"I'm sure Pepper would have told me if she was dating someone."

"We just thought we'd ask," Duke told her. "We didn't find anything else of note, unfortunately."

"That's too bad. I can't sleep at night thinking about what happened to her. It still seems like a nightmare I should wake up from. Then again, I should be used to this after what happened to my parents . . ." Her voice cracked as a sob lodged in her throat.

Simmy pulled the young woman into her arms, and Juniper nearly collapsed against her.

They gave her a few minutes to compose herself.

Then Duke asked, "Juniper, do you know where Caleb is now?"

"I haven't seen him in a while. I assume he's blowing off some steam."

"I was hoping to ask him a few more questions about the ice fishing."

"You could go to his cabin and see if he's there." Juniper sniffled again, still leaning into Simmy as she gave them directions.

———

While Simmy and Ranger stayed with Juniper, Duke and Andi headed toward Caleb's cabin to talk with him.

The man's smug face flashed in his mind as he walked. "Caleb is hiding something."

"I agree." Andi pulled the collar of her coat up higher around her neck as the breeze swept over them. "But what? He might not be a great guy or who he portrays himself to be, but that doesn't make him a killer."

"You're right." Duke's jaw tightened. "Maybe he'll give us some solid answers this time."

"I hope so."

They headed past the guest cabins until they reached some smaller, plainer cabins the workers utilized. From what Duke understood after talking to Juniper, four employees usually shared a small cabin with two sets of bunkbeds.

Which made the fact that Pepper had her own cabin even stranger, especially since she wasn't an employee. Apparently, Juniper had given her friend special privileges.

Did anyone here at the camp resent the woman for that?

As they reached the cabin—which was more of a rectangular metal pod—Duke climbed up some icy steps onto a narrow landing and pounded at the door.

Silence answered.

He knocked again.

Again, it was silent.

"Caleb, we know you're in there," Duke called. "Open up. We have questions for you."

There was no response. Did this guy think he could hide inside, pretend to be asleep, and that they'd go away? If so, Caleb had totally underestimated them.

Duke rattled the door handle—and it twisted.

The cabin was unlocked.

He and Andi exchanged a glance. He hadn't expected that.

"Caleb, I'm coming in." Duke slowly opened the door.

The last thing he wanted was for Caleb or one of his roommates to act out of fear and do something foolish—like try to attack them. For that reason, Duke remained on guard.

But instead of someone jumping out, an empty cabin greeted them. Two bunk beds. Clothes strewn across every surface. A TV in the corner with a jumble of cords spewing from it and a gaming system below. The stench of unwashed laundry wafted in the air.

It looked—and smelled—like a typical bachelor pad.

But there was no Caleb inside. So where had he gone?

"Since we're already here . . ." Andi raised her eyebrows and stepped in farther.

Duke gave her a look. "You're going to snoop, aren't you?"

"I'm just going to *browse*." She kept her voice casual. "It sounds much more innocent that way."

"Much more." He flashed a smile. "You should make it quick, just to be safe."

Duke watched as Andi wandered the perimeter of the room, looking for anything that might catch her eye.

Suddenly, she stilled.

Duke followed her gaze to a piece of paper sticking out from beneath one of the mattresses.

As Andi gently pulled it out, Duke stepped closer and peered over her shoulder for a better look at the handwritten words.

I've got to hand it to you, you've made a real mess of things. You've got one chance to make it right. Don't make me tear you apart.

Duke sucked in a breath. "Now *that* sounds suspicious."

Andi stared at the paper and shook her head. "You can say that again. What exactly is Caleb involved in? And is the use of the word *hand* a coincidence? And *tear you apart?*"

"I'm going to guess no."

Using her phone, Andi took a picture of the note before placing it in her pocket.

"I'll hand this over to Gibson." She moaned after the statement left her lips. "Bad word choice."

Duke gave her a wry look.

A pair of shoes beneath the bed caught her eye, and she pulled them out. The light caught something shoved inside one of them.

As Andi reached inside the boot, her fingers brushed something. She pulled the object out and held the bag toward the light.

Red liquid sloshed inside. Red liquid that looked an awful lot like blood.

Like *fake* blood.

Like the type that had been left on the fake hand outside their door.

Had Caleb been the one who'd left that?

Duke rubbed his jaw before shaking his head. "Let's get back to Juniper and see if she can radio Caleb. Caleb is somehow involved in all of this, and I need the truth."

Andi's gaze locked on his. "I couldn't agree more."

CHAPTER 25

aleb, are you there? I need to talk to you." Juniper's knuckles were white as she gripped the radio.

When there was no response, she lowered her device back into her lap.

Andi and Duke had come back, found her in her office, and told her what they'd discovered. Panic had fluttered through her gaze, and her face had gone pale.

"I don't know why he isn't responding," she murmured as she leaned against her desk. "It's not like him. Even when he's acting like a jerk, he's still usually pretty good at communicating."

"You said you saw him walking back to his cabin earlier, right?" Andi grabbed a paper cup and got some water from the dispenser in Juniper's office. She handed the drink to Juniper.

"That's right. He said he needed to be by himself a

while. That's what he does." Juniper took a sip of the water before running her hand over her face. "But he usually hangs out at his cabin. I don't know where else he would be."

"Is it like him to leave the camp without saying something?" Duke asked.

"He doesn't have a vehicle here so it would be hard for him to actually leave the property unless he went with someone else. I suppose he could have walked into the woods to have some alone time, but that doesn't seem like him either." Juniper frowned.

"What about the fake blood?" Andi asked. "Do you know anything about that?"

"Caleb did mention once that he has an older brother who works special effects on some low budget films. I didn't even think anything about it until just now. Caleb hasn't seen his brother in years so . . . I don't know. I didn't put it together. I have no idea why Caleb would leave a fake bloody hand on your door, though."

"Any guesses as to what might be going on?" Duke continued to press.

"I don't know what to say." Juniper ran a hand through her hair, tension seizing her expression. "I only know I'm fielding a lot of questions from guests about what's going on, and I'm trying my best to get through this. Probably 75 percent of the people staying here are leaving and asking for refunds. This is creeping them out, I guess."

"That's understandable." Andi squeezed her arm. "But I also know this situation has to be hard on you."

Juniper pressed her eyes closed as if fighting discouragement. "We need to have the majority of our cabins booked in order to make ends meet. Running this place isn't cheap. That's why I've been so thankful our bookings have been so consistent. But now with these things happening, it's going to cause bad press . . . and I don't know if we'll survive that."

"We're going to keep looking for answers," Duke assured her. "But first, we need to find Caleb."

"If I hear from him, I'll let you know. The rest of the guys on his team—who are also his roommates—should be out on the trails with guests. I'll check with them when they get back." She glanced at her radio as it crackled, and someone asked for her. "But right now, I have another guest who wants to leave. I should probably head to the front desk so I can handle this."

"You do that," Andi said. "We'll stay in touch with you as well."

Andi and Duke wandered away from the lodge. She wouldn't want to be in Juniper's position right now. She knew it wasn't easy.

But she needed to stay focused on finding Caleb. If he didn't have a car, then he couldn't have left the area unless he either caught a ride or borrowed someone's car—with or without their permission.

"I'd like to go back to Caleb's cabin one more time," she murmured to Duke.

"Then let's go."

The sun had sunk again, barely lingering on the edge of the horizon and creating an early twilight for them. The breeze was still brisk and cold. More than cold. It was freezing and attacked any exposed skin.

Andi tugged her coat closer around her face as they walked.

When they reached the cabin this time, they didn't go inside.

Instead, they paced the outside of the place. The snow was deep and soft near the edges of the building, and they sank to their knees—which made walking incredibly hard.

When they finally got to the back of the cabin, they both paused.

Andi's eyes widened when she saw the tracks stretching there.

Not only one set of footprints but two.

Had Caleb somehow escaped and disappeared into the woods?

Duke knelt beside the prints, examining them closer.

"What is it?" Andi could tell by the look on his face that he found something.

"I'm looking at the pattern of these footprints. Based on these tracks right here," he pointed to the set on the left, "one of these people didn't leave willingly."

"What?" The word came out as a gasp. "How can you tell?"

"If you ask me, this person was taken away kicking

and screaming. You can tell by the unevenness of the steps. By the drag marks. By how the indentations seem deeper and more erratic in places."

Andi glanced up and locked her gaze with his. "So what you're telling me is that you think Caleb took someone and ran?"

He twisted his head. "Or someone took Caleb and ran. It could go either way."

———

Duke and Andi followed the tracks into the forest, careful not to disturb any evidence.

Duke paused by a tree and stared at something on the white snow.

Andi followed his gaze and gasped. "Is that . . . ?"

He leaned toward it. "Blood—and it's fresh."

"Someone is in trouble," she murmured. "I don't like this."

"Me neither."

Someone had been hurt. He didn't know if the injury had been caused by someone else or by the consequences of walking through the forest. A branch could have cut someone's skin.

But he was leaning toward the former.

Foul play was involved with Caleb's disappearance. Duke just wasn't sure what side of things Caleb was on.

He had no loyalty toward Caleb. But Duke knew if

something happened to the man, it would be another loss for Juniper.

She'd already lost so many people.

He and Andi continued through the forest, following the trail of blood. They paused about a half a mile into their trek.

"We can go farther, but I don't think that's a good idea," Duke told Andi. "Let's get back to the camp. We need to call Gibson with the update."

"Definitely."

If Duke had his way, he'd whisk Andi away from here to somewhere safe.

But that wasn't a realistic option. Danger seemed to follow them wherever they went.

Besides, Andi wasn't one to run from conflict or danger, and that was one of the things he loved about her.

However, there was a killer lurking on these grounds. And Duke wasn't sure what it would take to stop this guy. Duke only knew he had to catch him before there were any more victims.

CHAPTER 26
DECEMBER, LAST YEAR

uniper dabbed beneath her eyes with a crumpled tissue as she stood outside, turning away from the frigid breeze sweeping across the tundra.

She still couldn't believe her parents were no longer here. Everything seemed surreal, like a bad dream she couldn't wake up from.

But she knew it wasn't. Her parents had been brutally murdered. Now she had to face the future without them.

She stroked Starla's face again as the reindeer stared at her from the other side of the fence, waiting for a treat.

Everything was always better when Starla and Tundra were around.

Her dad had nicknamed her Snow White because all the animals liked her. She was a favorite of the canines at the camp—they liked to follow her everywhere. The reindeer came running to the fence whenever she appeared.

Then last summer when a dark-eyed junco had landed on her shoulder, that had seemed to seal the deal. Snow White was her forever nickname.

She didn't mind the description. She'd do anything to hear her dad call her that now.

She'd wanted to go to college—maybe become a veterinarian. She definitely hadn't planned on taking over operations of this place at her age.

She supposed she could let Uncle Tim take the reins. It was what he wanted. But she didn't think that was what *she* wanted. Though she and her parents hadn't always seen eye to eye, she still wanted to honor them.

Caleb had encouraged her to not give up either.

Both Caleb and Peppermint had been such a support to her since her parents' deaths.

Sure, she had other friends, people she met up with on occasion when she went into the city to have a little fun. They were mostly people she knew from high school or from Scouts.

But right now, the thought of hanging out with them wasn't appealing. She'd just laid her parents to rest. Probably two hundred people had shown up at the small church her parents often attended.

Everyone had looked truly sorrowful. Several had looked scared.

The December Dismemberer was only supposed to be a legend, a killer other people encountered somewhere far away. He was never supposed to be a reality here. That fact had shaken this community to the core.

The hardest part was returning to life as normal. Because nothing felt normal. Usually in a time like this, Juniper would have relied on her parents.

Now, that was no longer an option . . .

Tears flooded her gaze, and she quickly wiped them away before they froze.

She looked up as footsteps crunched in the snow toward her. It was Caleb . . .

"Hey." He paused beside her, his gaze soft with compassion. "How's everything going?"

She shrugged and reached for the reindeer near the fence. "Starla is keeping me good company."

"You know I'm here for you if you need me," he reminded her.

"I know. And I appreciate that. Truly."

Caleb and Peppermint were the only ones who knew her secret.

Had that secret gotten her parents killed?

A sob lodged in her throat.

It had, hadn't it?

How could she ever live with herself?

Caleb pulled her into his arms and began to stroke her back. "It's going to be okay."

Juniper wanted to relax against him, but she couldn't. "Someone might see us."

"It doesn't matter anymore," he murmured. "Your

parents were the only ones who cared if we dated. Now they're not here to stop us."

His words sent a chill through her. Caleb almost sounded as if he were glad her mom and dad were gone, like their deaths had worked out in his favor.

She stiffened and took a step back. What kind of person said something like that?

"Juniper . . . I didn't mean it like that. You've got to know that." Caleb reached for her again, an apologetic look in his gaze.

She took another step away from him. "Then how did you mean it?"

"I just meant we don't have to keep things so complicated. No one is going to judge us for dating."

She wasn't so sure about that. Her uncle Tim wasn't going to love this.

And she didn't even want to think about romance right now.

Not after everything she'd lost.

But Caleb's words still echoed in her mind.

He didn't have anything to do with her parents' deaths . . . did he?

CHAPTER 27
DECEMBER, PRESENT DAY

efore Andi and Duke turned around, something up ahead caught her attention.

"Duke . . ." she murmured.

He followed her gaze and grunted.

They walked several steps farther before stopping at a clearing. A set of tire tracks stretched there.

Andi watched as Duke kneeled to examine them. "Based on the size of the tires and the distance between the wheels, these tracks most likely belong to a UTV."

"You think someone took off with Caleb?" she asked. "Had the UTV waiting here?"

"It's a theory." Duke rose. "We need to go check the garage. See how many vehicles the camp has and if they're all accounted for."

Andi nodded. "Assuming they keep the door locked . . . we need to talk to Juniper first to get access. Come on, we don't have any time to waste."

Quickly, she and Duke trudged back through the snow to the lodge.

Juniper looked up with hopeful eyes as they walked in.

Andi quickly shook her head to let her know there were no updates.

Juniper's shoulders instantly sagged.

"We need to see your UTVs." Duke got right to the point.

"What?" Surprise filled Juniper's gaze. "Why?"

"We think Caleb left on one—though we don't know if it was by his own free will or not," Duke explained.

Juniper gasped, and her hand flew over her mouth. "No . . ."

Andi squeezed her arm, trying to offer a measure of comfort. "I know that's hard to hear, but we don't have any time to waste right now. We need to figure out if this was one of the camp's UTVs or if we're dealing with an outsider."

Juniper's eyes widened as the reality of what they were asking seemed to hit. "Of course. Uncle Tim is probably the best one to talk to—other than Caleb." Her voice cracked.

"Can you radio him and have him meet us at the garage?" Duke asked.

"I'll do that now."

"And call the cops," Duke muttered. "I know you don't want to, but you need to. Caleb's life could be on the line."

Her skin pale, Juniper grabbed her phone and nodded.

"They're going to tell you not to let anyone leave," Duke continued. "Do your best to stop people. Everyone here should officially be questioned to see if they know anything."

"Got it." But Juniper's voice wavered as she said the words.

Tim was waiting at the garage when they arrived. He was already counting the UTVs and comparing the license numbers with those on a clipboard. The camp didn't have a large fleet—probably only eight, so checking didn't take long.

"All the vehicles are accounted for." He pulled his gaze away from the list and looked at them. "None are missing."

Did that mean someone who didn't live at the camp had shown up and abducted Caleb? Andi nibbled on her bottom lip. Was that what had also happened the day Calvin and Mary were killed?

Tim turned toward them, a frown forming deep creases at the corners of his mouth. "What now?"

"We wait for the police to get here," Duke said. "They have resources we don't. In the meantime, do you have any idea where the trail behind Caleb's cabin leads?"

Tim stared into the distance as if thinking through the question. "Well, they could pretty much go anywhere from there. They could follow the pipeline to the White Mountains. From there, there are numerous trails. It would be nearly impossible to track someone or to catch them at that point."

"That's too bad." Duke rubbed his chin as if he didn't like that answer.

Tim continued to stare at them. "You really think someone took Caleb?"

"Either that, or Caleb disappeared and took someone with him," Duke said. "But considering the fact a UTV from off campus was used, I'm thinking someone abducted Caleb."

"Why would anyone do that?" Tim fisted his hands at his sides, his expression hardening. "What exactly has that guy gotten himself caught up in?"

"That's what we're trying to figure out also," Andi said.

Tim's gaze sharpened. "I thought you were here to try to figure out who killed Calvin and Mary."

"We are," Andi said. "Now Pepper is dead also. Right now, we don't know how or if everything is connected."

"What if Caleb had something to do with their deaths?" Tim practically spat out the words as if they disgusted him. "What if we let him stay here all this time, welcoming him into our homes, when all along he's been a killer?"

Andi didn't know what to say, so she let his words hang in the air.

Relief filled Duke when he saw Gibson pull up to the camp.

Their friend looked serious as he climbed from his SUV and strode toward them as they all waited in the lobby of the lodge.

He paused when he reached them and glanced back and forth between Duke and Andi. "Someone is missing?"

Duke explained the situation to him.

Gibson clucked his tongue with each new detail. "I don't like hearing that."

"Believe me," Duke muttered. "We don't like sharing it."

"I take it you've all already done your own investigation?" Gibson stared at them, his expression making it clear he already knew the answer.

"We did what we could," Duke said. "We think either someone grabbed Caleb, managed to subdue him, and then took off with him in a UTV toward the White Mountains. Or Caleb grabbed someone and took off. There's no telling where he might be right now."

"And you have no idea why someone might have done this?"

"I have a couple of theories," Andi said. "Either Caleb was involved in Pepper's murder, or Caleb was involved in Calvin's and Mary's murders. Because of that, he wanted to run now that we're here investigating."

"There is a third possibility," Duke said. "Something could be going on here at the camp separate from last year's murders, and Caleb is caught up in that."

They gave Gibson the note they'd found and then ran through the details of what had been happening.

Gibson shook his head as they finished. "I'm going to need to talk to Ms. Burrows again."

"Juniper is in her office on the other side of the lodge," Andi said. "I can take you to her."

"That would be great."

"If it's okay, while you two do that, I'd like to wander the property," Duke told them. "I want to take another look at things."

There wasn't anything specific. But he wanted to get a better feel for this place and see if there was anything he'd missed earlier.

"Of course," Andi said. "Don't forget that the Carswells are coming later."

"Thanks for the reminder." He watched as Andi and Gibson walked toward the dining area where everyone had gathered.

As soon as Andi and Gibson disappeared from sight, Duke headed out to survey the property.

He stopped by the pen where the reindeer were kept. They were acting uneasy, pacing with skittering gazes.

They must sense something was wrong.

He paused to watch them. The creatures were majestic. They really were. If only they could speak. Maybe they had seen something.

This was also the area where they'd discovered Pepper's body. Crime scene tape still formed a square around the area where she'd been found, partly tied to the fence and partly to metal stakes in the ground.

Her death was still a mystery to him.

The method of her death didn't match that of the December Dismemberer. That seemed to point to the idea two different killers were at play here—not a comforting thought.

The hard part in situations like this was that snow and ice could obscure so many clues. When Duke had worked one case with the Army CID, his team had to wait until the landscape began to thaw out in the spring before they could uncover evidence without damaging it. Sure, they could use heat lamps. But that wasn't ideal for preserving fibers and other possible evidence.

He squinted as he looked down at the snow. What was that?

He leaned closer and realized it was some kind of glitter. The particles were contained to a small, two-foot-by-two-foot area. He was certain the specks hadn't been there yesterday.

Almost like . . . fairy dust.

He scoffed at himself. Fairy dust? To make the reindeer fly?

Yeah, right.

If that was what the substance was, then it had to be

a gimmick given to a child who'd then come over to the reindeer pen.

This didn't have anything to do with Pepper's death.

He frowned.

But what if it did? He needed to keep this finding in the back of his mind . . .

CHAPTER 28

I t seemed strange to continue on with life as normal with Caleb missing and Juniper in turmoil, Andi mused. However, the gang had already arranged for the Carswell family to come.

They'd barely had time to squeeze in a quick, late lunch when their guests had shown up.

When the Carswells arrived, they had no idea about everything that had transpired at the camp earlier. Andi didn't plan on telling them.

The cops had taken over the investigation into Caleb's disappearance—they had far more resources than the gang did. Ranger and Duke had volunteered to help in the search efforts, and Gibson had agreed.

The rest of the podcast team would talk to the Carswells.

Patricia Carswell had been Anderson's wife. She was in her fifties with salt-and-pepper hair, a plump figure, and notable circles beneath her eyes. She'd brought her thirty-year-old son, Jay, with her.

They both sat on the couch, Patricia gripping her son's hand.

Andi's heart went out to them. Their grief still felt heavy.

"Thank you so much for coming," Andi started as she sat across from them, a notepad and pen in hand. "Tell us about Anderson."

"He was a great family man." Patricia wiped beneath her eyes, her voice throaty with emotion. "He loved us and would do anything to make us happy."

"What about his job?" Andi asked. "What did he do for a living?"

"He worked for a garden center. He loved that also. The job didn't pay much, but that was okay. Some things are more important than money."

A better picture of Anderson formed in Andi's mind. "He sounds like a good man."

"He was." Jay's jaw flexed as if he held back emotion. "He was one of the best. He didn't deserve to die the way he did."

"No, he didn't," Andi agreed. "Can you tell us about the day he died?"

Patricia drew in a deep but shaky breath. "I've replayed it many times in my mind. It seemed like an ordinary day. There was really nothing special about it. I went to work as a teacher at the middle school as I always do. Jay was living in Anchorage."

"I have an accounting job at a firm down there," Jay explained. "Been there five years now."

"I noticed Anderson was working late a lot recently, but that wasn't all that unusual," Patricia continued. "There were things that needed to be done, and he was the type who didn't leave things unfinished."

"Not a bad quality to have." Andi offered a nod of encouragement.

"Not at all." Patricia paused as if gathering herself. "When Anderson didn't come home or answer his phone, I decided to go to the garden center. It was closed to the public at that point, but I decided to walk around to see if I could locate him. The store looked empty. But when I reached the greenhouse, I noticed that someone had built a snowman outside by the front door."

Andi braced herself, knowing exactly what was coming next. "Tell me about the snowman."

"It was probably four feet tall with charcoal eyes and a carrot nose." She paused and swallowed hard. "But it was what was on the side of his face that caught my attention. It was an ear. A bloody human ear."

As tears began to stream down her cheeks, Jay squeezed his mother's hand.

Andi could only imagine the horror. "I'm so sorry."

"When I went inside, I found him." Her voice cracked with every other word as more tears fell.

"Was there anything strange about the scene—other than the ear on the snowman?" Andi almost hated to ask the question in the midst of this woman's pain, but she had to.

"Not really. I mean, other than what you might expect."

"Dad wasn't even supposed to be at work that day," Jay added.

Andi straightened when she heard that tidbit. "What do you mean?"

"I mean, someone called in sick, so my dad went in. I can't help but wonder if he had said no, if we'd still have him with us right now."

Andi leaned back in her seat. Interesting thought.

Had someone followed Anderson to work, waiting for just the right opportunity to strike?

Or would whoever had been working at the garden center that night have been the victim?

The question lingered in Andi's mind.

———

Ranger drove the UTV down the icy trail, surrounded by snow-laden spruces on either side. Duke sat beside him, scanning everything in hopes of finding a clue about Caleb.

Gibson had cleared them to join in the search and given them a radio so they could communicate with everyone in the process. Three other pairs of searchers on UTVs had gone out, each covering a different section of the camp.

So far, no one had reported finding anything. Duke's best guess was that someone had a vehicle waiting somewhere outside this forest and that was how Caleb had disappeared. The jury was still out as to whether or not he had left on his own or if someone had forced him away.

The fact that Duke had seen that blood earlier raised all kinds of alarms in his mind, however.

He and Ranger had been out here for an hour so far but had discovered nothing. Not only that, but the temperature was dropping and the darkness was growing deeper. The fact they weren't familiar with this landscape made everything more dangerous.

He hoped the gang back at the cabin was having more luck questioning the Carswell family.

"Do you think we can squeeze down that path?" Duke pointed to a small opening between the trees. The route didn't appear to be an official path, maybe a game trail, but he thought the UTV would fit.

"Let's try." Ranger jerked the wheel, and they turned onto the path.

This one was definitely narrower and steeper. But he thought the UTV could handle it.

He kept his eyes peeled for signs of anything of interest. Though there were no fresh tracks down this trail, that didn't mean it hadn't been utilized recently. Fresh snow had begun to fall.

As they continued down the path, Duke prayed that they weren't wasting valuable time.

Then something out of place caught his eye. He strained for a better look through the trees. From his current vantage point, it almost looked like . . . a small building.

"Do you see that?" he asked.

Ranger narrowed his eyes. "It looks like an old cabin."

"I think we should check it out."

"I agree."

A few minutes later, they stopped in front of the place.

Duke got a better look. It was definitely a cabin. The wood covering the exterior was gray, and several pieces were crooked as if dry-rotted. If Duke had to guess, it was maybe four hundred square feet inside.

They climbed off the UTV to take a closer look.

Ranger scanned the building. "I'd guess this place goes back a good eighty years, maybe to when gold-miners were out here looking for their next big hot spot. I know there's a stream not far away. Maybe they were panning there."

"I wonder if other people are aware this building is here."

"Hard to say," Ranger said. "Even if they know, I'm not so sure it would matter. This cabin doesn't look inhabitable, especially in this cold."

"It does have a fireplace." Duke pointed to the pipe rising from the roof.

He noted how the snow right around the pipe had melted.

Was that indicative that someone had built a fire inside recently?

Was that person still here?

His muscles tightened at the thought.

Maybe there was more going on here than he'd initially assumed.

They would need to proceed with caution.

CHAPTER 29

As the Carswells' taillights faded in the distance, Andi turned to the rest of the team. They all stood near the door, where they'd told Patricia and her son goodbye only a few minutes ago.

"So what do you think?" she asked.

"I thought it was especially interesting that Anderson wasn't supposed to be working the day he was murdered." Mariella retreated into the living room and plopped down in an armchair, tucking her legs beneath her.

"Me too." Andi sat on the couch, needing a moment to deconstruct the conversation. "So the question is, was this killer watching Anderson and waiting for the right moment to strike? Did he find that moment when Anderson was working alone?"

"Or was this guy keeping his eye on the greenhouse for some reason?" Simmy leaned against the door frame with her arms crossed. "Maybe this guy targets people because of their location. Maybe he targeted the camp and the nursery."

"It is a theory worth considering," Andi said. "Remind me about the other locations?"

"A utility worker who worked in North Pole but lived near Eielson Air Force Base was found dead in his home. A gift shop owner was picking up some homemade candles from a vendor. A nurse was found dead in her car at the grocery store, and someone who works at the planetarium was found deceased in his backyard."

She frowned. "I'm not sure there are any connections there."

She wished Duke and Ranger were back so she could get their opinions. She also wondered if they'd discovered anything—if they'd figured out Caleb's location or what he might be up to. So far, they'd heard no updates.

Honestly, she was beginning to get worried. The weather was brutal, and they weren't supposed to be gone this long.

With a possible killer on the loose, too many things could go wrong. Duke and Ranger were capable, but bad things happened to capable people all the time.

That truth left her unsettled.

———

Duke drew his gun as they approached the cabin. Out of

caution, he stood on one side of the door while Ranger stood on the other.

With a nod, Duke threw the door open and swung around to see the inside.

He wasn't sure what to expect. Part of him imagined the place being taken over by nature. But to his surprise, the one-room cabin was neat and clean—and empty.

Duke and Ranger stepped inside to take a better look.

"Someone has definitely been here recently." Duke put his gun back into his holster at his waist.

Ranger held his hand over the cast iron stove in the corner. "This is cold. So recently could mean sometime in the past several days. It's dipped below zero."

"I agree." Duke continued to pace around the room to make sure his initial scan was correct.

There weren't many personal effects in the cabin. A beige blanket was strewn across a mattress on the wooden floor. Candles lined various surfaces—there was clearly no electricity.

The cabin was primitive, but for the right person, it could be a warm place to stay at night.

Was this where the December Dismemberer had been staying?

His throat tightened at the thought.

He paused near a dresser. Still wearing his winter gloves, he opened the drawer and squinted.

Two neatly folded flannel shirts waited inside. He picked up one.

It appeared, based on the size and shape, to belong to a woman.

A woman had been staying out here?

Duke was fairly certain this killer wasn't a woman. But he could be wrong.

So just who had been living out here? And where was this person now?

Before he could explore the questions too long, something snapped just outside the window.

His back tightened.

He and Ranger weren't here alone, he realized.

Ranger froze and glanced at him, clearly hearing the noise also.

Was the person lingering outside a friend or foe?

They needed to find out.

CHAPTER 30

tupid people.

Why couldn't they just leave things alone?

My life was so much better—so much simpler—before they showed up.

I'd seen those two go into the secluded, rundown cabin.

I'd been watching. I knew what they were thinking, what they were planning.

They wanted to find me. To stop me.

Too bad that wouldn't be happening.

Foolish idiots.

I knew I needed to send a message. So I had.

Then I'd left.

I couldn't be caught.

But if these people didn't start backing off soon, I'd have to up my means of scaring them away.

They did it to themselves. If they'd minded their business, none of this would be an issue.

Now I needed to make sure they left.

People could be such obstacles sometimes.

I knew what the most important thing was. My mission was all that mattered.

If these fools got on my bad side, I wasn't above killing them also.

Hunger began to stir inside me at the thought.

No . . .

I tried to push it away. I couldn't let the hunger continue. The hunger, after a while, would begin to control me. Then it would make me do things I didn't want to do, to behave in ways I didn't plan.

I liked to be more in control.

But sometimes, the urges were like animals clawing at my insides.

Once they were unleashed . . . everything was out of my control.

That wasn't my fault. I didn't care what people said.

People have been telling so many lies. Lies were the fuel some people ran on.

Those people deserve to die also. Was there anyone honest out there anymore?

If there was, I hadn't met them.

I ran my hand over my face, and a thought hit me.

A beard . . . I hadn't used a beard on my snowmen yet. Maybe that would be a nice touch.

It just so happened that both men inside the cabin had beards.

They weren't a part of my original plan. But people were always telling me I should be more flexible.

Maybe this would be a good start.

These men had practically given me the idea themselves.

Now I just needed to rearrange a few things on my plan.

My lips curled into a smile as I pulled my hat lower on my forehead and hurried through the woods.

CHAPTER 31

uke drew his gun and ducked behind the window. "You heard that too?"

Ranger already had his gun drawn also. "Sure did."

"It sounds like we have a visitor."

The question was, was this visitor the friendly or unfriendly type? Was it the person who'd been staying here? Or someone more sinister? Or maybe the people staying here *were* the sinister ones.

There were still entirely too many unknowns right now.

"I'm going to open the door on three," Duke told Ranger quietly.

Ranger nodded in acknowledgement.

Duke counted down and threw the door open, stepping outside as he did.

The dark, cold Alaskan landscape glared back at

him. But no one was there to bum rush him. No obvious signs of danger stared them down.

Just a still, snowy subarctic forest.

But Duke wasn't ready to let down his guard yet.

He'd definitely heard something out here.

"Hello?" he called.

There was no response.

Ranger handed him a flashlight. Then they split in opposite directions.

Duke's flashlight stopped at a new set of footprints in the snow. Footprints that led to one of the windows in the cabin.

Someone had been here while they checked out the cabin. The snow hadn't covered the prints yet. This person had most likely seen them inside.

Based on the tracks in the snow, as soon as this person had heard footsteps coming toward the door, he'd run.

The size of the print indicated the visitor had been a man. Possibly a woman with large feet, but Duke didn't think so.

After circling the cabin, Ranger met him. "We should follow the tracks."

Duke's thoughts exactly. "Let's go."

They followed the trail through the darkness, only to discover the footsteps ended at the path where Ranger and Duke had first started. A fresh set of UTV tire tracks stretched there. It was far enough away they wouldn't have heard a motor or the vehicle leaving.

"Whoever was out here is long gone." Duke shook his head as he stared at the tracks.

"Why would someone be following us?" Ranger asked. "If it was someone on the up and up, then he would have let us know about his presence. He wouldn't have run."

"That's true. And he wouldn't have been watching us through the window."

They started back to the cabin. When they reached it, Duke paused beside the UTV. The vehicle looked lopsided for some reason.

He took a step closer.

"Everything good?" Ranger asked.

"I'm not sure." He kneeled for a better look.

That was when he realized two of the tires had been slashed.

———

Andi paced the living room of her cabin, trying to keep her worries under control.

Why hadn't they heard from Duke and Ranger yet? It had been two hours.

Her mind had gone to worst-case scenarios—mostly a killer finding them and building a snowman in memory of their murders.

She didn't want to be that person.

But she was. Too many bad things had happened for

her to be an optimist in times like this. The familiar ache began in her head.

"Y'all . . ." She grabbed her coat and turned to the rest of the team. "I'm going to take a quick walk to the lodge. But I'll be back soon."

Maybe Gibson would be there and have an update. Or maybe Duke and Ranger had shown up and just not contacted the team yet.

"Do you want me to walk with you?" Matthew asked.

She shook her head. "I'll be fine, but thank you. I just need to clear my head a bit."

She shivered as soon as she stepped outside. It was dark and brutally cold. She hoped Duke and Ranger weren't stuck out in this. A person could die out in these conditions if they weren't properly prepared. Thankfully, she knew both Duke and Ranger could most likely handle themselves. Still . . .

As soon as she stepped into the lobby of the lodge, her gaze went to Gibson. He stood near the check-in desk, his phone to his ear. He lowered it when he saw her.

She paused in front of him. "No word from Duke?"

He shook his head. "I was just about to find you and ask you the same. We haven't heard from him or Ranger. The rest of the teams are back."

"Did you try him on the radio?" Andi had specifically seen Gibson give Duke a radio before he'd left.

"They're not responding."

Her thoughts continued to race. "What's the range on those things?"

"Usually about six miles."

She nodded slowly as she let that fact settle. "So if they got out of that range, there's a good chance they have no cell phone service or radio contact, am I right?"

Gibson frowned. "Unfortunately, yes. Knowing Duke and Ranger, there's a very good possibility they did just that."

Andi rubbed her arms as goosebumps covered her flesh. "What if they ran into trouble?"

His cheek twitched. "Let's hope that's not the case. They're both good at what they do. You know that."

She did know that. But it was good to hear the reminder also.

"What do we do now?" She tried to focus her thoughts instead of letting her fears run wild. That was never productive—though it was always tempting.

"I sent a couple of my guys out on the path where Duke and Ranger were assigned. I hope to hear something soon."

"Let me go," she insisted. "I want to help."

"That's a bad idea." He shook his head grimly. "I know you want to find him. But the best thing you can do right now is to stay here and hold tight. We don't want to lose track of anyone else."

Andi frowned, understanding his words—even if she didn't like them.

Instead, she stared out the window.

She prayed Duke and Ranger were okay.

CHAPTER 32

uke checked the UTV for a spare tire—not that he thought one spare would really help considering they had two flat tires.

There were none. Not only that, but his radio didn't work out here. He'd tried, but they must be too far away from the transponder.

He looked up at Ranger. "It looks like we're going to need an alternate plan."

"Yes, it does."

He glanced at the forest around them. "It's cold outside and dark. We wandered at least five or six miles away from the camp. It would be a long way to walk . . . but it is possible."

"Or we could just camp out here tonight," Ranger suggested with a nod toward the cabin.

That *was* another possibility. There had been wood outside the cabin, as well as some matches inside.

Starting a fire would keep them warm, which would be the smart thing. But Duke also knew Andi and the gang would be worried.

"I like your idea," Duke finally said. "I think our best bet is to stay here. Then we can set out again in the morning."

With that decision agreed on, they went back inside the small cabin. Ranger got busy starting a fire. While he did that, Duke tracked down a half-eaten canister of peanuts and some granola bars. It would be nice to have some food in their stomachs. Even nicer if the food was warm, but what he'd found would work for now.

Since he was stuck here, at least that might give him another chance to look around the place. Plus, he wasn't convinced they'd be here all night. Gibson would most likely send out another team once he realized they hadn't made it back.

The only problem was that they'd traveled off the path they were supposed to stay on. In one way, the risk had paid off because they'd found this place. On the other hand, it would make the search to find them take longer.

As Ranger continued to work on the fire, Duke opened more dresser drawers.

More women's clothing waited inside. Nothing fancy, just a pair of leggings and a couple of sweatshirts. If he had to guess by looking at the size and style of clothes, the woman who'd been living here was thin and on the younger side.

He couldn't imagine a young woman living out here by herself. This place was so secluded, and walking to town would be nearly impossible. Maybe this woman had a UTV or snowmobile she used. Still, living out here would be difficult.

Unless she had help.

That thought stopped him. Maybe that was it. Maybe this person did have help. Maybe someone knew she lived close by.

Could it be Tim? Could he have a secret girlfriend?

Duke couldn't rule it out.

Duke opened the last drawer and paused.

Men's clothing had been stuffed inside the drawer. He picked up a piece on top. Borealis Reindeer Camp was embroidered on the pocket of the shirt, and right below it was the name . . . Caleb.

Caleb had been staying out here?

An idea hit him, and Duke opened the top drawer again.

On a whim, he lifted one of the women's sweatshirts and brought it to his nose.

That was when he knew who the woman who'd been staying here was.

———

Andi couldn't sit still. She paced the dining hall of the lodge.

The rest of the gang had joined her after she told them the update.

It was better if they all stayed together. There had been too many close calls for them to relax. They needed to stick close to each other and be vigilant.

Simmy looked equally worried as she sat near the fire, staring at the flames.

A few guests milled around, instructed to remain inside. Juniper holed up in her office, catching up on paperwork, she'd said. Tim had driven into town because his son was having some type of emergency.

Everyone seemed on edge.

The door opened behind her, and she jerked her head to look.

Gibson stepped inside. Disappointment filled her—but the emotion was quickly replaced with hope. Maybe he was here with an update.

But one look at his face, and Andi knew it wasn't good news.

He paused in front of her. "There's still nothing."

Her shoulders sagged. "Duke and Ranger have to be out there somewhere."

"And my guys are looking for them."

"I know. And I appreciate that."

Gibson pulled out a chair at one of the tables and sat facing Andi. "As we wait, fill me in on everything that's been going on. And don't leave out any details . . . please."

She drew in a deep breath and pulled herself

together. Then she sat across from Gibson and began to go through everything they'd learned so far. Just as Gibson had asked, she didn't leave out any details, even the ones that didn't seem important.

As she talked, his radio crackled. Gibson held up a finger to pause their conversation and then put the device closer to his ear.

Andi tried to make out what was said, but it was hard to understand.

Finally, Gibson lowered the radio. "My guys found another trail off the main one, and it has some fresh tire tracks. They're going to check it out."

Her heart lifted. "That sounds promising."

He offered an affirming nod. "We should know something soon."

Andi hoped Gibson was right. Mostly, she prayed that Duke and Ranger were safe.

CHAPTER 33

uke heard the sound of snow crunching beneath an unseen weight outside the cabin and bristled.

What if the person who'd slit his tires was back?

He couldn't be sure. But he couldn't take any chances.

He drew his gun again as he approached the door.

"Someone's here." Ranger stood also, instantly going on alert.

The hum of a motor cut through the air.

Would whoever had been here earlier be brazen enough to return? He found it hard to believe.

But maybe.

He grabbed his flashlight and aimed it in front of him, and then cautiously opened the door.

Instead of seeing a person, a bright light blinded him.

He raised his hand to see beyond the glare.

"Duke McAllister?" a deep voice called. "Ranger Garrett?"

Duke remained stiff. "That's us."

"We're with the state police. We've been looking for you."

His shoulders softened as he let down his guard—some. "Someone slashed our tires," he explained. "We couldn't get back to the camp, so we started a fire to warm up here. Figured we might have to spend the night."

The man stepped into the light, and Duke recognized him as one of the officers he'd seen with Gibson earlier. Officer Winsome.

"I'm glad we found you," Officer Winsome said. "It's supposed to drop to twenty below tonight, and the snow is supposed to pick up. A storm is headed this way."

Ranger stepped toward them. "We're glad you found us also."

Duke glanced back inside the cabin. "You're going to want to check this place out."

"Why is that?"

"Because I believe Pepper Klinkhart was using this place for some kind of secret rendezvous before she was murdered."

————

"Good news," Gibson announced.

Andi and Simmy sat up from where they'd been seated at a table in the lobby—both attempting to work even though their concentration was shot.

Juniper wandered around, offering cookies and coffee to guests like a good hostess.

Some guests had been questioned and allowed to leave. Others had decided to stay, claiming they had nowhere else to go and weren't comfortable driving in the snow.

According to Gibson, none of them had anything to offer, however. Those potential leads had fizzled.

They turned toward Gibson as they waited to hear what he had to say.

"We found Duke and Ranger," Gibson told them. "They had some problems with their UTV, but they're on their way back now."

Relief swept through Andi. He was okay. Praise God!

At least this was a little bit of good news in the middle of a lot of bad news.

Andi hardly knew what to do with herself as she waited. So she did what she did best. She paced.

Finally, thirty minutes later, the doors opened again.

This time, Duke and Ranger stepped inside, two officers following them.

Andi and Simmy ran toward them, and Andi threw her arms around Duke.

Duke held Andi close.

"I was so worried," Andi whispered in his ear. "I kept fighting off the worst-case scenarios that wanted to play out in my mind. But they kept coming back."

"I'm sorry to scare you. I tried to radio in our location, but there was no service."

"I know." She pulled away from the hug and left her hands resting on his chest as she gazed up at him. "Did you find anything?"

His expression tightened. "We did. Everyone's going to want to hear this, though."

Almost as if everyone in the room had heard him say that, the rest of the gang appeared and gathered around, including Gibson.

"What happened out there?" Gibson placed his hands on his hips, his brow furrowed with curiosity.

"We found an old cabin out in the forest," Duke explained. "At first, we thought it was abandoned. When we went inside, it became obvious someone had been staying there."

"There are three or four of those old cabins out on our property," Juniper said. "They're left over from when goldminers were in this area. But they're mostly shacks."

"Any idea who would be staying there?"

"I have no idea." Juniper shrugged.

"I think I know," Duke stated. "It was your friend Pepper, wasn't it?"

Juniper swallowed hard. "It's complicated. She had a place to stay here at the camp. But when I first told her she could stay here, she did use one of the cabins. I couldn't let my parents know she was here, and it was only supposed to be temporary. After my parents died . . ."

"You let her take one of the staff accommodations," Andi finished.

"I had no reason not to." Juniper shrugged. "I felt a little guilty about it, like Peppermint was benefiting from my parents' death. Then I realized that was crazy. Circumstances had changed so there was no reason to keep her presence here a secret anymore."

"So why would she still be using it?" Duke asked. "It appears she'd been there recently."

Gibson glanced at Juniper. "Is there something you want to tell us?"

Juniper swung her head back and forth, guilt filling her gaze. "No . . . I didn't know she still went out there. Nor do I have any idea why."

"Maybe you should tell us everything you do know then," Andi said. "No more secrets."

CHAPTER 34
DECEMBER, LAST YEAR

have an idea," Peppermint told Juniper as they strolled among the reindeer in the pen.

It had been three weeks since Juniper's parents had died. After the funeral, she'd realized there was no reason to keep Peppermint in the secluded cabin.

The only reason Peppermint had been there was because Juniper knew her parents would be upset if they knew what Juniper had done, especially since they wanted nothing to do with the Klinkharts anymore.

Still, something had felt wrong about moving Peppermint out of that cabin and into a more secure space here at the camp.

However, they did have one staff cabin they weren't using. They could have let some of the female staff have more space and put two workers in one cabin and two in the other, even though each building was situated to handle four people.

Her parents hadn't wanted to do that in order to save money. Juniper guessed not running the heat in one of the cabins would save them a little on their bills. And every penny counted. That was what her mom always said.

Juniper knew her friend wanted to try out some projects using peppermint. She thought if she had some type of product to sell, the money that brought in might help her get back on solid ground. If she could get her own business up and running then she wouldn't have to depend on Juniper anymore. But she needed space to experiment.

Juniper, of course, had told Peppermint it wasn't a big deal if she stayed here. That she was in no hurry to run her off.

Those words were mostly true. Juniper did like having her friend around.

So why did she keep hearing her parents' voices in the back of her mind?

She was in charge at the camp now, and there was nothing wrong with her friend staying on campus. They should help each other out, after all.

But Juniper had heard some of the other staff members whispering, upset that Peppermint had gotten her own cabin. Uncle Tim especially hadn't liked it.

However, this wasn't Tim's decision. It was Juniper's.

Juniper threw more feed down for the reindeer. "What's your idea?"

Peppermint's eyes lit with excitement. "What would you think about letting these reindeer do special appearances in town?"

Juniper froze and squinted in confusion at her friend. "What do you mean?"

"I mean, so many places would love to have visits from the reindeer, especially at Christmastime. We could do some of the festivals in Fairbanks. Let kids meet the reindeer and get their pictures taken with them. I think it would be a real hit."

Juniper considered her words a moment before nodding. It really wasn't a bad idea. Even though the camp was doing okay financially, it would be nice to have some extra money in the bank for leaner times.

But she really needed to think through the logistics. What exactly would that idea involve?

She threw down another handful of feed. "I'd need someone to be in charge."

"I'd be happy to help." Peppermint shrugged, a hopeful look to her eyes. "Since my parents are no longer in the area, I don't see where it could hurt for me to leave the camp. Of course, I'd need at least one other person to go with me."

"I'm sure I could find another staff member to help, especially if it was only one or two days a week."

"That way I can also check out some of the craft fairs and festivals. Maybe even sell some of my peppermint products there." Her voice climbed with excitement.

"I think that sounds like a great idea." Juniper was proud of her friend for thinking ahead.

Movement in the distance caught her eye, and she looked toward the lodge.

It was Caleb.

He lifted a hand and waved toward them.

Peppermint followed her gaze but quickly looked away.

She'd been acting strange around Caleb lately. But Juniper thought it was because Caleb was the only one who knew all the history between their families. Well, Caleb and Tim.

Juniper figured those facts might make Peppermint feel self-conscious, which wasn't what she wanted for her friend.

No, Juniper would do whatever she could to help Peppermint. She'd do whatever she could to carry on the legacy her parents had started here at this camp also.

She only wished her mom and dad had been honest with her.

Because maybe then she could have been honest with them also.

CHAPTER 35

DECEMBER, PRESENT DAY

ibson directed the group to sit together at a nearby table, where they all waited to hear Juniper's explanation.

There was clearly more to this story.

"I know how this is going to sound." Juniper rubbed her hands together, her entire body tense and her actions jumpy.

That was never a good way to start a conversation, especially when a serial killer could be involved.

"Peppermint and I had been friends a long time. When we were in high school, our families had that big split, and we weren't sure we'd be able to be friends anymore. But at least we were able to see each other in school."

They waited in silence for her to continue.

"One day when we were eating lunch together in the school cafeteria, she told me that her dad wanted to move their family down to Seattle, where they could get a fresh start. She didn't want to go, but she was too young to stay here on her own. So I told her about the old cabin. I didn't want her to move either. She was like a sister to me."

"So you figured out a way to keep her here?" Andi asked.

"In a manner of speaking, yes. I mean, she was eighteen. A legal adult. Old enough to live on her own and make her own choices. She just didn't have any income to support herself."

"Okay, but why didn't she just move in with you?" Andi asked. "Why live in such a secluded cabin?"

"My parents would have never let her live with us. But Peppermint and I knew if she lived somewhere obvious that her mom and dad would find her. They would demand she go with them to Seattle. I suggested she live in the cabin."

"I was just inside that cabin," Duke said. "It's very rustic. How did she survive out there?"

Juniper shrugged. "I took wood, food, and other supplies to her as needed. I did whatever I could to help her out."

"Your parents never noticed what you were doing?" Gibson squinted as if skeptical about this story.

"I made sure they were busy doing something else whenever I went to visit. They liked the fact I had room to roam here, so they didn't ask a lot of questions."

"Pepper's parents never reported her missing?" Gibson asked.

"They did," Juniper said. "But she left a note saying she was moving out on her own, so there was nothing the police could do. She wasn't technically a missing person. And her parents knew she didn't want to move so . . ."

"Who's her secret boyfriend?" Andi asked.

Juniper froze, not responding.

"Juniper . . ." Simmy tilted her head at the woman.

She finally let out a breath and squeezed the skin between her eyes. "I only have suspicions. No proof. But I . . . wondered if she and Caleb were seeing each other."

Andi's eyebrows flew up. "Why do you think that?"

She squeezed her eyes shut again. "I suspected it a while. It was just the way the two of them were acting. But both of them denied it. I just can't believe that they'd sneak around behind my back. They were the two people I trusted most."

Simmy's hand went to Juniper's back again, and she rubbed it gently.

But Andi knew the question in everyone's mind.

Was Juniper upset enough about the cheating that she may have killed her friend and done something to Caleb?

CHAPTER 36

ndi walked beside Duke as he held a flashlight in front of the group while they trudged through the snow back to their cabin.

Gibson had told them they should turn in for the night. He still had more investigating to do, but a lot of it involved wrapping up loose ends.

Juniper had offered to let him and his colleagues stay at the camp tonight, since they now had empty rooms. Andi wasn't sure if he would take her up on the offer or not. Either way, Gibson had promised to be in touch in the morning.

Snow was still coming down lightly, and the clouds above prevented them from seeing any northern lights that might be dancing above them right now.

Something about the aurora still fascinated Andi to this day. It seemed otherworldly and reminded her of the vastness of the universe.

She wished it was out to distract her now.

"This has been some day, hasn't it?" Mariella finally broke the silence.

"You can say that again," Duke said. "Yet, even after everything that's happened, I'm not sure we're any closer to finding answers."

"Then we keep looking," Ranger said. "We'll get there."

"That is if all these crimes are connected with the December Dismemberer," Simmy said. "I mean, what's happened since we've been here breaks his pattern. I'm no profiler, but even I know that."

She had a point, Andi realized. If this serial killer was behind this, why was he deviating from his MO? Had something triggered him?

Was there more than one killer at play right now?

The question wasn't comforting.

Mariella started jabbering about some things they needed to do for the podcast, but Andi only half-listened. She had too many other thoughts running through her head instead.

When they reached their cabin, Duke stopped and threw his arms out to stop everyone behind him also.

Andi's breath caught. "What is it?"

He took his flashlight and shined it on the snowy ground. "Someone's been here."

Andi squinted, trying to see what he saw.

Then she realized what it was.

Footprints ran along the perimeter of the cabin.

Those tracks appeared to stop near each window, as if someone had peered inside to see if anyone was in there.

————

"Everyone, stay here," Duke grumbled. "Ranger, stay with them . . . just in case."

Ranger grunted and his shoulders broadened as he took on more of a bodyguard stance. "Good idea."

Duke held his flashlight in one hand and his gun in the other.

Then he quietly opened the front door and glanced around.

Silence greeted him. As far as he remembered, the place looked like the gang had left it. Nothing appeared out of place.

So who had been walking around outside the cabin?

The logical conclusion was . . . the killer. Had the man come to see what they were up to?

Based on what Duke had seen outside, there were no signs anyone had entered the cabin. Still, he needed to play it safe.

He checked the rest of the rooms, looking under every bed and behind every door.

He saw nothing.

Whatever that guy was doing outside, it didn't

appear he'd left them any surprises. Duke was thankful for that.

Maybe it wasn't the killer who had been out there. Maybe it was one of the state troopers checking to make sure everything was okay. Or maybe even a worker from the camp.

He could jump to any number of conclusions. But he wouldn't.

He had to remain objective.

He walked back to the door and signaled to the rest of the group, letting them know that they could come inside.

Slowly, they filed in. But everyone appeared on edge with their tight shoulders and darting gazes.

"Wait . . . you're sure it's safe?" Mariella's voice wavered.

"No one is hiding in here," Duke assured her.

"Good, because I need to run to the restroom."

She hurried down the hall.

As soon as she stepped through the bathroom door, she called, "You guys . . . you're going to want to see this."

They took off toward the bathroom, anxious to know what she was talking about.

Duke sucked in a breath when he glanced at the mirror.

Someone had drawn a beard on the mirror. No face. No body. Just a beard scrawled in black marker floating in the middle of the reflective glass.

He hadn't bothered to look at the mirror earlier. He was too busy looking for intruders.

Was this image some kind of warning? Or was it a sick joke?

CHAPTER 37

ibson showed up at their cabin a few minutes later.

Andi and the gang had known it was important for him to see this beard for himself. That he checked for any evidence the police might need in building a case.

But as soon as he saw what had been drawn on the mirror, he shook his head, a grim expression in his gaze. "I don't like the look of this."

"None of us do," Andi said as she stood in the hallway, trying to give him space.

Gibson turned and glanced first at Duke and then at Ranger. "This guy could be targeting either of you."

Andi watched as Duke ran a hand over his beard. Then she had visions of what the killer might do to him if he ever got his hands on Duke.

The blood drained from her face at the very thought.

They *had* to catch this guy before he struck again. They had no other choice. Because she couldn't stomach the thought of Duke or Ranger going through that kind of pain. Of either of them no longer being with them.

"This guy's clearly sending a message." She crossed her arms over her chest, trying to get the images out of her mind.

"But this doesn't fit his MO." Gibson remained in the bathroom but turned toward them as they gathered around the doorway. "The December Dismemberer doesn't normally give any type of hint about what is going on or what he's planning."

"I find that suspicious also," Duke said. "Why change now? Besides, he's never struck the same place twice."

"Maybe something changed," Gibson said. "Or maybe this is someone just trying to frighten you, to get you to leave this area."

Andi had thought of that also. "I can't help but think that someone is trying to shut this camp down."

Gibson's gaze darkened. "I've had that thought as well."

Andi studied his expression a moment.

He knew something they didn't, didn't he?

She waited to hear if he would share.

What wasn't Gibson telling them? Duke wondered. Because there was clearly something else on his mind.

"Gibson . . . ?" He stared at his friend.

Gibson let out a breath. "Look, I'm not supposed to share information like this. But all of us . . . we've been through some things together, haven't we?"

"That would be an understatement." Ranger offered a wry expression.

Gibson let out an exhausted chuckle. "Yes, it would be. The truth is, I did an extensive background check on Caleb Brinley."

"And?" Andi asked.

"Caleb Brinley from Montana died in 1979."

Duke's eyebrows shot up. "What?"

Gibson nodded. "Caleb Brinley, as we know him, does not legally exist."

"Wait . . . so Juniper's boyfriend found a dead man named Caleb Brinley and took on his identity?" Mariella's forehead wrinkled.

"That's how it appears."

"Was he in witness protection or something?" Simmy asked.

"It's really hard to find out that information," Gibson said. "My colleagues with the US Marshals usually don't like to share it with me. But I did put in a request. I'm waiting to hear back."

"Did you check Caleb's place?" Duke asked. "Andi and I saw some of it, but we didn't go through everything."

"We did check out his cabin, but we didn't find anything of note," Gibson said. "However, Caleb had an office in the garage where the UTVs are stored."

Duke's heart thumped in his ears. They'd found something, hadn't they?

He waited for his friend to continue.

"Under one of the floorboards, we found a box. Inside there was a thousand dollars cash, some fake IDs, a gun, and a knife."

"A knife? Could it be the one used to . . . ?" Duke couldn't finish the statement.

Gibson's expression remained grim. "We're going to test it for trace evidence."

Duke rubbed his jaw. "Fake IDs? Wads of cash? It sounds like something Ranger might have had at one time."

Ranger had worked for the CIA, where fake IDs and go-bags were an everyday part of his life.

"I thought about that, but this Caleb guy doesn't strike me as the CIA type," Gibson said. "Could be wrong."

"It's something to explore," Ranger said with a grunt. "But he doesn't strike me as a spook either."

"Caleb was definitely hiding something and definitely in some type of trouble." Gibson paused and let out a slow breath. "However, I don't think he's our serial killer."

Duke wanted to argue. He wanted to believe Caleb was guilty. But he knew the truth.

Caleb didn't fit the MO of the killer.

Two separate crimes were going on here.

Now they needed to comb through what was what.

CHAPTER 38

TWO DAYS UNTIL THE NEXT MURDER

Andi hadn't slept well last night. Not with knowing someone had been in the cabin and left that morbid image on the mirror.

Gibson had assigned another officer to stay inside the living room overnight, just in case.

Andi was thankful for that because she knew Duke or Ranger would have stayed up all night to keep an eye on things otherwise. They all needed their rest.

Today would be another busy day.

They all awoke early and got dressed. The cop staying with them was bright-eyed as if staying awake all night was normal. He told them it had been quiet before he left for the lodge.

Then the gang had bundled up and trudged through the snow toward the dining hall.

They could have probably thrown together something to eat at the cabin, but they were all anxious for an update, and the dining hall was the best place to hear one.

However, last night's snow had turned into today's winter storm. The icy precipitation came down so fast and thick that walls of white surrounded them outside, blocking their view of anything else. Only their instincts would get them safely to the lodge—and even that felt risky.

It would be easy for anyone to get lost in these conditions.

Finally, they reached the dining hall. The scent of bacon, sausage, and coffee immediately greeted them.

After peeling off her extra layers of clothing, Andi immediately went for coffee, needing something to warm her up. The rest of the gang either followed her to the pot or headed to the buffet to grab some food.

Andi had just taken her first sip when Juniper stepped out of her office, Tundra on her heels.

Based on the way she looked, she hadn't gotten any sleep last night either. Dark circles hung beneath her eyes, and her skin appeared listless and pale.

Andi paced closer. "Any updates?"

Juniper shook her head. "No. There's still no sign of Caleb. Not last I heard at least."

"I'm so sorry," Andi murmured. "I know that must be difficult for you."

Andi didn't know yet if the man was innocent or guilty. But she would give him the benefit of the doubt.

Plus, Juniper's distress was heartbreaking. She cared about the man.

Gibson had already talked to her and told her Caleb wasn't who he claimed to be. Juniper had been clueless. According to Gibson, she'd gone pale when she'd heard, like the fact had shaken her.

"Have you seen Gibson yet?" Duke took a sip of his coffee. "I heard he might spend the night here."

"He stayed in one of the cabins here at the camp." She nodded behind them. "It looks like he just came in."

They turned to see the state trooper step inside and stomp the snow off his shoes. He looked as if he'd gotten just as much sleep as the rest of them.

He headed toward them and paused. "Nothing new on my end. How about you guys? I heard it was pretty quiet."

"It *was* quiet," Andi told him, though she found little reassurance in the fact. Was this the quiet before the storm? That was what she feared.

"We have some corned beef hash, bacon, sausage, scrambled eggs, and fruit," Juniper told them, her voice dull. "Please, help yourself."

Juniper nodded toward the breakfast buffet in the distance. Matthew and Ranger were already eating.

Now that she mentioned it, Andi was kind of hungry —despite their dire circumstances. She hadn't eaten much yesterday, and now her stomach was reminding her of the fact.

They started toward the buffet.

Before they reached the food, the door flew open again.

Andi jerked her head toward it, curious about who was here now.

Her eyes widened when she spotted a man she'd never seen before.

Based on the fire shooting out of his eyes, he was angry. *Really* angry.

———

"Mr. Klinkhart . . ." Juniper muttered, taking a step back.

"Wait . . . who?" Mariella murmured.

"That's Heath," Duke told her, gripping an empty plate in his hands. "Pepper's dad. I saw his picture when I was doing research earlier."

The tall, broad-shouldered man stormed toward Juniper. His hands were fisted at his sides, and his face wore a fiery shade of red.

The man was seething.

"I just heard about my daughter," he announced. "From someone else. You didn't even have the nerve to tell me, even after all you've done?"

Even after all you've done? Was there more to this story? Or was the man simply referencing the fact that Juniper had helped Pepper start a new life for herself?

Duke edged closer to Juniper, ready to step in if things turned uglier.

He didn't need to, however. Gibson did instead. "I'm State Trooper Logan Gibson. Can I help you?"

The man's nostrils flared, and his gaze remained on Juniper. "I'm Heath Klinkhart. My daughter was found dead on this property. I flew in as soon as I heard."

"I'm sorry for your loss, Mr. Klinkhart." Gibson kept his voice professional. "But it wasn't Juniper's job to let you know about your daughter."

Heath only grunted.

"Traveling here was a risky move considering how bad the roads are," Gibson continued. "I'm surprised they didn't tell you to go to our office in Fairbanks."

"Nothing was going to keep me away. I haven't seen my daughter in a year, but I still had hopes I'd see her again one day." His gaze went back to Juniper, hatred rising in waves from his eyes. "Thanks to you, that isn't going to happen."

"Me? I just tried to help my friend. It's more than you ever did. You insisted she move with you. That she marry that man she didn't even like. It's not like we're in the 1800s or something. People don't do that anymore!"

"She wasn't making good decisions! We just wanted to help guide her. We wouldn't have forced the marriage. I'm not barbaric."

"She loved this place," Juniper countered. "She loved everything we represent, and she didn't want to leave."

"You shouldn't have interfered!"

As his voice thundered across the room, Juniper backed up and hit a dining table. A chair on the other side fell backward, causing a loud crash to echo in the room.

"You should have stayed out of it." Hatred came in invisible waves from the man.

"Do you want to tell me what's going on here?" Gibson stepped closer, placing himself between Heath and Juniper.

"The problem here is this woman." He glared at Juniper. "She's just like her parents—meddling, lying, and controlling."

"Don't talk about my parents." Some of the fear disappeared from Juniper's voice, replaced with defensiveness.

"I told your dad not to open this place. That it was bad news."

Juniper blinked in confusion. "That's not true. You wanted to go in with him!"

"Who told you that?"

"I overheard the conversation myself."

That was what Juniper had told them earlier also, Duke remembered. So what was this guy's take on the situation?

"Well, you heard wrong." Heath spit out the words. "I told your father this camp was a terrible idea. He wanted me to invest, but I told him no. He was furious with me for rejecting his idea."

Juniper shook her head, her gaze tumultuous with confusion. "No, that's not right."

"Did you come here just to tell Juniper that?" Gibson asked.

"No, I came here because it's her fault my daughter's dead. If Pepper had listened and moved with her mother and me, she'd still be alive right now!"

CHAPTER 39

While Duke and Gibson led Mr. Klinkhart away, Andi and Simmy led Juniper in the opposite direction.

It was clear these two needed to be separated. Juniper was upset—and rightfully so. That confrontation had been ugly and uncalled for.

Andi directed Juniper to a seat in the corner. Andi sat on one side of her and Simmy on the other.

"Are you okay?" Andi asked softly, truly concerned about Juniper's mental state after those accusations had been hurled at her.

Juniper shook her head, though her gaze still look bewildered with shock. "I can't believe he came here. I can't believe he said those things."

"Pepper's death is *not* your fault." Even as Andi said the words, she remembered her earlier suspicions—

suspicions that Juniper had discovered Pepper and Caleb were seeing each other and the murder could have been a jealous fit of rage.

She couldn't rule the theory out, though she didn't see Juniper as a killer.

Right now, she would put that idea aside.

"I know, but . . ." Juniper sniffled. "If I hadn't told Peppermint about the cabin and let her stay there, she would have moved away, and then none of this would have happened . . . her dad is right."

"Don't go there." Simmy squeezed Juniper's hand. "Something else could have happened to her if she did move. Her father obviously has anger problems and control issues."

Andi had noticed how quickly Simmy and Juniper had bonded. Simmy had almost stepped in as a motherly figure, and Andi sensed that was something Juniper desperately needed. The ability to love and care for others was a true gift, and Simmy had that in abundance.

Andi shifted her thoughts. "What about what Mr. Klinkhart said about the property? Do you think he's lying? Or do you think you misunderstood what was happening when your parents started this place?"

"What exactly did you hear, sweetie?" Simmy still gently gripped Juniper's forearm.

Juniper ran a hand roughly beneath her eyes before drawing in a breath. "My dad told Heath he was sorry this didn't work out. Then Heath said he was making a huge mistake. Then my dad insisted he wouldn't change his mind. I asked my parents later, and they confirmed what I heard. Why would they lie?"

"Maybe to protect themselves?" Andi suggested with a shrug. "To protect the image you had of them?"

"But if that's true . . ." Juniper blinked back tears as she shook her head. "Then that would change everything."

Andi knew those words were true. That would mean that Juniper's parents might have been keeping secrets. Not telling the whole truth. But what reason would they have to lie?

Questions swirled in her mind.

Juniper's phone buzzed, and she glanced at the screen. "It's the hospital. I should take this. It could be an update on Emmett."

Andi nodded and watched as she answered.

A few seconds into the conversation, Juniper's eyes brightened. "Is that right? Okay. Thank you. I appreciate it."

When Juniper ended the call, she looked at Andi and Simmy. "Emmett is awake, and he wants to talk to me."

———

Duke and Gibson had successfully gotten Heath Klinkhart to calm down.

Duke instinctively didn't like the man after he'd come in here acting so irate. But the man had also lost his daughter. He had to keep reminding himself of that fact.

He looked up as Andi walked over. She glanced at him and Gibson, then nodded in the distance, indicating she needed to tell them something.

They left Heath and followed Andi to the other side of the room.

"Juniper just got a call," Andi told them. "Emmett is awake and wants to talk."

"That's great news," Gibson said. "I'd like to talk to him as soon as possible. Do you think he saw something —or someone—before he found Pepper's body?"

"It makes sense to me," Duke said. "He basically said he had something to tell us, then started to say someone killed Pepper. He didn't have a chance to finish."

Gibson glanced at his watch. "I'll head back to the hospital. Even though the roads are slick, I think I can handle it."

Andi tilted her head. "Are you sure? It's pretty bad out there."

"I need to know what's going on," Gibson said. "People's lives may depend on those answers. Plus, there's a break in the storm for the next few hours, but it's supposed to get worse later."

"Do you want one of us to go with you?" Andi asked.

"No, the best bet is for you guys to stay here," Gibson said. "I'll take one of my troopers with me just in case. But I'll leave two of them here as well in case anything arises."

"That sounds like a plan." Andi glanced to Heath as he sulked in the corner. "And him?"

Gibson frowned as he studied the man. "I can't exactly send him on his way considering his current mental state."

"But I don't think he should be around Juniper either."

Almost as if he'd heard them, Heath stood. He almost seemed to growl as he stormed toward the door.

"Where are you going?" Gibson stepped toward him.

"I'm getting out of here. I can't stomach being at this place a moment longer. Besides, you have no reason to keep me here." Heath paused with his hand on the door as he stared at Gibson, challenge in his gaze. "So it's my right to leave."

The man had a point. There was no legal reason to hold him.

"That's true. But the roads are bad," Gibson reminded him.

"I'll be fine!" Without another word, Heath charged out the door.

They all stood in silence in his wake. The man was grieving, yes. But he also had some major anger issues.

No wonder Pepper had wanted to get away.

Gibson let out a sigh before turning back to them. "I'm going to head out now also. I'll let you know what I find out."

Duke nodded. This could be their chance to get some answers. He hoped Emmett truly did know something that proved helpful.

CHAPTER 40

Simmy had reminded the gang that they needed to eat in order to keep up their energy. Andi couldn't argue.

For that reason, the gang grabbed breakfast.

They were essentially the only ones in the dining hall, other than two cooks. Apparently, the kitchen staff hadn't quit and left like some of the other guests and employees.

Juniper had disappeared into one of the spare rooms at the lodge, saying she wanted to lie down a while but stay close. She had a lot to process, so maybe some sleep would be good for her.

Meanwhile, the Arctic Circle Murder Club found a table in the corner where they could figure out their next plan of action.

But Andi's thoughts had been racing all morning.

She forced herself to eat some eggs and toast. To drink her coffee.

As she finished eating, she stood, unable to sit still any longer. Instead, she placed her hands on her hips and began to pace. Meetings like these took her back to her days as an attorney when she and her colleagues would prep for a big case.

"Duke, did Heath say anything else when you guys were talking to him?" she started.

"Just that he'd flown in and landed this morning."

"Where is his wife?" Simmy asked. "Why didn't she come?"

"She's been sick with pneumonia and couldn't fly—even though she wanted to," Duke said. "So Heath came alone."

"I suppose that makes sense," Andi said before turning to Matthew. "Matthew, while you've been researching, did you find anything significant that may have happened on December 6 to trigger that specific date for these murders?"

He pushed his glasses higher on his nose as he peered up at her. "I've been looking into it, but I haven't made much progress. I'll keep looking."

"You do that," Andi said. "We also need to look up any stories from this area about snowmen. Maybe that plays a significant role in why this killer is doing what he's doing."

Mariella raised a manicured finger. "I can help Matthew with that."

"What about Jesse Burbach?" Duke sat back in his chair, appearing stiff from sitting for so long. "Has anybody looked at him again? He was the primary suspect when the police originally investigated."

"He had an alibi for the night of one or two of the murders," Ranger said. "I'm not sure what good it would do to continue looking into him."

"You're right." Andi didn't think they should waste their time if the man had already been cleared—especially since the countdown was on. "I'm also wondering what the connection is between the victims and the body parts left on these snowmen. It's been bugging me because I wonder if there's any significance to those choices."

"I don't see how there would be." Duke shrugged. "I mean, the woman that worked at the planetarium did lose an eye and the gardener lost a hand. But why in the world would hair be significant? It's not like the Burrows were barbers or hairstylists."

Andi frowned and slowly nodded. He was right. But . . . "I just feel as if we're missing something, and we need to figure out what it is."

"Let's review everything we have one more time," Duke suggested. "We won't be able to do much investigating outside this room today anyway, not unless these conditions outside clear up some."

Andi glanced at the window and saw the snow still coming down. She hoped Gibson got to the hospital safely.

"I say we start looking over these victims again," Andi said. "If we study the possible significance of the date and the snowmen, maybe something will click for us."

With that directive and all the tasks given out, the team got to work.

———

An hour later, the team was still researching. At least they still had an internet connection out here, but Duke wasn't sure how much longer that would last. The conditions outside were brutal, to say the least.

He and Andi had been studying the victim list, looking for any connections they might have missed. So far, they hadn't found anything of note.

What were they missing?

"This may or may not be significant." Matthew stared at his computer and tapped a few more things on the keyboard. "But I *did* find one thing about something happening on December 6."

They all turned toward him, giving him their full attention.

"Like I said, it might not be anything, but on December 6 twenty-one years ago, a man and woman were shot and killed in their home in Fairbanks. Their killer was never found."

"Keep going," Andi said.

"This couple left behind an eight-year-old son. Maybe this wouldn't be significant, but . . ."

"But what?" Ranger tapped his finger on the table.

"Their son, Hans, grew up to be an artist. I checked out some of his work. He does oil paintings." Matthew turned his computer around to show them the screen. "And is it just me . . . or does his favorite subject to paint about seem to be random body parts?"

Duke looked more closely at the screen. The paintings were abstract with bright colors and shapes. The one on the screen now was electric blue with some lime green mixed in, almost reminding him of the northern lights. Various black lines cut through the painting, almost like cracked glass.

But then, in various sections of the painting, ears floated randomly in the space.

The next painting was a tangerine orange and fluorescent yellow. The artwork had the same black lines stretching across it, almost as if Hans had wanted to imitate a shattered look. But this time instead of ears, there were eyes.

More paintings followed suit. There were hands, noses, mouths.

In the last one, there were mustaches and beards.

Duke remembered the beard drawn on the mirror in their bathroom.

The thought of it still left him unsettled. The drawing had been a threat, a warning that Duke and Ranger should watch their backs.

If the two of them were in danger, then the whole team was in danger.

His stomach knotted at the thought.

"I definitely think he's someone worth looking into." Andi nodded slowly as she stared at the paintings. "Good work, Matthew."

He practically beamed. "Thank you."

"Where is the guy located now?" Duke asked.

"He's in Fairbanks still. As far as I can tell, he's not married, nor is he especially successful as an artist—at least not from what I found online. In fact, it appears he works full-time doing car detailing."

Duke glanced out the window again at the whiteout. "The weather could make it difficult to go anywhere today—though I'm still hopeful it might clear up some. But we can search this guy's social media at least. Maybe even give him a call or talk to some of his friends. It's worth pursuing."

Duke's phone rang. It was Gibson. Maybe he had an update for them.

He quickly put the phone to his ear. "Did you make it to Fairbanks okay?"

"I did." Gibson's voice sounded grim and serious. "But I got here about ten minutes too late."

"What do you mean?" Duke braced himself for whatever bad news Gibson might be about to share. He sensed it coming.

"Right before I arrived, Emmett flatlined."

Duke's lungs froze. "What? I thought he was doing better?"

"That's what my impression was as well. I'm getting the hospital to do some additional tests to confirm his cause of death."

Duke's thoughts continued to race. Emmett had been on the verge of sharing something possibly significant to this case. Maybe he'd seen something at the camp. Maybe he knew something about Pepper's death.

Now, they'd never know.

If the wrong person found out Emmett had awoken and was about to share that information, this person could have wanted to silence Emmett for good.

But the logistics of that were tricky. This person would have needed to hear Emmett was awake. Then, in a short period of time, he would have needed to get to the hospital and kill him before authorities arrived.

As Gibson ended the call, Duke's thoughts continued to race over the possibilities of what might have happened.

CHAPTER 41

They're not in any hurry to leave, I mused.

I figured with everything that had happened, those silly podcasters would scurry away from this nightmare before Christmas.

But the Scooby-Doo gang was determined.

Yes, *they* could be referred to as the Scooby-Doo gang. But I, in no way, would be a Scooby-Doo villain.

And I would prove that.

Soon, and very soon.

People might not think I had a plan. But I did.

Things had already been set in motion.

I sat in a rickety wooden chair in the old cabin in the middle of the forest, only a few miles away from the camp.

No one ever knew when I stayed out here, and that was the way I liked it.

It was the perfect place to think through everything I

needed to do. And it was the perfect location so that when I needed to strike again I could.

I knew people all around town were wondering where I might strike again. I knew they were scared. That they'd change their schedules and routines because of it.

I smiled.

I liked having control over people. Fear was a powerful weapon.

I wondered if anyone questioned if I might strike in the same place twice.

That answer was yes.

This place was more personal. I needed to teach the people here a valuable lesson. But would they ever learn? I wasn't sure.

Eventually, someone might figure out my plan, but I wasn't holding my breath.

Could these people really be so dense? I thought I'd made the clues pretty obvious.

But apparently, I had not.

I took a sip of my drink. Peppermint hot chocolate.

The cabin had a small stove I'd been able to boil some water on. It had been a lifesaver on cold days like today—though I had to be careful not to let people see the smoke coming from the chimney.

This was my favorite treat.

Even if the memories of the person who'd created the powdery mix weren't good.

There were other advantages to living out here where no one could find me.

I'd seen other things too.

I knew what certain people were up to.

And I planned to hold those things over their heads.

Yet another part of me wanted them to continue on with their secretive deeds. I knew one day it would all blow up.

At that thought, I reached across the table and grabbed a bag I'd found.

I stared at the substance inside.

People weren't as smart as they thought they were.

CHAPTER 42

The gang worked throughout lunch. The kitchen staff had brought them turkey sandwiches, barbecue chips, and fruit salad. But nothing tasted good to Andi.

She needed answers first.

Mariella had stayed busy with the podcast. She tried to post several times a week in order to keep listeners' interest. It wasn't always about the big stories or investigations they were working on.

Sometimes she simply offered "Headline Highlights," which summarized other true crime stories going on in the country. She usually gave fans a peek at what they were currently working on as well.

The actual recording of the podcast was never Andi's favorite. But the end result was worth the pain of the process.

Mysteries were solved. Killers were identified. People were given closure.

Those things were what mattered most.

"I think I have an update for you guys," Matthew announced, leaning back in his chair but still staring at his computer screen.

"I could use an update right about now." Duke ran a hand over his face, appearing exhausted and frustrated.

"It's about Hans." Matthew pushed up his glasses again. "I've been looking at his socials trying to find some answers. And, yes, I do realize that people lie online. But . . ."

"What did you find?" Ranger leaned closer, looking as if he could use a mental break as well.

"Every December, Hans goes to Germany to spend the Christmas season there. He stays for the entire month."

"The entire month?" Andi's voice lilted with surprise. "So you're saying he's not in the States on December 6?"

"Yes, that's what I'm saying." Matthew nodded curtly. "He's been doing this for the past five years. It looks like his girlfriend lives in Germany, so he goes to see her."

Disappointment pressed on Andi's shoulders. Their most promising lead had evaporated as quickly as it had materialized.

"Is there any way to verify Hans was actually there and he's not faking his visits to Germany?" Duke asked.

Andi understood where his question came from. They couldn't afford to blindly trust something just because someone put it online. It was too easy to trick people.

"As a matter of fact, I *can* confirm his whereabouts. He posted several times on the date of December 6. Each time he claimed he was in Germany. But a couple of years in particular, he took a picture of himself on Saint Nicholas Day. The pictures of the celebrations in the background confirm those photos were actually taken on that date. I double-checked."

Andi frowned as she realized that yet another one of their leads had just gone up in smoke.

———

Duke felt they weren't getting anywhere. He'd never been one for a lot of desk work. He preferred to be out in the field searching for answers. But the storm right now made that difficult.

The few remaining guests at the camp came in and out of the lobby and dining hall. They couldn't get outside either. Even if they wanted to leave, it would be difficult. The camp wasn't running any shuttles to the airport right now.

Some of the staff had tried to relieve guests' boredom by offering Bingo and crafts.

But the general atmosphere in the lodge was one of restlessness.

Juniper emerged from her room shortly after lunch. Her face was still pale and, based on the way her arms were slung across her chest, she was still shaken by everything that had happened.

Despite that, they needed to talk to her.

Andi called her over, and Juniper trudged toward the table, her steps seeming to drag the floor.

She paused by their table, her gaze dull. "Any updates?"

Andi shook her head. "Unfortunately, no. But I was hoping to ask you a few more questions now that I've had time to think on things a bit more."

"About what?" She rubbed her arms, her motions still sluggish.

"About what Heath said," Andi told her. "He said he and his wife didn't want to invest in this place and that your parents didn't have enough money to start it. Do you know anything about that?"

A frown tugged at her lips. "It's been bugging me ever since he said that. I know what I heard. But now I'm questioning whether or not I truly did misunderstand something."

"Who might you be able to ask about it?" Duke asked. "Certainly, your parents had other friends they might have said something to."

"I suppose my mom and dad could have talked to a few people at the Caribou Club. I could give you a couple of names if you think that would help. The first people who come to mind are Dan and Jan—I mostly remember their names because they rhyme. But they were also a nice couple. He always gave me candy—butterscotch." Juniper shrugged. "But not in a weird way. In a grandfatherly way."

"If you could give us their last name, that would be great," Andi said.

"I can find it," Juniper said. "But I can't remember it off the top of my head."

"What about Tim?" Simmy tilted her head in a gentle manner. "Wouldn't your uncle know something?"

"Maybe." Juniper shrugged, the motion listless. "I tried to call him to ask him a few questions about a half an hour ago. He's not answering."

Tension immediately tightened Duke's chest. "What do you mean he's not answering?"

"He went into town to see his son, Jared, earlier this morning. Jared needed help with something. I can only assume he got there safely, considering this storm. When he left, it wasn't as bad outside."

Duke exchanged a look with Andi. "And I assume it's not like him to not answer his phone."

"No, it's not." Juniper frowned as worry stretched through her voice.

Another person missing? This wasn't a good sign, especially considering everything that had already happened.

CHAPTER 43

T he snowstorm eased, and forecasters said there would be a break in the snow for the next few hours.

Based on that, Andi and Duke had decided to head into Fairbanks.

The move was risky, but time was ticking away, and they needed answers.

Tim's son, Jared, might have some of those.

However, as Andi and Duke took off down the road, Andi couldn't deny the apprehension she felt.

Though she'd been trained as an ice road trucker, being out on these roads still felt unnerving. If anything happened, no one would be around to help them, and most likely they'd have no cell phone service.

However, she trusted Duke's driving skills. The man could handle himself in almost any situation—and he could handle himself around her. It took a strong man to do that.

"You doing okay?" Duke's voice pulled her from her thoughts.

"Doing fine."

The funny thing was that Andi felt as if she could tell Duke anything. But not about her anxiety and panic attacks.

The last thing she wanted was to hurt Duke. She wasn't sure that being brutally honest about her hangups would be good for him. She felt safer with her walls up.

She wasn't young and naive anymore. She knew relationships were complicated. Rarely was it boy meets girl, and boy and girl live happily ever after. Obstacles and conflict were a part of every relationship.

Not that Duke had done anything wrong. He hadn't.

However, Andi had never been in a position like this before, and she didn't know quite how to handle her uncertainties.

As the camp disappeared in the rearview mirror, Andi set her gaze on the road ahead. It was already a strange shade of grayish white outside, partly because of the snowstorm and partly because of the time of year. It was hard to believe that just last week it had been Thanksgiving.

In a surprising turn of events, the whole murder club gang had decided to stay in Alaska instead of going home. They'd celebrated the holiday together at Ranger and Simmy's house. Everyone had brought food and pitched in.

Instead of talking about true crime, they'd talked about what they were thankful for. They'd played games. They had laughed.

The whole evening had been good for all of them. It was one of the few times when they were reminded about how they were not just colleagues but friends. Here in Alaska, they were also family to each other.

The trees closed in as the road narrowed. This wasn't even the tough part of the drive. The tough part would be at the end of this lane when the road descended onto another road below. The grade was steeper. Even though they were in four-wheel-drive, it would be tricky.

As Duke reached that part of the street, he slowed but kept going at a steady pace.

"You've got this," Andi murmured.

He gripped the wheel. "Let's hope."

The road was essentially a sheet of ice beneath them.

She swallowed hard as Duke tapped on the brakes. The SUV slowed. Slowed some more.

She started to let out a breath of relief.

Then, just as they reached the bottom, the SUV began to slide downhill.

Toward the intersecting road.

The tires lost all traction.

"Hold on . . ." Duke murmured.

Andi glanced at the crossroad just in time to see a

truck plowing through the snow . . . headed directly toward them.

Duke saw the truck coming at them. He resisted the urge to follow his instincts—to slam on the brakes.

Instead, he gently pressed the brakes and turned the wheel.

He prayed the truck driver saw him in time and eased into the other lane, out of their way.

"Hold on," he murmured to Andi, bracing himself for the worst.

The SUV began to swerve, the back tires swinging out.

No! The timing couldn't be more terrible.

At any second, that truck was going to hit them.

Duke lay on his horn. Then he braced himself for the impact, praying everyone would be okay.

Then, just as it seemed the vehicles would collide, the truck veered out of the way, narrowly missing them.

Duke let out the breath he'd been holding.

"That was close." Andi rubbed her neck, looking ill at ease.

"You can say that again." He gripped the steering wheel as he continued down the road.

God had been watching out for them on that one. Duke lifted a prayer of thanks.

The rest of the drive was fairly quiet, which was fine.

He needed the silence to concentrate. They couldn't risk any more close calls like that.

Finally, they reached Fairbanks. The streets in town had been cleared more than the back roads. But Duke knew they didn't have much time before the snowstorm returned with a vengeance. If they didn't get back to the camp before that, they most likely wouldn't make it.

Andi called out directions, and several minutes later they pulled to a stop in front of Jared Burrows' house.

The place was small and painted a light purple. Similar-looking houses stretched up and down the streets and throughout the neighborhood.

A truck sat in the driveway.

"Is that Jared's or Tim's?" Andi asked as he followed her gaze.

"I have no idea." Duke opened his door. "Let's go find out."

CHAPTER 44

ndi and Duke hurried to the front door.

Andi wasn't sure what vehicle Tim usually drove. But only one vehicle was parked in the driveway, and she didn't recognize it from the camp—not that she'd been paying that much attention either.

She saw that the doorbell was cracked, so she knocked on the door instead.

Soon after, footsteps sounded, and the door opened.

A man who looked like a younger version of Tim stood there, staring at them with a confused expression on his face. He wore a beanie down over his ears, ripped jeans, and a flannel shirt. Based on his red nose, his heat either wasn't working or it was turned way down to save on electrical cost.

"Can I help you?" He brushed some potato chip crumbs from his chest.

"We were hoping to ask you a few questions. I'm Andi, and this is my friend, Duke. We're with the true crime podcast called *The Round Table*."

He remained unimpressed. "That's cool and all, but I don't listen to true crime podcasts."

"We're not here specifically to ask questions for our podcast," Andi started. "We're here to ask about your dad."

"What about my dad?" His eyes narrowed, and he shifted. "Did he do something?"

Andi tilted her head. "Do you think your dad did something?"

Jared sighed as if flabbergasted. "That's not what I meant. But you're true crime podcasters, and you show up here asking about my dad. What conclusions am I supposed to draw?"

"I could have worded that better," Andi conceded to his statement. "Duke and I are working on solving the murders of Calvin and Mary Burrows, your uncle and aunt."

Jared's eyes widened. "Oh, I see. I guess that makes sense. I still can't believe what happened to them. We were never especially close but . . . they didn't deserve to die that way."

"We actually came here looking for your dad," Duke said.

"Why would you come here to look for him?" His forehead wrinkled.

Andi paused at his question, realizing something

wasn't fitting. "Because you called him and said you needed his help with something."

Jared shook his head again. "No, I didn't. Sorry to disappoint you, but I haven't spoken to my dad in years. There's no way I would call that man to ask for help."

———

So Tim had lied to Juniper, Duke mused. Why would he do that unless he had something to cover up?

"I'm sorry," Andi said. "There must have been a misunderstanding. Because your dad left the camp and said he was coming to help you with something."

"Well, he made that up. He was clearly looking for an excuse to get away, though I couldn't tell you why."

The breeze swept across them, and Andi shivered.

Duke nodded at the house. "Listen, do you mind if we come in? Since we're already here, I'd love to get your take on what happened to your aunt and uncle."

Jared stared at them another moment as if weighing his options. Then he blew out a breath and sighed. "I guess so. But only for a few minutes. Then I have to go to work."

"What do you do for a living exactly?" Andi pulled her collar closer around her neck, her nose and cheeks red from the cold.

"I work at a big box store down the road. I figured we might close because of the snowstorm, but more people are coming to buy things in case they're trapped inside for an extended period. It's a catch twenty-two if you ask me."

"I can see that," Duke said. "I promise we won't take up too much of your time."

Jared opened the door wider, and they stepped inside. His house was unkempt, and the stench of dirty socks and old food permeated the air. And it was cold. It was *so* cold in here.

Was Jared struggling to pay for heat? Why else would he keep it so frigid inside?

Jared paused and glanced at his living room as if considering offering them a place to sit. But every visible surface was covered with piles of clothes, old pizza boxes, and stacks of junk mail.

"How about the kitchen instead?" Jared offered.

They went into the tiny kitchen and moved several things from the seats before sitting at an old table that rocked back and forth if you leaned on it.

"So what do you want to know?" Jared planted his elbows on the table as he sat across from them. "I don't really know how I can help you. And is this official—as in, is our conversation being recorded? I need to know if I should watch what I say."

"It's not official," Andi said. "Although, if you say something that's a turning point in our investigation, we'd love to come back later and officially get you on a recording."

He nodded slowly as if considering it. "I'll think about it. For now, what do you want to know?"

Duke shifted before diving in. "When you heard about what happened to your aunt and uncle, did your mind jump to any conclusions? Did you immediately think about a possibility of who could've done this to them?"

Jared blew out another breath. "I don't know, man. At first, I didn't know what to think. It's still hard to say. But . . ." He looked in the distance as if his mind were traveling back in time. "They were always kind of secretive."

"In what way?"

He shrugged. "I don't know. They didn't talk much about what they did before they moved here, but I think he had some high-paying job. It was their idea to move to Alaska almost twenty years ago. He said my dad should join them."

"Where did they move from?" Andi asked.

"New York, I think. We hadn't heard from them in years. Then one day, they reconnect with us. Tell us they've had a baby and want a change in scenery, that they're moving to Alaska."

"I didn't think your dad and uncle were close," Duke said.

"I didn't either. But my dad had fallen on some hard times. Uncle Calvin heard people could get jobs in Alaska in the oil field. Said my dad should apply. I was young at the time, but I remember bits and pieces."

"And it worked out for everyone to move?" Andi asked.

"It did. Course, only about five years later my parents divorced. Then my dad and uncle didn't talk for a while again."

Alaska didn't seem like a conventional choice when it came to places to move. But Duke had moved here also, so he had no room to talk.

However, he had to wonder if there was more to their story.

"I take it you and your dad aren't close," Andi said.

"He swindled my mom out of some money a few years ago," Jared said. "I haven't talked to him since. I don't trust him—and neither should you."

"Noted," Duke muttered.

"Anything else you need?" Jared glanced at his watch.

"Only if you can think of something you want to share." Andi waited.

"I've had nothing to do with that side of the family for years," Jared said. "The only time I've really thought about them was when that family friend came over a couple of months ago."

"Family friend?" Duke wondered who he was talking about.

"The Klinkhart guy." Jared shrugged as if annoyed. "He came asking about his daughter—as if I'd know where she was. Said he'd been searching for her."

That seemed to fit what Duke knew about the man.

He wasn't the type who liked it when things don't go according to his plan.

"Anything else?" Jared asked.

Duke shook his head. "I don't think so. I know you need to get to work. But if you think of anything else . . ."

Andi set her business card on the table.

Jared nodded. "I'll be in touch."

Duke happened to glance out the window as he turned to take a step from the room.

When he did, the snowman in the backyard made his blood go cold.

CHAPTER 45

ndi heard Duke suck in a breath, and she followed his gaze.

Her eyes widened when she saw the snowman in the center of Jared's backyard.

"You guys okay?" Confusion marred Jared's voice.

Andi pointed at the window, her arm trembling. "Did you build that?"

"The snowman?" A knot formed between his eyebrows. "No. Why are you asking?"

Duke and Andi glanced at each other.

"You *do* realize this killer leaves snowmen, right?" Andi asked, surprised at his cluelessness.

"Oh." Realization washed over Jared's features. "The December Dismemberer . . . but he doesn't leave every snowman. Neighborhood kids built that one."

"In your backyard?" Duke murmured in surprise.

Jared shrugged as if it weren't a big deal. "Their

backyard is full of junk their dad collects. I personally think he's a hoarder. Anyway, sometimes they like to play in my backyard—without my permission, usually. It doesn't really matter to me, and since there's no fence up, they probably don't even think about property lines. That said, they built a snowman earlier today."

Andi studied Jared's face, determined to make sure he was thinking this through. "Are you *sure* they're the ones who built it?"

He shrugged. "I'm pretty sure. I mean, I wasn't watching them the whole time. But when I saw the snowman, that's what I assumed."

"Do you mind if we take a closer look?" Duke asked.

"Feel free."

He and Andi went to the back door and carefully stepped outside. They trudged toward the snowman, knowing they shouldn't disturb the scene in case it turned out to be something.

Andi stopped in front of the snowman to examine it.

This one was bigger than the others left at the crime scenes. Those had all been around four feet tall. This one was closer to six feet.

The first thing she looked for was any body parts— the real kind that the killer took from his victims.

This snowman had stick arms. Two mismatched rocks for the eyes. An old, stained towel for the scarf. No nose.

Andi glanced at the snowy ground to make sure nothing had fallen off.

She saw nothing, but it *had* snowed this morning. The evidence could be buried.

Using her foot, she carefully brushed away some snow from the ground, just to be certain.

But there was nothing hiding beneath the white mounds other than some leaves and twigs.

"Maybe this *was* just the neighborhood kids having some fun," Duke muttered.

"There's nothing inherently dangerous about a snowman," Andi said. "Especially for the young and innocent."

Plenty of kids had built them over the years. Plenty would build them in the future.

But in this case, Andi wanted to proceed with caution.

However, it looked like this particular snowman was nothing to be concerned about.

———

Duke glanced at Andi as they climbed back into his SUV. He cranked the engine and started the heat. They definitely hadn't warmed up when they went into Jared's house.

He probably had the thermostat set on fifty-five, if Duke had to guess—just high enough that the pipes wouldn't freeze.

Duke didn't bother to start driving anywhere yet.

Instead, he turned to Andi. "What do you think?"

She shook her head. "I don't get the impression Jared has anything to do with the murders. Nor do I think he knows anything about them. What concerns me the most is the fact that Tim said he was coming here and he didn't."

"It definitely sounds like Tim is hiding something."

"For sure. Why did he want to leave the camp? Was he running away? Trying to cover up some evidence?"

Duke blew out a long breath. "It's hard to say without knowing more details about where he might be. He didn't have anywhere else to go from the sounds of it."

"I'd still like to talk to Dan and Jan," Andi said. "The members of the Caribou Club that Juniper mentioned. Maybe they have some insight. While we're in town we might as well . . ."

"I'm in favor of that too," Duke said. "Why don't you see if you can find out their last name or their address, and we'll pay them a visit."

Sometimes they might call people before stopping by. In this case, the element of surprise could work in their favor.

It only took Andi a few minutes to find out the information they needed, and they took off.

CHAPTER 46

Andi stared at the house in front of them. The home of Dan and Jan Price.

This neighborhood was a nice upgrade from Jared's place, with houses probably four times as large as his and better maintained.

Andi and Duke still had a couple of hours before the next round of snow was supposed to hit, so they might as well make the best of their trip. However, they didn't want to take too much time either.

Just like at Jared's, they climbed out and walked to the porch.

But unlike Jared's house, when they reached it, Andi saw the front door was ajar.

She and Duke exchanged a glance. That wasn't a good sign.

Duke reached for his gun. Then he pushed the door open and called, "Hello? Anybody here?"

They waited for an answer.

When there was none, a bad feeling lingered in Andi.

Had something happened to these people? Why else would they leave their door open at this time of year with temperatures below zero?

Duke took a hesitant step inside when a figure appeared down the hallway.

Andi froze as she waited for a better glimpse of the man. Had they stumbled upon the killer? Her nerves were on edge after everything that happened, and she prepared herself for the worst.

A moment later, an older gentleman with white hair, wire-framed glasses, and a large belly came into focus. "Can I help you? What are you doing in my house?"

She released the breath she'd been holding.

This man didn't appear to be a killer. *Praise the Lord!*

"Your house?" Duke jammed his gun back into his waistband. "The door was open, so we thought something was wrong."

The man paced closer and squinted. "Do I know you?"

"No, sir," Andi said. "We're investigating the death of Calvin and Mary Burrows, and we came by to talk to you. We saw the door was open and were concerned."

"The door was open? I don't know why that door was open." Then he paused, his lips twisting into a frown. "Or maybe I do. My wife . . . I'm afraid she's getting a touch of dementia. Sometimes, I find the flour in the oven instead of the pantry. The other day, she accidentally used toothpaste on top of a cake she was decorating instead of icing. I'm going to guess she may not have closed this door when she came in from taking the trash out. I told her I would take it out, but she insisted. She's a stubborn one."

At least that explanation made a little more sense.

"I see," Duke said. "I'm sorry if we frightened you."

"You should get out of the cold." Dan ushered them inside.

They stepped inside the living room, which was warm and cozy with its homemade quilts, bearskin rug, and a fire blazing in the fireplace.

Dan paused and turned toward them. "Can I get you some coffee?"

"I wouldn't turn that down," Andi said. "But I don't want to impose either."

"I don't mind." Dan walked to the pot, which had already been brewed.

He poured two cups and handed them each one. As he did, a pleasantly plump woman with a coif of gray hair appeared from upstairs.

Her gaze flickered between Duke and Andi as if trying to figure out who they were.

"Dan?" she finally asked.

"Jan, we have some friends visiting," Dan said. "They're here about . . ."

"About Calvin and Mary Burrows," Andi said.

Jan's eyes lit. "Calvin and Mary? I haven't talked to them in years. How are they doing? I really need to get together with them again sometime soon."

Grief clutched Duke's heart. His grandmother had dementia, and he knew just how hard that could be on loved ones. The mental decline was heartbreaking.

Maybe coming here hadn't been a good idea after all.

———

Andi sipped her coffee as she sat on a blue-and-red-plaid couch. A shiny coffee table stretched in front of them, a glass dish with butterscotch candy in the center.

Dan had insisted they sit in the living room. He'd asked Jan if she would grab some butter cookies from the pantry. She had agreed.

When she disappeared from the room, Dan leaned closer and whispered, "I'm not sure she'll be much help to you."

"We can leave if you need us to." Andi pointed behind her at the front door. "I hate to make things harder for you."

"No, Calvin and Mary were good people. I've been saddened by their passing ever since it happened. The fact that the person who did it hasn't been tossed in jail with the key thrown away only makes things worse. Whatever you need to ask me, I'll try to answer. It had been a couple of years since I talked to them before they died."

"We're most curious about what happened with them at the Caribou Club," Andi started. "I heard their departure wasn't an easy one."

As soon as those words left her lips, Jan appeared again with a plate of cookies and a wide smile. "Please, have one. I would have baked something myself if I'd known you were coming. Maybe you can take some back for Calvin and Mary also?"

Andi's heart lodged in her throat. "I'm sure they'd love that."

Jan then sat down in the chair next to her husband. "You mentioned the Caribou Club. I love that place. Such lovely people."

Dan glanced at his wife, concern and sadness in his gaze. "You always did love our gatherings there."

"I heard Calvin and Mary had some conflicts with some people in the club." Andi picked up a butter cookie and nibbled on it. The treat took her back to her childhood visits to her grandma's house.

"Unfortunately, they did." Dan rubbed his jaw. "But they had every reason to have butt heads with Baylor and Barney."

"Who are Baylor and Barney?" Duke asked. "We haven't come across their names yet."

"Baylor Boykins and Barney Holder." Dan's gaze darkened. "They were on the board several years ago, and they liked to call all the shots."

"Why did Calvin and Mary have a dispute with them?" Andi asked.

"Those men were up to no good," Dan said. "They wanted to appear altruistic, like they were doing things for the good of the community. But all the while they were actually just watching out for themselves."

"Is that confirmed?" Duke asked.

"As confirmed as a supreme court justice." Dan offered a confident nod. "They were misappropriating funds is what I believe the official term is."

"What about Edwin Standard?" Andi asked. "I thought he was involved in that."

"He was also," Dan said. "But since he passed, I didn't figure I'd bring him up."

"What did the club do when they found out what was going on?" Duke asked.

"The club never made those facts public," Dan said. "We thought it would bring too much negative attention to us. Then again, if we don't tell people, then we don't have transparency, and that doesn't make us trustworthy either. Their actions put us in a difficult position, but that was ultimately what the board chose to do."

"So the Burrows' suspicions were correct?" Andi asked as she wiped cookie crumbs from her fingers. "Baylor and Barney were skimming money to have their own lavish parties?"

"That's right," Dan said. "But since then, we have new leadership, and the club's not like that anymore."

"Do you think that Baylor and Barney were upset

enough to want to do something to the Burrows?" Andi chose her words carefully, not wanting to set Jan off, especially if she thought they were still alive.

Andi waited to hear Dan's answer, hoping she and Duke might finally find one of the elusive leads they desperately needed.

CHAPTER 47

"Oh no," Dan said. "Everyone loved Calvin and Mary. Everyone except Calvin's brother."

Those words got Duke's attention. "You mean Tim?"

Dan nodded. "That man was nothing but trouble. He was always coming around asking for money. Couldn't hold down a job. Drank too much."

Andi shifted on the couch, her coffee seemingly forgotten. "Did things ever escalate between Calvin and his brother?"

"Escalate?" Dan scratched his head. "I can't say if they did. But Tim always seemed to be giving Calvin and Mary trouble. He couldn't ever stand on his own two feet, and he always came crawling back to his brother to ask for help."

"But things never got violent, right?" Duke clarified.

"Not that I know of." Dan sighed and shrugged. "But who knows what happened behind the scenes."

Duke stored that information away. As Jan began to wander the room, Duke saw the weariness on Dan's face and knew it was time for him and Andi to go.

"Thank you so much for everything you shared." Duke rose and picked up his coffee mug. "And thanks for the coffee, of course."

"No problem." Dan's expression tightened as he glanced at his wife.

"We should be hitting the road before the storm gets much worse." Duke nodded toward the door.

Andi stood also and followed Duke's lead.

"Come back and see us sometime," Jan said. "Next time bring Calvin and Mary with you."

"Of course." Andi offered a tight smile.

After placing their cups in the kitchen sink, they exited the house.

Had Caleb moved out of first place on their suspect list? Maybe *Tim* was the one they should be looking at.

But, first, they'd need to find a connection between Tim and the other murder victims.

"So Tim disappears," Duke talked through his thoughts. "It sounds as if he was pretty demanding of his brother and sister-in-law. Now he lives at the camp his brother started, and he seems to want to push Juniper out as owner and manager of the camp."

Andi gave Duke a look. "It sounds like *he's* the one we should be investigating."

"I agree. What if he grabbed Caleb and did something to him? I wonder if he has an alibi for the moment Caleb disappeared."

"It's a possibility we should look into." Andi shook her head. "What's with all these secrets everyone seems to have?"

"I don't know." Duke shrugged. "Maybe everyone is trying to protect someone else."

"Or maybe everyone is trying to protect themselves." She shot him a look.

"Maybe." He breathed out through his nose and then glanced out the window at the snow covering everything in sight. "I guess we should get back before it gets worse out here."

"Let me check the weather first." Andi quickly looked on an online app. "The storm is moving more slowly than forecasters predicted. But it is going to hit hard later. What do you say we swing by the hospital?"

"For what?"

"To see if Gibson has any updates on Emmett."

Duke narrowed his eyes with thought. "Do you think Gibson is still there?"

She shrugged. "I think it's a possibility. Besides, once we get back to camp, I don't know when we'll be able to leave again. Thankfully, Juniper is okay with us staying longer. I'd hate to leave now after everything that's happened."

"Same here."

"Let's go to the hospital," Andi said. "Then we'll head back to the camp . . . most likely."

He knew what that meant: unless something else came up.

Duke eased away from their spot on the side of the street and headed toward the hospital.

Andi couldn't stop thinking about whether or not Emmett's death had been natural . . . or if someone else had caused it.

What if Tim had been monitoring Emmett because Emmett had seen the man do something? Would Tim have known how to make Emmett's death look natural?

It was hard to say. But it was definitely a theory worth exploring.

Duke and Andi walked into the hospital and practically ran into Gibson as he headed out.

Gibson's brow furrowed as he paused in front of them. "Duke and Andi? I wasn't expecting to see you guys here. I'm surprised you came out in this weather."

"When the weather cleared, we decided to drive into Fairbanks to question a few people," Duke explained. "We're heading back soon before the storm gets worse, but we thought we would stop by first."

"To ask about Emmett?" Gibson raised an eyebrow, making it clear he wasn't surprised.

"We've been anxious to hear about him," Duke said. "Any updates you're allowed to share?"

Gibson glanced from side to side before stepping closer. "Between us, the hospital did a quick blood test, and they *did* find something surprising. Potassium chloride."

"What does potassium chloride do exactly?" Duke asked.

"To keep things simple, it can stop the heart."

"So you think Emmett was murdered?" Andi whispered, keeping her voice low as a family with a young child walked by.

"That's my guess. I think Emmett knew something about Pepper's killer, so the perpetrator ended Emmett's life before he could share anything."

Duke raised his eyebrows as he let that theory settle in his mind.

A second later, he asked, "Did anyone see anyone suspicious come to visit him?"

"Tim stayed with Emmett a while when he was first admitted. Then Emmett had some relatives come. But they weren't here at the time he passed. With the snowstorm coming, they decided to hunker down in their hotel instead."

"So where does that leave you?" Andi asked.

Gibson hesitated before saying, "There was one other person who came to see Emmett. We spotted this guy on the security footage, but we're still trying to identify him."

"You have that security footage handy?" Duke asked. "Maybe we can help."

Gibson pulled out his phone and tapped the screen. Then he turned the device toward them as a video started to play.

Duke and Andi leaned in as they watched.

As soon as Duke saw the man's face, he knew exactly who he was.

"That's Jared," Duke told Gibson. "Tim's son."

Maybe the man wasn't as innocent as they'd thought. Maybe he'd made that snowman after all— maybe as a practice run for his big night.

The thought was chilling, but something worth exploring.

CHAPTER 48

ibson went to question Jared. He hadn't let Andi and Duke go with him—not that Andi had expected him to.

While he did that, she and Duke had decided to grab a quick bite to eat before heading back. She knew cell phone service at the camp would be sketchy, and she desperately wanted an update from Gibson before they left Fairbanks.

What if Jared was behind this? If he'd killed Emmett? Maybe he was even working with his father.

Andi had to wonder if they were next in line to inherit the camp. That might be motive enough for murder. Although . . . if they wanted the place to turn a profit, they probably shouldn't want too many dead bodies to turn up.

Tim did have money problems, according to what people had said.

There were so many possibilities right now.

She and Duke went to an old boathouse restaurant located on the Tanana River. The rustic place had fantastic salmon chowder, which sounded good on a cold day like today. The savory scent of the fish and the stew filled the air and made Andi's stomach rumble.

They were seated by the window overlooking the snowy, white river. She had no doubt the water was frozen over by now. This whole area was a frozen wonderland.

As soon as the waitress had taken their orders, the sound of a TV blaring overhead caught Andi's ear. The weather report was talking about the onslaught of snow coming their way.

She shivered.

They really didn't have much time to get back to the camp. And even then, once they got there, they'd probably be stuck for a while. But they needed to be there to keep investigating.

The killer would strike again soon if they didn't stop him.

Then the news story changed. As soon as Andi heard the name Victor Goodman, she tensed.

She hadn't listened to the news in a couple of days. It had been a nice break, truthfully. She tended to listen to news whenever she could, which didn't always leave her in a great state of mind.

"The upcoming trial of oil tycoon and business mogul Victor Goodman is slated to start in three months," the reporter said. "Many experts think this will be the trial of the decade, and the media storm around the event has already begun."

His picture flashed on the screen, and her gut churned with revulsion. If that monster had his way, she'd be dead right now.

Duke squeezed her hand. "He's behind bars. He's going to pay for everything he did. You don't have to worry about him anymore."

Andi offered a faint smile, wishing she believed him. But Victor was clever, and she wouldn't put it past him to figure out a way to be cleared of the charges—including witness intimidation.

She'd been keeping her eyes open for any signs of trouble, knowing good and well the lengths Victor would go through.

"I know," Andi finally said. "I just put so much energy into bringing him down . . . now that it's done, I hardly know what to do with myself."

"You got your license to practice law back. You've been busy with new cases. I'd say you're adjusting pretty well."

She couldn't argue with his statement. Duke always knew how to help ground her when her thoughts got out of control.

Was she beginning to need him? She'd never felt that way before. She'd always prided herself on being self-sufficient. But so much had changed in the past couple of years.

Andi studied his face a moment. The familiar rush of attraction swept through her—the one she always felt when she looked at him. She'd never felt this way about anyone before.

But right now, she felt damaged. She hated that feeling. The sentiment was foreign to her. She'd always been the confident one who'd charged forward, even when it was foolhardy.

"What are you thinking?" Duke took a sip of his water.

Her heart pounded harder. Was he talking about their relationship?

When he didn't explain, she realized he was referring to the case.

She nearly laughed at herself. Why was she acting so paranoid?

"There's so much to sort through, really," she finally said. "I feel like we're looking for Calvin and Mary's killer. But I still have trouble connecting him with the person who murdered Pepper. Something is missing, and I really don't understand why."

"It *is* perplexing. This guy has to have some type of reason for what he's doing."

She used her index finger to absently trace the condensation on her glass. "If we don't figure it out soon, he'll strike again."

"Maybe the gang found something back at the camp."

"We can hope," Andi said. "Or maybe Jared will

have more answers for Gibson than he had for us. Maybe he even knows where his father is."

Duke's phone rang. "It's Ranger. Maybe they discovered something."

She listened to the one-sided conversation with bated breath.

When the call ended, Duke locked gazes with her. She knew whatever Ranger had told Duke excited him.

"It turns out that Tim has a history of being a bit of a nomad. He worked as a janitor at the planetarium for a while, and he worked maintenance for the hospital—both places where the December Dismemberer's victims worked."

"And he works at the camp. Now he's missing . . ." Her voice caught.

His eyes glimmered with hope. "Maybe the killer has been right under our nose the whole time . . . only we didn't realize it until too late because now he's missing."

———

As Duke ate his salmon and baked potato, his mind raced with possibilities. Maybe they were finally onto something.

They just needed to figure out where Tim had gone.

But they could do none of that right now. Instead, he decided to relax a moment and enjoy this time with Andi. Between the holidays and how hard Andi had been working on passing the Alaska Bar Exam, they hadn't had a lot of quality time together in recent weeks. Plus, signing over ownership of his travel company to the man who'd bought it had been more time-consuming than he'd thought.

"We've come a long way, haven't we?" Duke studied Andi's face from across the table as the gentle candlelight softened her features.

She offered a lazy but sad smile. "We really have, and it hasn't even been a year yet."

For a moment, Duke forgot about their circumstances. He wanted to pretend like everything was right in his world.

And it almost was . . . other than a killer being after them.

And other than the walls Andi had put up, walls he didn't understand.

Why wasn't she letting him in? Had he done something to make Andi think she couldn't trust him?

"Who would have thought that day I came across your truck broken down on the side of the Dalton Highway that we'd be here right now?" Maybe reminiscing would make things feel normal for a moment.

"And that we would solve so many crimes together." Her smile widened.

Duke reached across the table and squeezed her hand. "In case I haven't told you, I'm really proud of you."

Her cheeks practically glowed. "Thank you. I could have never done all this without you."

"I beg to differ. You would have *totally* done this without me."

Her smile gave away the truth. She would have foolhardily charged ahead to bring down Victor with or without him. She would have also fought with every last lick of energy she had to restore all the wrongs around her.

But it had probably been easier with his encouragement.

Just then, Duke's phone rang. He glanced at the screen.

"It's Gibson calling back."

Then he answered.

CHAPTER 49

ared went to the hospital to visit one of his coworkers who was in a car accident," Gibson told them. "We already confirmed his story."

"I thought he went into Emmett's room?" Andi said.

"If you look at the video, a nurse walks in front of him as he's headed down the hallway," Gibson explained. "It's hard to tell exactly where he went. His friend's room was right beside Emmett's."

Andi fought a frown. She'd hoped to get somewhere with this case, to find some type of answer.

Jared could still be a suspect, she supposed.

"Thanks for letting us know," Duke said.

"Of course," Gibson said. "We did find one thing that was interesting."

Andi sat up straighter. "What's that?"

"We looked through some of the photos Barb had posted on social media."

"Barb is the woman who fell through the ice, right?" Duke clarified.

"That's right. She was a nature photographer. Anyway, we were just doing our due diligence. But one of the photos she took at the camp was of the northern lights with the reindeer."

"So what about it caught your eye?" Duke's gaze narrowed with thought.

"If you blow it up and look in the background, you can see someone walking in the woods behind the reindeer."

"What's suspicious about that, exactly?" Andi tried to put things together in her mind.

"It appears to be a man with a bag. Based on the way he's glaring at the camera, I think he was up to no good."

Andi's breath caught.

"Could you tell from the photo if he was doing something wrong?" Duke asked.

"No, we couldn't. But if the person who was photographed knew that photo could later be used as evidence, they might have wanted to silence Barb. Maybe they feared she saw more than she did, so they wanted to keep her quiet."

"She's still alive, right?" Andi didn't want to ask the question, but she had to.

"She's fine, but she already left to go back home. Apparently, she said she'd had enough of Alaska."

That move may have saved her life.

"Can you tell who this guy was?" Andi held her breath as she waited for Gibson's response.

"As a matter of fact, we can," Gibson said. "He's the man we know as Caleb Brinley."

———

Duke's thoughts raced as they headed back to the camp.

He reminded himself to stay focused on the road. It was slick, and snow had started to fall again. He couldn't afford to be distracted.

"So is Caleb the one behind these murders?" Andi's question echoed Duke's own thoughts. "He was at the camp last year when Calvin and Mary were killed. He was there when Pepper was found dead."

"And we can't forget the fake blood found in his cabin along with that mysterious note," Duke said.

"Maybe we're looking at it wrong," Andi suggested. "Maybe Caleb wrote that note to give to someone else, and he just hadn't delivered it yet. What did it say again? 'I've got to hand it to you, you've made a real mess of things. You've got one chance to make it right. Don't make me tear you apart.'"

Duke nodded slowly. "You could be right. Everything does seem to point to him. The fact he's using a false identity only confirms our theory."

Caleb Brinley from Montana didn't exist. Without knowing what his true name was, it would be hard to track his history. To see where he'd been living the past several years. To see if he might be responsible for the other murders.

He was definitely their number one suspect right now.

Then there was Tim. The fact he'd disappeared was also suspicious.

But what if Tim had caught on to what Caleb was doing? What if he'd gone to confront Caleb, and Caleb had threatened him?

The signs of struggle they'd seen in the snow behind Caleb's cabin could have been Caleb forcing Tim to an awaiting UTV.

Caleb could have done something to Tim.

Right now, this was their most plausible theory. The fact they didn't know where Caleb was only solidified that thought.

"Why?" Duke asked aloud. "Why would Caleb do this? I mean, other than the fact that maybe he's a little psycho. But even psychos usually have some reason for why they choose who they do."

Andi nibbled on her lip before shaking her head. "That is something I don't know, especially since we don't know anything about Caleb's past, including his real name. But maybe there's some type of link we've missed."

"I still get the sense as well that there's something Juniper isn't telling us. I'm just not sure why she would be hiding something, considering the stakes."

"I agree. I've thought that from the start. And I'm

still thinking about the birth certificate I saw. About the fact Juniper's parents had trouble conceiving. That they moved here from New York twenty years ago. They apparently have had some secrets of their own."

"It looks like we have more investigating to do."

Andi nodded. "But first, we need to get back to the camp—in one piece." She groaned. "Poor word choice."

Right as she said the words, the SUV lost traction again.

This time, Duke quickly gained control of the vehicle, and they continued down the road.

It would be a tense drive. But he was anxious to check in with everyone to see if they'd discovered anything.

They only had twenty-four more hours to figure out who the next victim might be and to stop this killer.

CHAPTER 50

y the time they reached the camp, Andi could hardly see the road in front of them. Thankfully, she and Duke arrived safely—even if her nerves felt shot.

"I think we should swing by the lodge," Andi told Duke as the SUV tires rumbled over clumps of snow. "I want to talk to Juniper. Plus, I don't feel like she should be by herself this evening."

"I agree that's probably a good idea, especially with Caleb still being out there. And Tim. And even Jared."

"Exactly," Andi said. "There are too many dangerous possibilities. Plus, I'd like to ask her a few more questions."

Suddenly, the ache on top of her head began again. Without realizing what she was doing, she reached for it.

"You keep touching the top of your head lately," Duke murmured. "What's going on?"

"Nothing."

"Andi . . ." His voice trailed.

He clearly knew something was wrong. Was this her chance to open up?

"It's just a headache."

"A headache at the exact same area where someone almost sawed open your skull?"

She swallowed hard but said nothing.

"You can talk to me, you know," Duke said quietly.

"I know."

"You don't have to shut me out. I want to be there for you."

"I know." Her voice came out sharper than she'd intended. "I don't want to talk about this anymore."

"Understood." His voice sounded defeated.

Andi immediately disliked herself for what she'd said, for the tone she'd used.

But it was too late to take it back.

Duke pulled to a stop in front of the lodge.

Andi cast a lingering glance at him before hurrying inside. Later, she promised herself. She'd talk to him later—when they didn't have so many other things pressing on them.

———

It didn't take much to convince Juniper to stay at the cabin with them—as long as Tundra could come. Andi had said of course.

Apparently, at the direction of the police, all the guests and the rest of the staff had been sent home during a break in the snow. It only made sense given the circumstances.

Juniper climbed into the SUV with them, and they headed to the cabin. The rest of the gang had already gone back there a couple of hours ago.

"Why do I sense you guys have bad news?" Juniper started, glancing back and forth between them from the back seat.

Andi stole a glance at Duke as she contemplated what to say.

"Why don't we wait until we get back to the cabin first before we share?" she finally said.

"Okay." Juniper began to pet Tundra, her hand moving almost frantically across his back. "But you're making me nervous."

Andi hated to put her in that spot. But it was better if they shared the update once instead of multiple times.

Once Duke parked, the three of them—plus Tundra —rushed through the onslaught of snow toward the front door. Thankfully, someone had thought ahead enough to place a shovel outside and to refill the firewood near the door.

They burst inside.

The gang had gathered around the fireplace. Some of

them had pen and paper in hand. Others had files in their laps. Matthew had his laptop. They were all working and drinking coffee, and several bowls of popcorn sat between them.

Everyone's eyes brightened when Andi, Duke, Juniper, and Tundra came inside.

"I'm so glad you made it." Simmy rose and gave them each a hug. "We were so worried. The weather out there has been atrocious."

"We had a couple of close calls on the road, but thankfully Duke knows what he's doing." Andi flashed him a soft grin.

"I don't know about that. Maybe it was just God's grace that got us there and back in one piece." Duke paused. "By the way, Juniper and Tundra are going to stay here tonight just to be safe."

"Sounds smart," Simmy said. "Let me get you something warm to drink and maybe a blanket."

"Did you learn something else?" Ranger's voice sounded dead serious and all business as he stood near the fireplace, a hulking look to his stance.

"Maybe. But first . . ." Andi took her boots off and found an empty seat on the couch.

Then she and Duke explained everything they'd learned today, ending with the revelation that Caleb was their most likely suspect due to the photo Barb had taken.

Andi glanced over at Juniper and saw she looked pale. "What do you think about all that?"

Juniper shook her head. "I'm stunned. At one time I thought he was my Prince Charming. But as I got to know him, I realized he definitely wasn't perfect and that he definitely wasn't Prince Charming. But I figured everyone has their flaws, right?"

In a sense, she was correct, Andi mused. But there was being imperfect, and then there was being secretive and a liar. There was a difference.

"I've been so distracted with running this camp . . ." Juniper continued. "I wasn't able to spend that much time with him—or even monitor him, for that matter. Then he and Peppermint started doing these appearances together with the reindeer. I suppose the two of them bonded because of that."

"That could have happened," Simmy said. "If they were spending a lot of time together, feelings could have developed. But I'm sure that's not easy to hear, and it doesn't make what they did right."

"I guess it doesn't matter. Peppermint's not here anymore, and Caleb was a cheating jerk." Juniper swallowed hard. "But this leaves me with no one."

"Oh, sweetie." Simmy sat beside her and squeezed her hand. "I know this is hard right now, but you're going to get through it."

Before they could talk any more, Tundra suddenly rose and began growling at the front door.

———

Duke and Ranger both strode to the windows.

As they did, Duke flipped on the outdoor lights so they could see.

He peered outside, but snow was the only thing filling the air.

It would take a lot for someone to be out in this weather just to threaten them.

But Tundra had clearly heard something.

"What is it, boy?" Juniper rubbed the dog's head.

He let out a whine and then lay down, almost as if whatever sound he'd heard was forgotten.

Strange. But dogs did strange things sometimes.

Just to be on the safe side, Duke checked all the windows again. They were all locked, and he saw nothing outside.

He and Ranger nodded at each other as they took their places back with the group around the fire. The cabin appeared secure.

"False alarm," Duke announced.

Tundra stood and began to turn in circles to get comfortable. As he did, his tail swept the coffee table, and a folder fell off, scattering papers everywhere.

Simmy quickly reached down to grab them and stuff them back into the folder.

But as she did, her gaze stopped at one. She held it in her hands, staring at it.

Her hand began to tremble.

"Simmy?" Andi seemed to sense that something was wrong as she frowned and leaned toward her friend.

But Simmy didn't seem to hear Andi.

She tore her eyes away from the paper in her hands, her gaze laser focused on Juniper. "This is yours, isn't it?"

Duke glanced at Juniper, wondering what exactly was going on. He hated being in the dark about it, but he hoped to hear an explanation soon.

Juniper nodded. If it was possible, her face went even paler.

Simmy stared at her, an unreadable emotion dancing in her gaze. "Is this what I think it is?"

Juniper ran a hand over her face, her expression crumpling. "Yes. I think it is."

"Does somebody want to explain what's going on?" Ranger finally asked. "Because I, for one, have no idea."

But it was as if Simmy and Juniper didn't hear him. They kept staring at each other.

Then finally Juniper mumbled, "I think you're my mother."

CHAPTER 51

ndi took a moment to comprehend what had just been said, unsure if she'd heard correctly.

Instead of jumping in with questions—which was her nature—she waited to hear what the two women had to say. Whatever the truth was, this was Simmy and Juniper's story. Not Andi's or anyone else's in the group.

"Did you say you think I'm your mom?" Simmy stared at her, a stunned look in her gaze. "I mean, I very well could be the surrogate who gave birth to you. It's hard to say for sure, but your birth date matches. That's the date I gave birth to my first baby via surrogacy. I remember all those dates."

"I've been trying to figure out the truth for the past year and a half or so, ever since I realized my parents may not be my parents."

Simmy shook her head, her gaze a mix of compassion and confusion. "No, sweetie. As a surrogate, I carried you. But I'm not your biological mother. I'm sorry."

"In most cases, that's true." Juniper swallowed hard as she paused. "But not in mine."

The gang sat in stunned silence as they waited to hear the rest of the story.

Juniper swallowed again and fanned her face as if unable to speak.

"I don't understand how you could be mine," Simmy finally said. "The embryo . . . it may or may not have belonged to your mom and dad. There was a big scandal with—"

"I know," Juniper finished, moisture rushing to her eyes. "I heard about it. About how the man who was brokering the deals was actually using embryos from himself and his first wife."

Simmy nodded slowly as if carefully treading water.

Juniper let out a sigh. "I guess maybe I should start at the beginning."

"Please do," Simmy said quietly.

She pressed her eyes closed as if gathering her courage. Then she opened them again, a new determination staining her gaze before she began. "A year and a half ago, Peppermint convinced me I should do one of those DNA tests. She thought it would be fun. She'd done one herself and found out her family was from Germany and that she's eight generations removed from being royalty or something crazy. I didn't really put much stock into anything she said. But just for kicks, I decided to do a DNA test also. However, I didn't tell my parents."

"Why not?" Ranger asked.

"Because I told them that Peppermint had done one, and they thought it was stupid. Said that the government was going to get ahold of those DNA records and put her in a database. They were adamantly against me doing it."

"But you did it anyway?" Andi clarified.

"I had a little money saved up, and I decided to use that. I suppose I halfway did it out of rebellion. My parents had a lot of rules for me, and they drove me crazy at times. This one seemed so harmless, not like something that could hurt anybody."

"So you got the results back? How did that point to the fact that your parents weren't your parents?" Andi knew the details of what happened to Simmy, and the facts weren't adding up in her mind.

Juniper's gaze stopped on Simmy. "You were registered with one of those ancestry websites."

Simmy's cheeks flushed, but she nodded. "I signed up several years ago. My boss gave it to me as a Christmas present. I'm not sure why I did that even. I guess I was curious if I had other family out there. Nothing ever came of it, though. In fact, I forgot I even did it."

"You were a match with me. So I started digging a little deeper. I knew my parents' DNA wouldn't be in the system since they were so against testing. But that led me down a rabbit hole that eventually led me to you."

Simmy quickly shook her head, an almost panicked look in her eyes—and Simmy never looked panicked. "That's not possible. The DNA would have to belong to someone else."

"I struck up a conversation with my father. He admitted that he and my mom used a surrogate—but that was all he admitted. I began to do my own research into surrogates in the New York area that same year. That's when I found an article about that surrogacy scandal."

Simmy stared at Juniper in shock.

She took some time to process before asking, "What happened next?"

Juniper glanced at her lap. "What happened next is where things get a little complicated."

———

Duke waited patiently to hear whatever Juniper would say next.

He hadn't expected this twist. Did her story tie in with her parents' murders somehow? He wasn't sure yet.

"I felt betrayed, like I didn't even know my own parents," Juniper explained. "But I'd hit a dead end. I didn't know how to find out the truth. So I hired someone to find some answers for me."

Duke's eyebrows shot up. "That doesn't sound cheap."

"It wasn't. I couldn't afford to do it. Not really. I had to borrow money out of my parents' safe." She frowned and pressed her eyes closed. "Before I could pay them back, they discovered the money was missing. They blamed Caleb, which I hated. But I couldn't correct them. I didn't want them to know. Besides, they'd lied to me so I figured I could lie to them too. Looking back, it was so immature."

"And that's how you discovered Simmy?" Ranger's voice still held an edge of protectiveness. No doubt, he didn't want Simmy to get hurt in the midst of this.

"It is. The guy I hired was able to figure out that Simmy had changed her name after giving birth to me. That's why I got confused." Juniper's gaze fluttered from her lap to Simmy as if she wasn't sure how Simmy would react.

Did she fear Simmy would reject her?

Duke knew Simmy wouldn't. But he could see where Juniper might be uncertain.

"I kept researching and discovered Simmy was a part of this true crime podcast." She paused. "For the longest time, I didn't want to dredge up anything about my parents' murders. I wanted to forget what I'd learned. But then I realized you could help me find answers, that it was a win-win. That's when I started trying to contact you."

"I remember we got some emails from you a couple of months before we were able to respond." Simmy tilted her head almost apologetically. "We've been getting an overwhelming amount of correspondence."

"I understand." Juniper glanced at her hands again. "I never told my parents any of this. I didn't know how to. But I felt bad about deceiving them. I even wondered for a while if me digging up the past is what got them killed."

"Why would you think that, sweetie?" Simmy squeezed Juniper's hand again.

The motion seemed to give her another surge of strength, and Juniper sucked in a breath as if pulling herself together. "I knew the man who hired you to be the surrogate was a bad person. I knew he probably wasn't operating alone, and when I started digging into my past, I wondered if that triggered something. I wondered if my parents had been killed to keep their silence and protect this guy's secrets."

A tear trickled down Simmy's cheek. "Oh, sweetie. That's a big weight for you to carry."

Tears streamed from Juniper's cheeks now too, and she quickly wiped them. "It has been."

"Your parents' deaths had nothing to do with you, Juniper," Duke reassured her.

"I'm beginning to realize that. But there's so much going on here, and I can't help but wonder if I'd handled myself differently if my parents would still be alive."

"There's far more at play right now than you realize," Ranger said.

Silence fell as everyone seemed to process the conversation.

Then Simmy brushed Juniper's hair behind her ear. "You're really my daughter?"

She nodded. "That's what I was told."

"I wouldn't put it past Mark to have done something to me. I was naive back then. They told me it was in vitro. But I suppose I could have been artificially inseminated. I don't remember any of it. I wasn't allowed to ask questions." Simmy tilted her head, all her attention on Juniper. "I was on a quest to find my real father also. It led me here. I understand your desire to take a deep dive into your past."

"My parents also had secrets," Mariella added. "It seems like every family does."

Duke rose, sensing some smaller, more private conversations needed to take place—conversations that not everyone needed to hear. "Maybe we should call it a night and get some rest. Then we can talk again in the morning. I have a feeling Simmy and Juniper may want some time alone."

Both women nodded as if grateful for his suggestion.

Yes, they still had a lot to talk about. A lot to think about.

But the best thing the team could do right now was

to rest their minds and restart these conversations in the morning.

CHAPTER 52
ONE DAY UNTIL THE NEXT MURDER

Andi awoke early. She hadn't been able to sleep anyway. Not with everything going on.

Instead of tossing and turning in bed, she quietly got up, threw on a sweatshirt and some slippers, and padded out into the living room.

She wasn't sure where Juniper had slept during the night, and she didn't want to disturb her in case she was on the couch.

Andi spotted Juniper sitting in front of the fire staring at it. Tundra raised his head above the back of the couch to look at Andi as she walked into the room.

Juniper glanced over her shoulder, her hair piled high in a messy bun.

"Good morning." Her voice didn't sound as perky as it once had. As a matter of fact, it sounded a little raw and hoarse as if she'd been crying again.

Andi took a hesitant step closer. "I hope I'm not bothering you."

"I've just been sitting here thinking. I welcome a distraction from my thoughts."

Andi quietly walked toward her and lowered herself on the other end of the couch. She gave Tundra a quick rub on his back before turning to Juniper. "How are you doing?"

"It's really hard to say." Juniper shrugged. "On one hand, I'm still devastated about everything that happened. But on the other hand, getting to know Simmy has been pretty amazing."

"I didn't realize it until you said something, but now that I know you could be related, I can see the resemblance. Simmy is a wonderful woman."

Juniper absently began to pet Tundra again. "She seems amazing. I didn't want to say anything at first because I just wasn't sure. I didn't know what she'd be like or if I'd want to tell her. But now I'm glad I did."

"You're going to love getting to know her better," Andi said softly.

"I'm sure you're right. For the past year, I've been consumed with guilt. I've wondered if my secrets played a role in my parents' deaths. I lied to them about what I knew, about what happened to the money." She paused. "Having this guilt in my life is a terrible way to live."

Andi thought about her own life. About the guilt she'd felt because of her own issues.

In her quest to protect Duke, she may have ended up hurting him more instead.

She absolutely hated that thought.

She looked back at Juniper. "Living requires taking risks. Sometimes we don't know if our decisions are right or wrong. In some cases, there is no right or wrong. It's just one way or another. Often, we won't know the consequences of our choices until after the fact."

Juniper glanced at her. "You sound like you understand."

"I do."

Something about the conversation made it clear to Andi that she needed to talk to Duke. She needed to let him know what was going on in her head.

Because if anything ever happened to her, she hated to think about him being unsure concerning where she stood on her feelings for him. It wouldn't be fair.

Now she just needed to find the right moment to tell him.

———

Duke heard people murmuring in the other room. But he waited until his alarm showed that it was 7:00 a.m. before he got out of bed.

Instead of heading right into the living room, he took a quick shower, enjoying the warm water. The cabin had gotten cold last night despite the heat being on. That was what happened when it was below zero outside. They hadn't even seen the worst of winter yet.

Today was a new day.

The day they needed to find some answers—a task that sometimes felt impossible.

He opened the door and saw Andi and Juniper talking on the couch. His heart lodged into his throat at the sight.

He wished he could get past the walls Andi had put up. He wanted to believe he could. But he'd rather she let them down on her own terms than him breaching the walls himself like an overeager rescuer.

However, a question had hit him last night: What if he tried to break past them but couldn't?

He didn't want to think about it, but it was a possibility.

However, being here right now at this cabin didn't seem like the time or the place to address any of those issues. Too much was going on already.

The women heard him step out, and Andi called, "Good morning."

"You ladies okay this morning?" Right away, he headed toward a window at the front of the cabin.

They'd drawn the shades last night, so he had no idea what it looked like outside right now. But if forecasters were right, the snow was supposed to have stopped a few hours ago.

"I'm feeling much better today," Juniper said. "I'm

glad everything is out in the open—even though I was terrified about it."

"Secrets can be big burdens to carry." Duke shoved the curtain aside.

A layer of snow was plastered against the window, not allowing him to see anything beyond it.

He moved to a couple of other windows, but they were all the same.

Finally, he went to the front door. He mostly wanted to see how deep the snow was so he could figure out a plan for today.

But as soon as he opened the door, something on the porch caught his eye.

It was a snowman. Four feet high. Freshly made.

Dread pooled in his stomach as he muttered, "It looks like we've got company."

CHAPTER 53

ndi's heart nearly thumped out of control when she heard Duke's words.

Who could possibly be here?

She leapt to her feet and peered out the door.

The snowman stared at her.

The blood drained from her face so quickly she felt lightheaded. She reached for the chair behind her to keep her balance.

Was there a . . . body part?

The faces of the rest of her team slammed into her head. Had this killer hurt one of her friends?

Duke seemed to think the same thing.

He shut and locked the door, rushed toward Ranger and Simmy's room, and pounded on their door. "Are you guys in there? Are you okay?"

As he did that, Andi hurried back toward her room, where she'd left Mariella. Her roommate had been sleeping when Andi had gotten up, but she still wanted to see with her own eyes that Mariella was okay.

As Andi threw the door open, Mariella stirred from her slumber. "Andi? What's going on?"

"You're okay?"

"I'm fine. Why wouldn't I be?"

"You're going to want to get dressed and come out here."

Andi ran back into the living room just as Duke jogged toward his bedroom.

He mumbled a few things inside the door and then joined her.

"Everyone is here, safe and accounted for," he announced.

Relief swept through her. Her mind had gone straight to worst-case scenarios. Scenarios where one of their team members had been injured . . . or worse.

Knowing everyone was okay, she hurried back to the front door and opened it again to look at the snowman. She inspected it and realized there was nothing gruesome about this snowman. It was typical in every sense of the word—from the coal eyes, the carrot nose, and the stick arms.

Except . . . there was no mouth. The other snowmen had mouths, right?

A sick feeling swirled in her gut.

Was this a sign? The beard, mustache, and now the mouth?

"Someone had to have done this in the past couple of

hours after it stopped snowing," Duke said as he joined her.

She agreed with Duke's assessment. Any footprints left by the person who'd done this were now gone. Because even though the blizzard was done, the wind still blew, causing the snow to drift.

Andi shivered.

Someone had left this snowman to send a message.

And it had worked. Her blood felt as cold as the figure built on their front porch.

———

Simmy fixed everyone a simple breakfast of pancakes and fruit. Juniper had loaded them down with food yesterday when she'd sent them back to the cabin for the night.

Despite the good food, everyone was on edge.

Duke had already called Gibson and told him about the snowman. He had also taken pictures. But the person who'd left this sick calling card was clearly long gone at this point.

"So what do we do now?" Juniper had cut up her pancake and poured syrup all over it. But it didn't look as if she'd taken a bite. "Do we all sit around and wait for this guy to strike tonight? Because I don't know about you, but that snowman seems like a warning to me. It's like this guy is telling us he's going to kill one of us next."

A pit formed in Duke's stomach. He'd thought the same thing, though he didn't want to vocalize it.

"Maybe we should get out of here." Ranger leaned back in his chair and took a sip of his coffee, his food long gone. "Besides, I told Karen we'd just be gone a few nights at the most. I'm anxious to see Anastasia. We can keep investigating, just not from right here."

"At this point, does it matter?" Mariella shrugged. "This guy's going to strike tomorrow. We can move the investigation wherever we want, but if we don't figure out something today, then someone will die tomorrow."

Her words hung in the air. But Duke knew she was right. Right now, they'd be wise to give this case every last ounce of their energy.

Everyone was quiet as they finished eating their breakfast, no doubt lost in their thoughts.

Until Juniper abruptly rose. "I know this seems unimportant considering everything else that's going on. But I need to feed the reindeer. I can't leave them to their own devices."

Duke stood, placing his napkin on the table. "I'll go with you. I don't mind."

"Would it be okay if I came too?" Simmy stole a lingering glance at Juniper as she asked the question.

"I would love that." Juniper flashed a grateful smile.

They would feed the reindeer.

Then they needed to put their heads together and figure out how to stop this killer—possibly Caleb—before he carried out his loathsome Christmas wishes.

CHAPTER 54

Duke, Simmy, and Juniper bundled up to go outside. The wind was frigid, and the snow was deep, which would make the walk difficult.

Duke double-checked his gun before they left. It was locked and loaded—and jammed into a holster at his waist.

He had no idea what was waiting out there for them. But they'd need to be careful. All of them.

He was thankful the guests and the rest of the staff had gone into Fairbanks for the night. It was only wise —at least until they could figure out what was going on. The more people who were here, the more people who were at risk.

Simmy and Juniper chatted behind him as they walked, and Duke let them have their moment. He knew they had a lot of bonding to catch up on.

There were still unanswered questions in the whole scenario. But Duke had no reason to think Juniper wasn't telling the truth about what she'd learned. He knew about the situation with Simmy. She'd been taken advantage of. The man behind the scheme was evil.

When they reached the reindeer pen, Juniper used a key to unlock the padlock on the shed. As she did, Duke took the shovel and scooped the snow away from the door so she could get inside.

The lock clicked, and Juniper tugged it off. She opened the door just enough for them all to squeeze in.

Duke, for one, was happy to get out of the cold. Even if the shed wasn't heated, at least the walls blocked the frosty wind.

Juniper tugged a light on before walking to a tub to check the pellets inside. "I need to grab some feed from this container. Reindeer can take care of themselves out in the wild, but we've kind of spoiled them here," she explained. "The good news is that the cold doesn't bother them too much. But they'll need to eat, and they're not going to find food while trapped in their pen."

Juniper seemed to be talking more than usual, probably out of nerves.

"I think it's wonderful how much you care for the animals," Simmy told her. "You remind me of Snow White."

Juniper's gaze jerked toward Simmy. "That's what my dad used to call me too."

Simmy smiled softly. "I can see why."

So could Duke. Juniper cared for animals like Simmy cared for people—another way the two of them were alike. Now that Duke knew, he couldn't stop thinking about the similarities.

He glanced around before his gaze stopped at something in the corner. "What's in this tub over here?"

"Should be the magic Christmas dust the kids sprinkle on the reindeer to help them fly. It's really just oatmeal that's been ground up with some sparkles. It's safe for the reindeer if they eat it." Juniper took a scoop and loaded pellets into a canvas bag. "Why do you ask?"

"It's on the bottom of the stack, so I'd think it would be used last. However, it's cleaner than the rest, almost like it's been used more frequently."

Juniper observed the tub. "You're right. I'm surprised you'd notice a minor detail like that."

"I was in the Army CID. Old habits die hard, I suppose."

Out of curiosity, he moved the other bins aside and opened the one on the bottom.

Sure enough, bags of reindeer dust were inside.

But he squinted when he saw the bags had been disturbed.

Out of curiosity, he moved some of the magic dust away to see what was under them.

His heart skipped a beat when he realized what was hiding beneath the magic dust in the bin. It was magic all right . . . but not in the way Juniper had probably intended.

———

As Duke stared into the tub, Gibson called.

"Hey, man." Duke kept his eyes glued to the tub.

"Everything okay?" Gibson asked. "You don't sound like yourself."

Duke carefully picked up one of the hidden bags inside the tub and held it up for a better look. "I think I may know what's been going on here. At least part of it."

"What's that?"

"It looks like someone may have been using the camp to smuggle drugs."

Juniper gasped behind him. "What?"

He hadn't had a chance to explain anything yet, and all he had were theories.

"Let me put you on speaker." Duke did that and placed the phone on a nearby shelf.

As he did, Juniper and Simmy walked to the bin and peered inside. Juniper moved more of the magic dust aside, revealing more bags.

Her eyes grew wide. "What is that? And how did it get in there? It's definitely not reindeer feed."

"Looks like crystal meth, if you ask me," Duke stated.

"Crystal meth?" Juniper's voice climbed a few notches as she backed away. "Why are drugs in there?"

He turned toward Juniper. "Didn't you say you set up some reindeer appearances around town?"

She nodded.

"Whose idea was it originally?" he asked.

"Peppermint brought the idea up to me. Why?" She shook her head as if confused.

"I'm guessing part of the reason she dreamed up this idea was so she'd have an innocuous way to hand off these drugs to people."

"What?" Juniper's hand flew over her mouth. "Peppermint wouldn't . . ."

"Who was responsible for the appearances?" Duke continued.

"Peppermint and Caleb were in charge of them." Her face paled as her voice drifted off.

"That would explain the fairy dust I saw by one of the reindeer also," Duke said. "I assumed it was some type of reindeer food you used as a gimmick for the kids."

"We do have that. But . . . the drugs are what got Peppermint killed, aren't they?" As Juniper seemed to go weak at the knees, Simmy wrapped her arms around her. Juniper sagged against her. "Then she got Caleb involved. Or maybe this was all Caleb's idea. I don't even know. But they were in on this together. They had to be. I was being played this whole time—being played for a fool."

"You all need to get out away from that camp," Gibson said through the phone. "I don't like anything I'm hearing right now."

Duke agreed. "How are the roads?"

"They're bad. A sheet of ice, and the city can't keep up—they're freezing over just as quickly as the crews can treat them. The backroads are especially dangerous."

Duke frowned and rubbed his jaw. "That's what I thought. I'll see what we can do to get us out of here."

"I have another update," Gibson continued. "But why don't you call me when you get back to the cabin? My update can wait."

Duke promised to be in touch once he was back with the rest of the gang, and then he ended the call.

"Does Officer Gibson think that the people buying these drugs are going to come back to get them?" Juniper's voice rose with anxiety.

"It's a possibility," Duke said. "We should leave just to be on the safe side. Let's get these reindeer fed. Then let's get back. Because if I had to guess, we're sitting on at least a hundred thousand dollars' worth of meth. That's something a lot of people would kill for."

CHAPTER 55

ndi listened to Duke's update when he returned to the cabin after feeding the reindeer.

After he finished, she shook her head. "I can't believe that's what was going on this whole time. Are we sure it was Caleb and Pepper?"

"They're the only ones who make sense." Juniper sat on the couch with a blanket pulled around her and a cup of cocoa in her hands. Simmy had made the drink for her. "I just can't believe this."

She'd already spoken those words of disbelief several times since she'd come back into the cabin.

"Aren't there better ways they could have distributed these drugs?" Andi paused near the fire, relishing the warmth of the flames. "And where were they even getting the drugs to begin with?"

"Things aren't monitored out here," Juniper said. "I could see where someone who was up to no good would want to use this location. They packaged it with the magic Christmas dust, and no one suspected a thing."

"My guess is that Pepper died because of this," Duke said. "That note said: *I told you this would happen.*"

"Someone wanted to send a message, not only to Pepper but to Caleb also," Andi murmured. "Maybe they were trying to take too large of a cut for themselves."

Duke grabbed his phone. "I told Gibson I'd call him back. He said he has another update for us."

"Can you put it on speaker?" Andi said.

"You got it." He dialed the number, and the sound of ringing came through the device.

Gibson answered on the first ring. "Hey, Duke. Thanks for calling me back."

"You have the whole gang here listening."

"That's fine. I wanted to let you know I've been doing some digging into Caleb's background. As I told you before, Caleb Brinley, as people at the camp knew him, does not exist. He stole someone's identity."

"Did you find out who he really is?" Andi asked.

"I did. His name is Caleb Michaels, and he was involved in the drug scene down by the US/Canadian border. He made some enemies—on both sides—and went on the lam about three years ago. He's used various identities since then."

"I can't believe that." Juniper shook her head, her eyes pressed closed as if she were mentally chiding herself for trusting the man.

"You guys are going to try to get out of there still, right?" Gibson asked. "If Caleb's enemies are close, and they know the stash of drugs is there, there's no telling what they will do to get their hands on it."

"That's the plan," Duke said. "We'll let you know when we're on the road. We just need to grab a few things."

As Duke ended the call, Andi ground her teeth.

She hadn't been sure if Pepper's death was related to what was going on here or not. But she definitely hadn't expected drug smuggling. Nor had she expected Juniper to be Simmy's long-lost daughter.

They had some answers, but they still had so much to figure out.

According to Gibson, they needed to get out of here.

She wasn't one to question him.

Actually, she *was*.

But not right now. Right now, she knew without a doubt they needed to leave—before it was too late.

———

Duke, Ranger, and Matthew all went outside to shovel snow so their vehicles could get out of the driveway.

As they did that, the rest of the gang packed. When they finished that, Juniper and Andi went back to put out extra food for the reindeer. Then everyone was ready to load the bags into the vehicles and take off.

Juniper and Tundra rode with Simmy and Ranger, while the rest of them rode in Duke's SUV.

Part of Duke was relieved to get away from this place. Too much had happened here. He had no idea what kind of people Caleb had mixed himself up with. Until they had more answers, it wasn't safe.

These guys could have been the ones who killed Pepper. Because no one knew for certain that Caleb had killed her. Maybe it was someone Caleb had made mad with his behind-the-scenes drug deals.

Either way, Duke had a feeling Pepper's death and Caleb's disappearance was somehow related to the drugs.

As they headed down the snowy lane, he remembered how his vehicle had slid out of control yesterday. The conditions today were even more precarious.

But as he saw something on the road in front of them, he tapped his brakes.

Quickly, he glanced in the rearview mirror to make sure that Ranger saw him slowing.

Thankfully, his friend slowed also.

"What happened here?" Andi leaned closer to the windshield for a better look.

Duke crept closer before fully braking and throwing his SUV into Park.

Then he stared at the mess in front of him.

At least four trees had fallen and blocked the only road leading from the camp.

Was this a coincidence?

Somehow, he doubted it.

CHAPTER 56

s Andi climbed out of the SUV, she sank up to her knees in the snow.

The icy precipitation instantly penetrated her jeans, and her skin stung from the biting cold.

But she didn't care.

Instead, she trudged toward the trees blocking the road. Duke joined her.

Though they were all spruce and not especially large, there were enough trees blocking them that they'd need equipment to get beyond them. She wasn't an expert on tree removal, but that much was obvious.

Ranger had climbed out also and stalked toward the downed trees. He grunted as he stared at one of them.

"What is it?" Duke paused in the middle of the drive and turned toward Ranger.

"These trees didn't just all fall across the road because of the storm." Ranger pointed to one of the tree trunks. The cuts near the base were clean, not splintered. "They were intentionally cut down—with an ax, if I had to guess."

Andi's breath caught, and shivers raced up and down her spine.

She knew what that meant.

Someone had wanted to trap them at the camp.

Someone had wanted Andi and her friends to be at his mercy.

Someone had wanted them to be afraid.

And that someone was a devious serial killer.

This guy had something planned—something she didn't even want to think about.

———

"We just need to make the best of this until Gibson can get out here to help us." Duke crossed his arms as he stood in front of the couch.

They'd gone back to the cabin, where they could stay warm. They simply didn't have the equipment they needed to clear those trees from the road. They could take a few snowmobiles out of here, but even that was risky. They would need enough gas to get to Fairbanks.

At least Gibson knew what had happened. They'd called him, and he was on his way. However, it might take longer than usual due to road conditions.

While they waited, they decided to make good use of their time. They reviewed everything they knew while they ate lunch—lunch simply being sandwiches and coffee.

All the information they'd gathered was spread on the table in front of them.

What were they missing?

Everyone was quiet as they stared at the papers, and Andi resorted to doing her normal pacing.

"I want to examine the victims again," Andi murmured. "There has to be a connection we're not seeing."

"We've already been through all of them." Duke leaned back in his seat and crossed his arms, exhaustion pressing on his shoulders until they ached.

"There has to be something we're missing."

Duke stared at her a moment and then nodded slowly. "Okay then. Let's go through each of these victims again and see if we overlooked anything."

Mariella tapped her fingers together. "The first victim was a utility worker in North Pole."

They went through the rest. A gardener. A gift shop owner. A neonatal nurse. Someone who worked for a planetarium. And the owners of the reindeer farm.

"It seems pretty random to me," Simmy murmured.

"Let's talk about our first victim." Andi paused and stared at his photo on the murder board. He was in his fifties with long white hair. In the photo, he stood proudly near a canvas sign proclaiming, "North Pole." "What do we know about him?"

"His name was Robin Carson." Mariella flipped

through the papers until she found the sheet on him. "I actually talked to his wife this week. Said he was a quiet man who liked working with his hands. On the day he died, he'd been wrapping utility poles in North Pole."

The whole town of North Pole was decorated for Christmas, including the signs around the community that looked like candy canes.

Andi froze and straightened. She sounded breathless as she asked, "What did you say he was doing?"

"He was wrapping utility poles to look like candy canes," Mariella repeated, narrowing her eyes with confusion. "Why?"

Andi raised her head toward the ceiling and closed her eyes. "I might know the connection."

Duke's breath caught. "Then please share."

They could use something encouraging.

CHAPTER 57

ndi's thoughts raced. "I can't believe we didn't see it."

"Please, tell us what you're thinking." Duke's intense gaze met hers, an urgency to his tone.

She stared at the pictures once more. Robert Elon with his T-shirt proudly proclaiming the name of his gift shop. Nurse Brianna Jenson holding a coffee mug from the hospital and grinning. Calvin and Mary beside one of the reindeer.

Each victim a life prematurely cut short.

She quickly shuffled through the facts to make sure she wasn't off-base.

She wasn't.

"The utility worker—the week he died, he was working on candy cane light poles," Andi started. "The gardener grew poinsettias. The planetarium guy liked stars."

Realization rippled through Duke's gaze. "The gift shop owner represented gifts, and the neonatal nurse represented babies."

"My parents represented reindeer." Juniper's voice cracked as she said the words.

Andi nodded. "Everyone who's died has represented a different aspect of Christmas."

Silence stretched a moment.

Finally, Ranger leaned forward and said, "So this killer . . . he really hates Christmas for some reason. But how does that help us to find this guy?"

"That's a good question." Andi began pacing again. "Why would he still be focusing on this reindeer camp? Why repeat an element he's already covered?"

"What else hasn't he covered?" Simmy asked. "What symbol of Christmas?"

"I'm not sure," Andi said. "Wise men? Shepherds? Wreaths?"

"It's anyone's guess," Mariella said. "But he seems determined to strike here again."

"He did draw that beard on the mirror," Matthew reminded them. "Could that represent Santa?"

"None of us have any connections with Santa," Andi said. "Am I right?"

Everyone nodded in agreement.

"The beard, to me, indicated that this guy would be targeting either Duke or Ranger," Matthew said. "Maybe he sees one of you two as the kingly types."

"Why would he think that?" Duke sounded earnestly confused.

"I don't know," Matthew said. "Maybe because you're tough and strong. You're natural leaders. You're confident. Who knows?"

"Anything is a possibility," Andi said. "But I stand behind the idea that this guy has a personal connection with this place."

"Like Caleb or Tim." Juniper crossed her arms and frowned.

"They're our best guesses right now," Andi said. "Unless you have other ideas."

"I don't."

Before they could talk about it anymore, the cabin went dark.

Any sounds around them went silent—the hum of the refrigerator, the heat blowing through the air vents, the whirring of the dishwasher.

Someone had cut the electricity, she realized.

Most likely, the killer.

———

As soon as the cabin went dim, Duke rose. So did Ranger.

Without saying a word, they both stalked toward the windows. Peered outside. Looked for a sign of anything suspicious.

All Duke saw was snow.

"The storm could have taken down a power line," Juniper offered.

That *was* a plausible explanation. But given everything that had happened, they needed to be on guard.

"Isn't there a backup generator?" Duke asked.

"I . . . I thought there was one." Juniper shrugged. "But wouldn't it have come on by now?"

It would have . . . unless someone had tampered with it also.

Duke's jaw tightened.

"What should we do?" Andi stared up at him from her seat on the couch.

Duke didn't like the fact they were trapped here. That they could be at a killer's mercy.

For all he knew, this guy could be watching them right now as he plotted his next move.

However, there were seven of them in this cabin plus Tundra, and only one killer. How did this guy think he would take them all down? If they all stuck together, they should be okay.

In theory.

Matthew closed his computer. "And there goes the internet as well."

If the internet was down, there was a good chance the phones wouldn't work either.

Duke disliked this more and more all the time.

Thankfully, they had the fire and a decent amount of wood outside. At least they could stay warm.

"Maybe we should get one of the snowmobiles and

try to get out of here?" Juniper said. "I almost think I'd rather take my chances that way."

"You said you're not sure if you have enough gas to make it back to Fairbanks, though," Duke said. "It sounds risky to me. Plus, there's Tundra."

At his words, Juniper began to stroke her dog's fur.

The lights flickered back on above them.

Duke glanced at the ceiling. Maybe the power hadn't gone out for a nefarious reason after all. Maybe it truly had been weather related, and they were all just over-reacting.

But nearly as soon as that thought crossed his mind, music began to blare again from the HomePod.

This time, it was the song from the Disney movie *Frozen*. The one about wanting to build a snowman.

Duke knew *that* wasn't a coincidence.

CHAPTER 58

ndi charged toward the HomePod and yanked the cord from the wall.

Hadn't she read an article once about how people or companies could eavesdrop using these things? She was pretty sure she had.

Either way, they couldn't take any chances right now. The stakes were too high.

She'd been on the verge of dismissing the power outage as being a fluke.

Until this.

Someone was playing with them, wasn't he?

Now they were trapped here and at this guy's mercy.

"What's this guy's next move?" Andi allowed herself to ask the question aloud even though she didn't want to. She didn't want to acknowledge the truth in the words.

But they'd be wise to think this through.

"Wait . . . did you say Gibson was on his way?" Mariella tucked her legs beneath her and pulled her blanket closer.

"Yes, he's on his way," Duke said. "I hope he gets here in time."

Andi swallowed hard. She thought the same thing.

"As long as we stay together and we stay here, we should be okay." Ranger's voice rang through the air, the assuredness of his words grounding them.

Juniper leaned into Simmy, and Simmy gave her a hug.

They all felt like prisoners here. No one had to say it aloud for Andi to know it was true.

They were trapped.

Andi paused near the Christmas tree and sniffed. "Does anyone smell that?"

"The smoke?" Simmy asked. "It's coming from the fireplace, right?"

"I'm not sure," Andi said. "This smells different somehow."

At her words, Duke rose. Without saying anything, he walked to the other side of the cabin and started opening doors.

That was when she saw it.

Smoke beginning to gather at the ceiling.

She prayed that her worst fears wouldn't be confirmed.

As soon as Duke opened the door to the bedroom where Mariella and Andi had been staying, he knew exactly what was wrong.

Someone had set this place on fire.

He quickly closed the door, praying it would contain the flames.

But they couldn't stay here any longer.

He charged back toward the gang. "Grab whatever you can. We've got to get out of here."

Juniper gasped. "Is that what I think it is?"

He didn't mince his words. "The cabin is on fire."

Just as the statement left his lips, flames began to lick from beneath the bedroom door. The fire was spreading entirely faster than Duke had thought it would. With the wind outside, maybe it shouldn't be surprising.

"We have to leave!" Duke motioned toward the front door. "Now!"

Wasting no more time, they grabbed their things and hurried outside.

They could get in their SUVs and drive to the lodge. Head away from the flames that threatened to destroy them.

But as soon as they stepped onto the porch, Duke's gaze went to the two SUVs parked out front.

All four tires on each vehicle had been slashed.

A lump formed in his throat.

They wouldn't be driving anywhere—just as the killer had intended.

CHAPTER 59

The killer had them right where he wanted them, didn't he? Andi thought to herself as she stared at the flattened tires on their vehicles.

He'd managed to run them out of the cabin. Trapped them at the camp.

Even if they were able to get to the UTVs and snow machines, she had a strange feeling they wouldn't be able to use them.

Would they all be out of gas? Would the shed be locked and inaccessible?

She didn't know. But someone had put a lot of thought into this.

"What should we do?" Simmy asked as she grasped Ranger's arm with one hand and held onto Juniper with the other.

"We could walk to the lodge." Juniper's voice quavered as she stared at the building in the distance.

"We'll have to walk across the field in the snow, but at least it will be warm once we get there."

"It's going to be a tough walk." Duke followed her gaze, knowing how long the hike would be. "The snow is deep. But you might be right. That might be our only choice."

As if to confirm those words, a crash sounded beside them. The ceiling beams of the cabin had collapsed.

Duke raised his arms and urged the group away from the flames. "We gotta get moving."

As he began to trudge through the snow, the group stayed with him.

Thankfully, they'd had time to grab their coats and boots. A person could freeze out here fast.

"I just had a thought," Juniper murmured.

"About what?" Andi looked back at her as they started through the snow.

"A story someone told me. About how a fire on Christmas made them never want to celebrate again. I don't know why I never thought about it earlier."

"Who told you that story?" Duke asked.

Before Juniper could answer, movement in the distance caught her eye.

Someone else was here.

———

Duke watched as a snowman stepped from the woods.

No, it wasn't a snowman.

It was a man wearing all white, from his snowsuit to the white mask on his face.

But that wasn't what captured Duke's attention.

It was the AR rifle in his hands and the second one strapped over his chest—and a third gun at his waist.

Whoever that man was, he was prepared for battle.

Duke started to reach for his own gun.

"I wouldn't do that if I were you," the man said, his voice deep and slightly familiar.

Where had Duke heard that voice before?

As the man's gun pointed at Duke, Duke raised his hands in the air to show he wasn't reaching for his weapon.

This guy could shoot them all within seconds if he wanted to. He just had to pull the trigger and sweep his gun down the line.

The cabin crackled as flames consumed it and more timbers fell.

Simmy gasped and jumped closer to Ranger. Tension rippled through the air as fire and ice mixed.

Duke didn't take his eyes off the man.

Just what was this guy planning to do with them? He'd gone through a lot of trouble to get them here.

The man walked closer before stopping in front of them. Duke still couldn't see who the man was because of the mask he wore.

But he didn't think it was Caleb. Something about his build and voice didn't fit.

Could it be Tim?

Maybe.

Jared?

Another possibility.

"You guys should have never come here," the man said. "You only stirred up trouble."

"You don't have to do this." Duke tried to reason with him, though he knew his efforts would most likely be futile.

"Don't tell me what I do and don't have to do!" the man snapped.

This guy was already on edge. Duke needed to be careful what he said and did. He hoped the rest of the team would be as well.

"What do you want from us?" Andi's voice sounded steady and confident as she called out to the man.

"You guys are going to be my most talked about December 6 murder ever," he said. "I kept going back and forth as to which one of you would be the best. I even picked out one of you. Then I decided it should be all of you. But the best part? I never expected to get all of you at once."

"What do we represent about Christmas to you?" Andi said.

His eyes widened. "So someone finally put that together, I see."

"We did."

"You all represent family," the man stated. "You represent family that sticks together through thick and thin. Something I never had. Now, enough talking.

Throw your guns on the ground. Don't make me tell you again!"

Duke glanced at Ranger, who nodded at him. Then they did as the man said. They didn't have much choice right now.

As much as Duke might want to charge the guy and tackle him, he knew how futile that would be. The man would simply shoot him, then finish everyone else off.

With one hand still on his rifle, the man reached into his pocket and tossed something into the snow.

"You." He nodded at Duke. "Get those. Tie everybody up."

Duke glanced at the object in the snow and saw it was a bundle of zip ties.

Once he tied his friends up, it would all be over.

He couldn't let that happen.

He needed to figure out a way to stop this, and he didn't have much time.

CHAPTER 60

he pain pulsating on top of Andi's head nearly brought her to her knees. She tried to ignore it. She couldn't deal with it right now—not when she was facing a killer.

Who was the man behind the white mask? Had he planned the outfit he wore just so he could look like a snowman?

And what would Duke do? Would he tie everyone up? Or put himself at risk and try something?

Both prospects terrified her.

Flames shot from the cabin as the building beside them continued to burn. The orange and yellow fire offered a stark contrast to the otherwise white surroundings.

Andi's feet and legs felt frozen while her right arm and one side of her face nearly melted from the heat of the blaze.

She needed to buy some time, however. Swallowing hard, she asked, "Why the snowmen?"

Her question seemed to startle the man—he flinched and looked away from the zip ties.

Duke hadn't made any attempt to grab them yet, and Andi hoped he wouldn't have to.

"My family home burned down on December sixth." Bitterness stained the man's voice. "I was only twelve, and my family was celebrating an early Christmas with extended family. Someone didn't attend to the fire as they were supposed to. While we were all sleeping, my childhood home went up in flames. By the time the rescue workers got there, I was the only one left alive."

"That sounds terrible." It truly did; Andi's words were honest.

"When I was rescued, I was taken outside. That's when I saw that the snowman my brother and I had built earlier in the day was still standing. Melting but standing. My dad's hat had somehow escaped the fire and blown out of the house. It landed beside the snowman. I remember reaching down and putting it on the snowman's head."

Andi despised this guy, but she had to admit his story was gut-wrenching.

She'd figured that whatever had happened to the killer to set this chain of events into action had been traumatic, and she was right.

"I was placed in foster care, and the first family to take me in loved Christmas," the man continued. "Said the best way for me to 'get over' what had happened was by celebrating big. Everything was all about Christmas, starting in October. They played Christmas music, had advent calendars, saw Christmas miracles wherever they went. It was *pathetic*."

"That must have been hard for you," Andi said. "I'm sorry."

The man glared into space as if his mind had gone into a different world. "I've hated Christmas ever since then. Despised it. Despised all the happy people. Despised everything the holiday represents. Every time I see a Christmas movie or a commercial about the holidays I get a sick feeling in my stomach. I needed something to make me feel better."

"Don't you think you took things to the extreme?" Andi resisted the urge to touch the top of her head, to show any pain or fear. But sweat began to run down the side of her face, and heart beat so hard she couldn't ignore it.

Flashbacks of being tied to that operating table hit her. Memories of seeing the doctor come toward her with the scalp. Recollections of the panic she'd felt.

She had to get a grip!

The man's nostrils flared. "It's only fair that others suffer the way I've suffered. I wanted to leave my mark —and I think I've been effective."

Andi took a deep breath, trying to focus on this situation. She could do this. She could manage her panic, her emotions.

She just needed to focus on the facts instead.

"Why did you wait so many years to start your killing spree?" Andi would guess this man was in his forties or fifties, based on his voice and stance. What had triggered his actions six years ago?

"Seeing this place and hearing about everything it represented . . . it reminded me of everything I'd lost. It reminded me of that foster family that forced Christmas on me. Who worshipped Christmas like it was their god. Being here triggered something inside me until it was all I could think about." He paused. "Then I saw the snowman."

"The snowman?" Juniper asked. "What snowman?"

"The first time I saw this property, there was a snowman. Your dad built it, Juniper. Said it represented everything happy about the season."

"My dad?" Juniper's lips parted in surprise. "You knew him? You came to this property before now?"

"That's right." The man swallowed hard. "To me, that snowman represented all my loss. I kept seeing my father's hat on the melting snowman outside our home. The image has always haunted me, always been a reminder of my pain."

"So now you want to make sure you ruin Christmas for everybody else?" Disgust dripped from Andi's voice. She didn't hide it.

This guy's mind was warped. His pain had transformed him into a monster.

She couldn't let her pain do the same. Not turn her

into a monster. But turn her into someone she didn't recognize.

"I do this in honor of my family." His voice rose sharply. "To keep their memories alive. To remind others that life isn't always fun and games!"

"Yet, wasn't this a game?" Andi wished she could slap some logic into the man. It was too late for that. His motives made perfect sense to him. He'd justified every murder. "You were just waiting for someone to figure out how you chose your victims. It sounds like you were having some fun with it."

"I was making a point!"

"There has to be a better way," Simmy murmured. "Killing others won't bring your family back."

"I have no one! Don't you understand that?"

Juniper stepped forward, a new confidence in her gaze. "You had someone, but you lost her."

Was Juniper talking about herself? Was this man Caleb? How had she figured out his identity?

Then she said, "Please, tell me you're not the one who killed Peppermint. I've always known you weren't a good man, but tell me you didn't kill your own daughter."

The breath left Andi's lungs.

Wait . . . was Juniper saying that this man was . . . Heath Klinkhart?

At Juniper's words, the man pulled off his mask.

Duke sucked in a breath when he saw Heath Klinkhart staring back at them.

"I offered all the signs you needed to figure this out, but no one did," Heath muttered.

All the signs? Something about his words triggered a realization.

They *had* missed something, hadn't they?

Duke suddenly remembered the photos of the victims on the murder board.

The canvas sign. The T-shirt. The coffee mug.

Heath had first encountered his victims through his screen-printing business, hadn't he? Why hadn't they seen that earlier? He *had* interacted with the victims before murdering them.

"Why couldn't you and your family just have minded your own business?" Heath snapped. "None of this would have happened."

"This wasn't my parents' fault." Juniper's hands fisted at her sides and her jaw hardened.

"Did you know they weren't really your parents?" A smirk formed on Heath's lips, almost as if he wanted to hurt Juniper, to give her that emotional punch in the gut.

"As a matter of fact, I did." She lifted her chin higher.

"They were scammed," he continued as if he hadn't heard her. "They were devastated when they found out you weren't their flesh and blood. But for some reason, they still loved you. That's why they fled here to Alaska —they didn't want you to be taken away from them. My wife and I were the only other people they ever told."

"How did they find out about the mix-up?"

"They had no idea someone else's embryo had been used for the surrogacy—not until they realized you were nothing like them."

"Why did they hide the truth from me? My dad hardly even wanted to admit I was born via a surrogate. Why so many secrets?"

"They struggled with whether or not to tell you all the details. My guess is that they would have eventually admitted that you weren't their flesh and blood."

Juniper grasped Simmy's arm as she stared at Heath with an incredulous look in her gaze. "So you're doing all this because you had a falling out with my parents?"

"It's more complicated than that. I told them I would keep this secret quiet—all they had to do was give me some money."

"That's dirty," Juniper muttered.

"That's what happens when you trust the wrong person. Besides, they're not the reason I've killed these other people. I just thought they'd be the icing on the cake."

"You're sick." Juniper's voice cracked as she said the words.

"Enough talking!" Heath aimed his gun at all of them before glancing at Duke. "I told you to tie everyone up. Don't make me repeat myself."

Duke cast his gaze to the rest of the group. He hoped they understood his silent message.

Because he needed to make his move now. It was his only chance.

When he did, they would need to run to safety.

He prayed they'd get to shelter in time.

CHAPTER 61

ndi stared at Duke.

What was he thinking? He was planning something. She just wasn't sure what.

She held her breath, wishing he wouldn't put himself on the line. But she knew him well enough to know he would.

She watched Duke take a step forward. Reach down to grab the zip ties.

As he did, Ranger suddenly had a coughing fit.

Heath's gaze darted to him.

As it did, Duke dove for the man's gun. He tackled Heath as he shoved the man's gun away.

Then he called over his shoulder, "Run!"

Andi remained frozen.

She didn't want to leave him.

But Ranger grabbed her arm. "Come on!"

With one last glance at Duke, she took off with the rest of the gang. Tears wanted to blur her eyes, but it was too cold outside for tears.

Right now, she needed to keep moving. This was what Duke wanted.

But where would they go?

"This way!" Juniper called.

They took off toward the reindeer pen.

The reindeer pen? Why in the world would they go this way? They should be headed to the lodge. Somewhere with walls. Somewhere it was warm.

Andi glanced behind her.

She saw Duke rise to his feet. As he did, Heath gripped his gun and slapped Duke across the face with the barrel.

Duke fell to the ground.

"No!" she muttered.

She tried to stop and turn around, but Ranger grabbed her arm, holding her in place.

As gunfire sounded, grief clutched her chest. Duke . . .

Then Heath started toward them.

Ranger gripped her arm tighter. "Duke would want you to keep going."

But all Andi could think about was how much she loved him. How she couldn't see her future without him. She should have let him in. Shouldn't have been so stubborn or prideful.

She looked at the rest of the group across the field and saw that Juniper had darted into the reindeer pen.

"What are you doing?" Ranger called as he paused a moment.

But Juniper didn't slow down. "Come with me. Trust me. Please!"

The rest of the gang had no choice but to follow.

Maybe Juniper knew something that they didn't.

Their lives depended on that fact.

———

Andi could barely think as Ranger pulled her over the fence.

The rest of the gang ran ahead of them, following Juniper.

More gunfire rang out.

Heath was shooting at them!

She glanced ahead. Saw Juniper motioning toward them as she stood in the center of the field.

Staying out in the open seemed like a terrible plan.

Andi trudged through the snow anyway, trying to get to the rest of the gang. Part of her didn't care. Not if Duke was dead.

Was he dead? Could he have survived that gunshot?

More bullets rang out behind her.

But Heath was apparently a terrible shot, perhaps more skilled with a knife.

Just when she didn't think she could run a step farther, Andi finally reached the rest of the group.

She sucked in icy breaths that hurt her lungs.

"Juniper, what's your plan?" Ranger paused, his jaw muscle thumping with tension.

"You'll see." She glanced around.

There was nothing to see. Only a few random reindeer wandering about.

"We should see if we can get to the lodge." Ranger sounded no-nonsense. "Before it's too late."

"He'll just find us there and hunt us down one by one," Juniper stated.

"And what's he going to do right here?" Mariella asked. "He's going to make human snowmen out of us or something."

Andi shivered at the thought.

She glanced up.

Saw Heath had reached the fence and started to climb over.

It was only a matter of time before he reached them. Before they became easy targets. Targets that even an unskilled marksman could hit.

Oh, Lord . . . help us. Please! Be with Duke also. I'm begging You. Please!

"I don't know what you all were thinking," Heath muttered as he lumbered through the snow drifts toward them. "But thanks for sticking together and making this easy on me."

He was going to kill them all, wasn't he?

And Gibson was probably still ten minutes away, at least.

There was no one to help them.

Nowhere to hide.

They'd made a fatal choice by coming out here, Andi realized. Why had Juniper led them this way? Was she in on this also?

CHAPTER 62

uke moaned as he sat up.

He gripped his chest, trying to pinpoint the pain. Where had the bullet pierced his body?

He glanced down, searching for the blood. For the wound.

Then he saw it.

The bloody hole in his coat near his shoulder.

He grimaced as he pulled his coat away, carefully peeling the fabric from his skin.

Relief whooshed through him.

The bullet had just skimmed his skin.

He would be okay.

Praise God!

Because he had other things to do right now.

He dragged his gaze around until he spotted his friends.

In the field.

The field?

Why were they out there? They needed shelter!

Heath hobbled toward them, his gun raised.

The man called out something to them, something Duke couldn't understand—threats, no doubt.

Duke needed to get to them. He needed to help.

He rose to his feet, feeling unsteady for a moment.

Then he found his balance and took a staggering step forward.

He only hoped he reached them in time.

———

"We can't just stand here!" Andi said. "He's going to kill us all."

But as she took a step away, she saw it.

The reindeer. They knew something was going on, and the creatures had been stirred up.

Her mind swirled as she realized what was happening.

All the reindeer had begun to walk in the same direction. In a circle. Around them.

"What on God's green earth is happening right now?" Ranger muttered as he glanced around.

"That's right, guys," Juniper whispered to the reindeer. "I knew you wouldn't fail me."

"I'm so confused." Mariella glanced around, fear filling her gaze.

"It's a reindeer cyclone," Andi muttered as she remembered what Juniper had told her. "They do it to protect their own."

A few minutes later, all thirty-five or so of the reindeer had gathered and walked in circles.

Andi watched as the reindeer formed a living, breathing whirlpool around them.

They were protecting them—Juniper, specifically—like she was one of them.

The picture of community, of being stronger together filled her mind, and tears wanted to escape from Andi's eyes.

But this wasn't over yet. She had to stay focused.

"What kind of witchcraft are you practicing?" Heath yelled.

He tried to creep closer, but the reindeer stopped him, nudging him back, not allowing him in.

Finally, he scowled and stepped back.

He raised his gun instead.

"Get down!" Ranger yelled.

Andi and everyone in the center of the circle ducked, huddling together amongst the sound of stomping reindeer hooves and snorts.

But Heath was too discombobulated to pull the trigger.

The reindeer confused him—just as nature had designed.

Andi lifted a prayer of thanks.

But how long would this protection last?

How long could Andi and the rest of the gang make it out here in the cold? Could they wait it out until Heath found another way?

She wasn't sure.

CHAPTER 63

uke paused.

What were those reindeer doing?

He didn't know. He only knew the creatures' actions were preventing Heath from reaching the rest of the gang.

The pattern they were walking in had distracted the killer from the fact Duke wasn't dead.

This was his chance to make a move.

He grabbed one of the guns left in the snow.

Then he took a heavy step toward the reindeer pen. His body ached—and his shoulder.

But he could push through this.

He had no other choice—especially when he remembered what this guy would do to his friends if he carried out his ultimate plan.

No way would pieces of his friends end up on a snowman.

Heath was yelling something. But every time he took a step closer, the reindeer pushed him out of the way and disoriented him.

Brilliant.

Duke climbed the fence and landed silently on the other side.

A jolt of pain went through his shoulder, and he grimaced.

He'd get that taken care of later.

As he continued forward, he watched as Heath raised his gun.

Was this man going to try to shoot his friends, despite the fact that reindeer were blocking them?

Duke couldn't let that happen.

Instead of running after the man, he raised his own gun.

More pain shot through his arm, making his aim unsteady.

He could do this. He had no choice.

———

Andi saw Duke appear. Saw the cabin going up in flames behind him.

Heath was clueless. He was too focused on getting through the reindeer to notice anything else.

She held her breath.

Duke raised his gun.

As he did, Heath turned.

Saw Duke.

Raised his gun.

"No!" she shouted.

Then someone pulled the trigger.

Both men fell to the ground.

"No!" The word escaped before she could stop it.

Who had fired that shot? Heath or Duke?

CHAPTER 64

Andi tried to run toward Duke. But too many reindeer paced between the two of them.

The animals that had once provided protection now formed a barrier.

Panic raced through her.

She had to know if Duke was okay!

She started to run through the creatures again. Then she realized what a truly impenetrable wall they had formed. The reindeer might trample her if she wasn't careful.

"I've got this," Juniper murmured as she stepped up next to Andi.

Andi watched as Juniper raised her hand to one of the reindeer. It took the animal a moment to pause. To sniff her.

But once one reindeer stopped walking, the rest of the creatures slowly began to stop also. The pause gave

Andi just enough time to dart between the animals and run toward Duke. Ranger followed on her heels.

Finally, she managed to weave her way in and out of the reindeer, to get beyond them to the two men lying on the ground.

Just as Andi reached them, she looked up. Four men in uniform raced toward them from the entrance of the camp.

State troopers, she realized.

Gibson was here.

She prayed he wasn't too late.

She dropped onto her knees into the snow beside Duke.

He moaned as he lay there.

"Are you okay?" She scanned him. Saw the blood on his shoulder.

Then she continued to rake her eyes over him, looking for any more telltale signs that he'd been hit by that bullet—and hit somewhere critical.

"It was Heath," Ranger muttered as he hovered near the man.

Andi looked behind her and saw the blood on Heath's chest.

Tears of relief tried to spring to her eyes, but the frigid temperatures wouldn't allow them to flow.

She leaned toward Duke and ran her hand along the side of his face. The force of the gunfire must have thrown him back. In his injured state, he'd been unsteady.

"Can you hear me?" Andi murmured.

He moaned, then his eyes fluttered open. He started to push himself up before grimacing.

Before he answered, his gaze went to Heath.

Once he saw that the man was down and no longer a threat, Duke's expression relaxed. "Now I'm okay."

As Gibson and his men surrounded them, Andi pulled Duke's head to her chest and held him.

———

An hour later, paramedics and more police officers had arrived on the scene. They'd had a crew move the trees out of the way so vehicles could get to them.

Duke sat in the back of an ambulance, a paramedic tending to his wound. The bullet hadn't fully pierced his skin but only grazed it. Stitches should suffice.

Andi had hardly left his side since everything went down.

As they sat in the back of the heated ambulance together, a paramedic in front of them, the doors opened.

Gibson appeared. "Can I have a moment?"

The paramedic nodded and climbed out. Gibson shut the doors behind him to keep the heat in before taking the paramedic's seat across from them.

"That was some showdown back there," he said. "At least from what I've heard."

"I've never seen reindeer act like that," Duke muttered.

"They pretty much saved our lives," Andi said.

"A Christmas miracle?" Gibson grinned. "Although I *have* heard that reindeer do things like that. I've just never seen it with my own eyes before. It was pretty spectacular."

"Do you have any other updates for us?" Andi asked as she reached over and squeezed Duke's hand.

Duke squeezed back, not wanting to ever let go.

"Actually, I do." Gibson's grin faded. "Some of my guys managed to track down Caleb."

Duke's eyes widened. "That's good news. How did you find him?"

"He was hiding out at a local hotel, and somebody spotted him. Said he was acting suspicious. He had Tim with him and was holding the man hostage. Apparently, Tim discovered what Caleb was up to concerning the drugs and confronted him. That's when things started to fall apart."

"Did Caleb tell you anything else?" Andi asked.

"As a matter of fact, he did." Gibson leaned forward with his elbows on his legs. "Apparently, there was a guest here last week who recognized him from back when he lived in Washington State and was involved in drug trafficking. He began to threaten Caleb, which made him nervous."

"Did Caleb confess to all this?" Duke asked.

"He did. Once he started talking, he spilled everything. About how he was involved with hauling drugs over the border and selling them. He'd been doing it since he was fourteen, he said. He had a guy who helped him with the fake IDs. He made a lot of enemies in the process of doing that."

"I assume when one of those enemies found him here that he was in big trouble," Andi said.

"For sure. Apparently, Caleb owed this guy money. But the man eventually left the camp, and Caleb thought he was in the clear. He believes this guy came back and confronted Pepper. He thinks this man killed her as a way of making good on his threat to Caleb, and that Emmett must have seen something."

"Another casualty . . ." Andi murmured.

"This guy was also the one who compromised the ice because he knew Caleb would be going out there."

"What about the things that happened to us while we were here?" Duke asked. "The beard someone drew on the mirror, the snowman on the Christmas tree . . ."

"We believe Heath was responsible for those things," Gibson said. "He was feeling a little braver this time around because he didn't do anything like that with his other murders."

"And Caleb?" Andi asked.

"Caleb left the bloody hand—he admitted to that, plus you found the fake blood. He said he was afraid you might catch on to what was going on with him, so he tried to scare you away. Little did he know that the actual December Dismemberer was here at the camp and planning his next murder."

Andi glanced at Duke and squeezed his hand again. "At least we can be thankful that this is all over."

"If you guys hadn't been here, I have no doubt Heath would have struck again. That he would have claimed another victim. The state of Alaska may not realize this, but they owe you a lot of thanks."

"I'm just glad that this guy has been stopped," Andi said. "Maybe people can rest easier now and truly enjoy the upcoming holiday."

"Let's hope." Gibson stood. "I need to continue to get some statements and look into things. What are you guys going to do now?"

Duke and Andi glanced at each other.

Duke knew what he wanted. He wanted to have a nice long talk with Andi. To get some things out in the open.

"As soon as we're cleared to leave, I suppose we can go back to Fairbanks," Duke said.

"It should only be a few more hours. I know they're setting up in the lodge area for now. That's where the rest of the gang went."

"We'll head there in a second," Duke said. "Thanks."

"Take as much time as you need," Gibson said before waving and stepping from the vehicle.

Maybe this was the moment he'd been waiting for— the moment he and Andi could really talk.

CHAPTER 65

There was so much on Andi's mind. So much she wanted to tell Duke.

Being in the back of an ambulance didn't seem like the best time or place. But this was what she had right now, and she didn't want to waste another moment.

"I'm sorry for the way I've been acting lately," Andi said.

"What's been going on in that head of yours?" Duke's soft gaze met hers. "It's been so hard not knowing or being able to help."

She rubbed the skin between her eyes as she tried to gather her thoughts. "I've been having these panic attacks lately. I didn't want to tell you because I don't want to seem weak. I don't want everybody else to see me like this either."

"Struggling isn't a sign of weakness," Duke said.

"In my head I know you're right, but that's not what my mentor taught me. He told me that leaders should always be strong. I didn't want to burden you guys anymore. Everyone has been through so much. It's not just me."

"What causes these panic attacks?"

Andi blew out a breath. "Anytime something reminds me of being captured and strapped down to that operating table." Her voice sounded strained, even to her own ears. "The top of my head aches every time."

Duke squinted. "It does?"

She nodded. "I even panicked to the point where I went to the doctor. It was on the day you were meeting with everyone to finalize the sale of your travel business. I didn't want to mention it—not unless they found something."

Duke squeezed her hand tighter. "Did they find anything?"

She shook her head. "No, they didn't. I was afraid those guys really had managed to somehow insert something into me that was changing my thoughts. I couldn't get that idea out of my head."

"But there was nothing," Duke confirmed.

"I'm all clear. The panic I'm feeling is all a result of the trauma."

"I know you've been seeing a therapist."

"And he's been helping me a lot. He really has. But it's going to take a while to talk through some of the PTSD I'm dealing with." She paused and frowned. "I hate to even use that term because I don't know if I've earned it. I feel like it's something that should be reserved for people who've been through war zones or something."

"In your own way, you *have* been through a war zone."

She nodded, though the motion felt lackluster. Then she dragged her gaze back up to meet Duke's. "I'm sorry."

"Don't apologize. I just want you to know that you can always talk to me. I won't think less of you if you're going through something and don't have all the answers."

"I appreciate that unconditional love and support I have from you. I'm going to try to do better."

Duke leaned toward her and planted a kiss on her forehead, letting his lips linger there a moment. Andi leaned into him, relishing his touch.

Then the doors to the ambulance opened, and they knew that their moment was over. But at least they'd talked. At least Andi had gotten everything out into the open.

It felt good not to keep it inside anymore. Maybe she'd just been silly by wanting to stay quiet about it. Exposing her deepest fears to others was something totally out of her comfort zone.

But she was going to work on that.

Right now, they needed to check on the rest of their team.

his is for you." Andi handed Mariella a present. "It's from me and Duke."

She watched as Mariella gingerly opened it, a grin on her face.

After Mariella pulled off the colorful wrapping paper, she tugged off a box top and pulled out a . . . reindeer stuffed animal.

She squinted as if confused. But as she turned the reindeer around, she seemed to notice it wore a pink sweater with a name embroidered across the front.

Slasher.

Mariella burst into laughter. "I'm not going to live that one down, am I?"

"No, you're not," Duke confirmed.

The whole group laughed.

Christmas was still five days away, but the murder

club had decided to have an early Christmas celebration together.

Everyone had gone to Ranger and Simmy's house. Anastasia was here with them, as well as Juniper. Jason had joined them from Salmon-by-the-Sea. Tim had been invited, but he was currently trying to make things right with Jared.

The DNA test had come back, confirming Juniper was indeed Simmy's daughter.

The only explanation they'd come up with to explain the twist was that IVF treatments were too expensive and so Mark, Simmy's first husband, had opted for artificial insemination instead. But only for Simmy's first pregnancy.

He'd been anxious for this baby to be born—probably because the sooner the baby came, the sooner he would get paid. Therefore, he hadn't wanted to go through the longer IVF process.

Simmy and Juniper had been bonding ever since the news was confirmed—actually, before that. In fact, Juniper had come to live with Ranger and Simmy until she could get things figured out.

Operations at the reindeer camp had been temporarily shut down. But Ranger and Simmy were working with Juniper to help her figure out exactly what she wanted to do with the place—if she wanted to continue to run it or if she had other plans.

Like becoming a veterinarian.

There were still the reindeer at the camp to take care

of. But there were several investors interested in taking over the camp. Andi was working with Juniper on the legal aspects of that—and to make sure if she took any deals, she wouldn't get cheated. Right now, Juniper was leaning toward keeping her family's cabin and retaining a small ownership in the property.

She didn't want to leave the animals she cared about so much.

Animals that had saved the gang's lives.

Thankfully, the families of the victims of the December Dismemberer finally had some answers. Maybe with the answers, they would also have some closure and peace.

The same wouldn't be said for Claire Klinkhart. Gibson had told them that Claire had left Heath two months ago, unable to take his temper any longer. She'd gone into hiding. When she'd been located and questioned, she'd admitted she had no idea Heath was a killer.

According to Claire, Heath had gone back to Alaska last year after their move to Seattle. He'd said he had some loose ends to tie up after their move. She'd never imagined the loose ends were Calvin and Mary.

She would have a long road of grief and recovery ahead for her, and Andi prayed she'd have strength and a good support system in the process. In many ways, Claire was a victim also.

The Arctic Circle Murder Club had put the finishing touches on their latest podcast, and it had been a big hit.

Now they'd moved on to their next case.

The doorbell rang, and Ranger rose to answer. A moment later Gibson walked in and joined in the fun. "I heard I was invited to stop by, so here I am."

Everyone welcomed him, motioning for him to join their circle around the fireplace.

Simmy really had done a great job decorating. Not only were there the normal Christmas decorations—the tree, the garland, the wreaths on the doors. But on the coffee table in front of them was a wooden nativity set that Ranger had gotten for Simmy.

Every time Andi glanced at the scene, a surge of warmth rushed through her.

The set was a nice reminder that Christmas wasn't just about traditions and gifts and materialism.

Christmas was about remembering the birth of God's Son here on earth.

Duke caught her staring at the nativity and squeezed her hand.

Ever since Andi had told him what she was going through, her panic attacks had lessened. She felt she was doing so much better.

But she was going to continue to go to therapy, just to make sure she was still on track.

As everyone broke off into their own conversations, Andi looked up in time to see Matthew slip something to Juniper.

Juniper's eyebrows flew up at the unexpected gift.

Andi knew she should look away and give them

privacy, yet she couldn't seem to tear her gaze away from them.

Juniper opened the gift and held up a Christmas ornament.

From *Lord of the Rings*.

"An Evenstar . . ." she murmured. "I love it!"

Was something brewing between the two of them? Andi wasn't sure. But the idea was intriguing, at least.

She prayed for Matthew, that one day he would find his match. That he wouldn't always feel like the seventh wheel.

She prayed for everyone on their team. They were doing a good work together . . . but there would always be obstacles to overcome, forces that tried to stop them.

For now, she would celebrate Christmas with her Alaska family. Then Duke was going home with her to Texas to meet her father. Mariella and Matthew were going to California to see family. Ranger and Simmy would celebrate their first Christmas as husband and wife . . . along with Anastasia and Juniper.

She squeezed Duke's hand as he sat beside her and prayed she'd never stop counting her blessings.

~~~

Thank you for reading **Only One More Lie**. If you enjoyed this book, please consider leaving a review!
~~~

making it clear the killer will stop at nothing to get what he wants.

Margin of Error

Some secrets have deadly consequences. Brynlee Parker thought her biggest challenge would be hiking to Dead Man's Bluff and fulfilling her dad's last wishes. She never thought she'd witness two men being viciously murdered while on a mountainous trail. Even worse, the deadly predator is now hunting her. Boone Wilder wants nothing to do with Dead Man's Bluff, not after his wife died there. But he can't seem to mind his own business when a mysterious out-of-towner burst into his camp store in a frenzied panic. Something—or someone—deadly is out there. The killer's hunger for blood seems to be growing at a brutal pace. Can Brynlee and Boone figure out who's behind these murders? Or will the hurts and secrets from their past not allow for even a margin of error?

Brink of Danger

Ansley Wilder has always lived life on the wild side, using thrills to numb the pain from her past and escape her mistakes. But a near-death experience two years ago changed everything. When another incident nearly claims her life, she turns her thrill-seeking ways into a fight for survival. Ryan Philips left Fog Lake to chase adventure far from home. Now he's returned as the new fire chief in town, but the slower paced life he seeks is nowhere to be found. Not only is a wildfire blazing out of control, but a malicious killer known as "The Woodsman" is enacting crimes that appear accidental. Plus, there seems to be a strange connection with these incidents and his best friend's little sister, Ansley Wilder. As a killer watches their every move and the forest fire threatens to destroy their scenic town, both Ryan and Ansley hover on the brink of danger. One wrong move could send them tumbling over the edge . . . permanently.

Line of Duty

Jaxon Wilder didn't plan on returning home to Fog Lake, Tennessee, following his tour of duty in Iraq. But after a gut-wrenching failure during his stint in the Army, he now faces a new challenge: his family. Abby Brennan always did her best to be the good girl and to live by the rules. When a wrong decision changes her entire life, she tries to hide from the world. However, a madman known as the Executioner is determined to find her and enact his own brand of justice. When Jaxon and Abby are thrown together in the killer's crosshairs, they're forced to depend on one another to survive. Will Jaxon's sense of duty be enough to help keep Abby safe? Or will deadly secrets lead to the penalty of death?

Legacy of Lies

The justice system failed her family—and so did her hometown. Madison Colson knows deep down that her father—a convicted serial killer—is innocent. But believing it and proving it are two entirely different things. Unable to help her father, Madison has spent most of her adult life overcompensating by helping others. When her aunt dies unexpectantly, duty calls her back to Fog Lake, Tennessee, a beautiful but painful place she'd rather forget. Terrifying events begin to unfold once she arrives, unleashing her worst night-mares. The Good Samaritan Killer—or a copycat—is back, and now Madison Colson is his target. FBI Special Agent Shane Townsend is determined to stop the deadly rampage that has sent the tightknit community into a frenzy. But he needs to earn Madison's trust first. The task feels impossible, especially considering his father is the one who put her dad in prison. With the whole town on edge and pointing fingers, tension escalates out of control. Madison and Shane must sort the facts from the lies—and fight for a legacy of truth—before The Good Samaritan Killer has the final say.

Secrets of Shame

A killer has a promise to keep . . . Attorney Isaac Colson only wants to put his tumultuous past in Fog Lake behind him and return to his life in Memphis. But when an ominous text threatens that he must come back or there will be deadly consequences, he knows he can't take any chances. Rebecca Moreno has only ever loved one man—her high school sweetheart, Isaac Colson. But when his dad went to prison for murder, Rebecca's father forbade them from seeing each other again. Years later, Isaac is back in town and old feelings are stirring. But Rebecca is harboring a secret that could change everything. When The Good Samaritan Killer strikes again, guilt pummels her. She has to tell Isaac the truth. But as events unfold, she has more to lose than ever. Isaac and Rebecca must find answers—their lives depend on it. But everyone seems to have secrets, each that forms an obstacle to finding the truth . . . and to staying alive.

Refuge of Redemption

Home is a place of refuge—unless it's a killer's playground. For years, Bear Colson has been known as the serial killer's son. But now, someone else is behind bars for the crimes his father was accused of committing. Bear wants to believe hope for a brighter future is in sight, but he has reason to suspect more than one killer was involved. Forensic photographer Piper Stephens' career crashed and burned when she trusted the wrong man. Now, after discovering an alarming secret about the infamous Good Samaritan Killer, she sets out to find both answers and redemption. But things go awry when her assistant becomes the next victim. As fear batters Fog Lake residents once again, Bear and Piper join forces to track down the truth. But the killer is determined to remain in the shadows—and he'll destroy anyone who stands in his way.

COMPLETE BOOK LIST

Squeaky Clean Mysteries
#1 Hazardous Duty
Half Witted (Squeaky Clean In Between Mysteries Book
1, novella)
#2 Suspicious Minds
#2.5 It Came Upon a Midnight Crime (novella)
Half Truth (Squeaky Clean In Between Mysteries Book
2, novella)
#3 Organized Grime
#4 Dirty Deeds
#5 The Scum of All Fears
#6 To Love, Honor and Perish
#7 Mucky Streak
#8 Foul Play
#9 Broom & Gloom
#10 Dust and Obey

#11 Thrill Squeaker
#11.5 Swept Away (novella)
#12 Cunning Attractions
#13 Cold Case: Clean Getaway
#14 Cold Case: Clean Sweep
#15 Cold Case: Clean Break
#16 Cleans to an End
While You Were Sweeping, A Riley Thomas Spinoff

The Sierra Files
#1 Pounced
#2 Hunted
#3 Pranced
#4 Rattled

Lantern Beach Mysteries
#1 Hidden Currents
#2 Flood Watch
#3 Storm Surge
#4 Dangerous Waters
#5 Perilous Riptide
#6 Deadly Undertow

Lantern Beach Romantic Suspense
#1 Tides of Deception
#2 Shadow of Intrigue
#3 Storm of Doubt
#4 Winds of Danger
#5 Rains of Remorse

#6 Torrents of Fear

Lantern Beach P.D.
#1 On the Lookout
#2 Attempt to Locate
#3 First Degree Murder
#4 Dead on Arrival
#5 Plan of Action

Lantern Beach Escape
Afterglow (a novelette)

Lantern Beach Blackout
#1 Dark Water
#2 Safe Harbor
#3 Ripple Effect
#4 Rising Tide

Lantern Beach Guardians
#1 Hide and Seek
#2 Shock and Awe
#3 Safe and Sound

Lantern Beach Blackout: The New Recruits
#1 Rocco
#2 Axel
#3 Beckett
#4 Gabe

Lantern Beach Mayday
#1 Run Aground
#2 Dead Reckoning
#3 Tipping Point

Lantern Beach Christmas
Silent Night

Lantern Beach Blackout: Danger Rising
#1 Brandon
#2 Dylan
#3 Maddox
#4 Titus

Beach Bound Books and Beans Mysteries
#1 Bound by Murder
#2 Bound by Disaster
#3 Bound by Mystery
#4 Bound by Trouble
#5 Bound by Mayhem

Lantern Beach Exposure
#1 Fractured Lies
#2 Shattered Whispers
#3 Unsteady Ground
#4 Troubled Graves
#5 Deceptive Shallows
#6 Secret Shores

True Crime Junkies
#1 Just the Nicest Person
#2 He Walks Among Us
#3 Never Happen to You
#4 The Dead of Night
#5 Leave the Lights On
#6 The End of the Road
#7 The Secrets She Kept
#8 Most Likely to Die

The Shadow Agency
#1 Shadow Operative
#2 Shadow Chaser
#3 Shadow Assignment
#4 Shadow Collateral
#5 Shadow Survivor

Fog Lake Suspense
#1 Edge of Peril
#2 Margin of Error
#3 Brink of Danger
#4 Line of Duty
#5 Legacy of Lies
#6 Secrets of Shame
#7 Refuge of Redemption

Vanishing Ranch
#1 Forgotten Secrets
#2 Necessary Risk

#3 Risky Ambition
#4 Deadly Intent
#5 Lethal Betrayal
#6 High Stakes Deception
#7 Fatal Vendetta
#8 Troubled Tidings
#9 Narrow Escape
#10 Desperate Rescue

Saltwater Cowboys
#1 Saltwater Cowboy
#2 Breakwater Protector
#3 Cape Corral Keeper
#4 Seagrass Secrets
#5 Driftwood Danger
#6 Unwavering Security

Beach House Mysteries
#1 The Cottage on Ghost Lane
#2 The Inn on Hanging Hill
#3 The House on Dagger Point
#4 The Bungalow on Shadow Road

The Worst Detective Ever
#1 Ready to Fumble
#2 Reign of Error
#3 Safety in Blunders
#4 Join the Flub
#5 Blooper Freak

Raven Remington Relentless
#6 Flaw Abiding Citizen
#7 Gaffe Out Loud
#8 Joke and Dagger
#9 Wreck the Halls
#10 Glitch and Famous
#11 Not on My Botch
#12 One Hit Blunder

Holly Anna Paladin Mysteries
#1 Random Acts of Murder
#2 Random Acts of Deceit
#2.5 Random Acts of Scrooge
#3 Random Acts of Malice
#4 Random Acts of Greed
#5 Random Acts of Fraud
#6 Random Acts of Outrage
#7 Random Acts of Iniquity

Cape Thomas Series
#1 Dubiosity
#2 Disillusioned
#3 Distorted

Carolina Moon Series
#1 Home Before Dark
#2 Gone By Dark
#3 Wait Until Dark
#4 Light the Dark

#5 Taken By Dark

The Sidekick's Survival Guide
#1 The Art of Eavesdropping
#2 The Perks of Meddling
#3 The Exercise of Interfering
#4 The Practice of Prying
#5 The Skill of Snooping
#6 The Craft of Being Covert

School of Hard Rocks Mysteries
#1 The Treble with Murder
#2 Crime Strikes a Chord
#3 Tone Death

Standalone Romantic Suspense
Keeping Guard
The Last Target
Race Against Time
Ricochet
Key Witness
Lifeline
High-Stakes Holiday Reunion
Desperate Measures
Hidden Agenda
Mountain Hideaway
Dark Harbor
Shadow of Suspicion
The Baby Assignment

The Cradle Conspiracy
Trained to Defend
Mountain Survival
Dangerous Mountain Rescue
Lethal Mountain Pursuit

Crime á la Mode Mysteries
#1 Dead Man's Float
#2 Milkshake Up
#3 Bomb Pop Threat
#4 Banana Split Personalities

Standalone Novels
Vacation Friends
Death of the Couch Potato's Wife
Imperfect
The Good Girl
The Wrecking

Standalone Sweet Christmas Novellas
Home to Chestnut Grove
How Her Ex Stole Christmas

The Gabby St. Claire Diaries (a Tween Mystery series)
#1 The Curtain Call Caper
#2 The Disappearing Dog Dilemma
#3 The Bungled Bike Burglaries

Nonfiction

Characters in the Kitchen

Changed: True Stories of Finding God through Christian Music (out of print)

The Novel in Me: The Beginner's Guide to Writing and Publishing a Novel (out of print)

ABOUT THE AUTHOR

USA Today has called Christy Barritt's books "scary, funny, passionate, and quirky."

Christy writes both mystery and romantic suspense novels that are clean with underlying messages of faith. Her books have sold more than four million copies and have won the Daphne du Maurier Award for Excellence in Suspense and Mystery, have been twice nominated for the Romantic Times Reviewers' Choice Award, and have finaled for both a Carol Award and Foreword Magazine's Book of the Year.

She is married to her Prince Charming, a man who thinks she's hilarious—but only when she's not trying to be. Christy is a self-proclaimed klutz, an avid music lover who's known for spontaneously bursting into song, and a road trip aficionado.

When she's not working or spending time with her family, she enjoys singing, playing the guitar, and exploring small, unsuspecting towns where people have no idea how accident-prone she is.

Find Christy online at:
www.christybarritt.com
www.facebook.com/christybarritt
www.twitter.com/cbarritt

Sign up for Christy's newsletter to get information on all of her latest releases here: **www.christybarritt.com/newsletter-sign-up/**

facebook.com / AuthorChristyBarritt
x.com / christybarritt
instagram.com / cebarritt